Pride Publishing books by C F White

Responsible Adult
Misdemeanor
Hard Time
Reformed

St. Cross
Won't Feel a Thing
Won't Be Fooled Again

Pink Rock
Love & Tea Bags

Pink Rock

LOVE & TEA BAGS

C F WHITE

Love & Tea Bags
ISBN # 978-1-83943-835-6

Interior text design by Claire Siemaszkiewicz
Pride Publishing

Published in 2019 by Pride Publishing, United Kingdom.

Pride Publishing is an imprint of Totally Entwined Group Limited.

LOVE & TEA BAGS

Dedication

To Joe.
Who has unfortunately got to grow old with me.

Chapter One

It Always Starts With Tea

The slurp was loud and rather obnoxious, especially when the man was sipping from one of Mark's grandmother's dainty china tea cups that Mark saved for special occasions. Since Mark hadn't had any need for the guest china in quite some time, he'd let Grammy's cardinal rule slide for the strapping workman clambering up in his loft.

"Yup, I see the problem," the workman yelled down the open hatch in Mark's landing ceiling that led to the over-cluttered store of stuff that Mark hadn't set foot in for…well, quite some time.

Mark wished he hadn't offered the man a brew. He really hadn't had the time to wait for the kettle to boil, for a start. But he'd been brought up well, and one must offer one's tradesmen a cuppa in the hope they'll knock a few quid off the call-out charge. He suspected he would have to delve deep into his already ravine-like pockets, so anything that could be considered mates-rates would really help at this point in his life. Mark wished he did have mates. Ones that were handy, anyway.

"Oh, yes?" Mark called back, his voice echoing through the square hole in his ceiling. He closed his eyes, for some reason, as if that would soften the blow of what was going to come out of the man's mouth next.

"Gonna need coupla new roof tiles, mate. A lotta this stuff is gonna get ruined."

"Bugger," Mark muttered into his own mug of piping-hot tea. Well, it was rude not to join the man in a beverage.

"What was that?" The man's round, if somewhat flushed, face appeared at the hole.

"Nothing, nothing." Mark shook his head. He didn't much fancy repeating himself. The man might take it seriously and give him a whack. Or, which would be much worse, not take the job of fixing Mark's leaking roof. "Thank you." He smiled.

Mark had been told, on occasion, that he had quite a nice smile. One that relaxed people. Mark, however, believed it to be far more useful to allow people to walk all over him. Or pass by him. *Through him…*

With a grunt, the workman set his steel-toe-capped boots on two metal rungs of the ladder, revealing the tip of his rounded behind popping out of the elastic waistband that appeared to be failing in its one basic function. Normally, on an average Saturday night, Mark wouldn't have minded the view, as his internet history would evidence. But today was a Monday and the man didn't look like he would appreciate Mark's ogling. Not that Mark was ogling. He just had nowhere else to look. *Honest.*

On reaching the landing, the workman crashed back into Mark. Stumbling, Mark gripped his cup with both hands to prevent the utter travesty of spillage onto the carpet. Not only did he not have time to clear up any stains—not that any would show on the swirling patterns of the seventies-design stitch work—but he also hated to waste a cup of the good stuff.

The workman hefted up his jogging bottoms, his hands empty of the china tea cup he had been avidly slurping from up in the loft. And that meant Mark would now either have to venture up into the space he avoided like the seaside lido on a May bank holiday afternoon, or leave it up there to breed new life. He knew which he would rather.

"Right." The man scratched his stubbled chin. "See, you're gonna need a coupla new tiles. Tha's what the leak is. The rain we been 'avin is comin' in frou ta 'ole in ya roof. Travelling daan the walls and dripping aaat ya ceiling."

"Good-oh." Mark nodded, not letting on for a single second that he had no idea what the man had just said. "Uh, can you fix it?" He mentally crossed his fingers in the hope that he hadn't just said that he could. Or couldn't.

"Yeah, no sweat. I can do two tiles at a ton."

"A what now?"

"A ton."

"A ton of what? *Tiles*?"

"No. A hundred smackers."

Mark blanked, shaking his head.

"Paand?"

"Oh, I see. Well, that's not too bad then." Mark smiled. And phewed. Mentally.

"But that won't fix ya problem."

"Oh dear." Mark furrowed his brow, which he didn't like to do all that often as the lines weren't smoothing out after so much anymore.

"Dunno which bleedin' cowboy did ya roof last, but they didn't felt it." The man tucked a tiny pencil behind his ear. Where he'd got the pencil from was Mark's first question. Quickly followed by, *do I really want to know?*

"That cowboy would be my grandfather." Mark attempted to add a hint of pride to his voice, but the vacant expression of the workman before him just made him slink into a guilty, wincing admission. "He built the house."

"Ah. Right. 'Nover 'and-me-down was it?"

"Hand-me-down?" More deep-set wrinkles formed on Mark's brow. He must remember to use that skincare range for men he'd got as a Secret Santa present at work last year, the one that claimed to defy even the deepest-set wrinkles. He had a hunch who'd been bold enough to buy that for him. *Bloody Yvonne.*

The man waved, indicating Mark's attire. "The clothes."

Mark held out his arms, still clutching his mug of tea, and peered down at himself. Trusty grey corduroy trousers, wonderful and comfy, and rather warm considering the current climate, matched with a white button-down shirt. The vest underneath was simply due to the fact that his dark nipples tended to show through the thin material of cheap cotton. He'd discovered that tidbit of information back at secondary school when the popular boys used to poke his nipples through his school shirt, many twisting for added effect. *And people say all-boy grammar schools are a safe haven from bullying.*

Mark ran a hand through his thick dark hair, sliding it across his forehead in a floppy fringe, ignoring the jibe at his attire and moving on to the pressing transaction at hand. "So you were saying about the roof?"

"Yeah. Gonna need ta replace it." The man sniffed, his chest rising with the inhale of breath, then shrugged. "Set ya back 'bout five grand."

The fact that Mark had chosen the man's pause to take a sip of tea probably summed up his entire existence. It had been, of course, the wrong decision. He spat the tea out, liquid escaping from his nose, and coughed, gasping to get air, rather than the delightful Twinings English Breakfast, into his lungs.

The workman slapped him on the back. Perhaps he thought that would help the situation. It didn't. It only exacerbated it, knocking Mark off his feet and forcing him to grapple for the banister to prevent a rather tragic tumble down the stairs.

"Better out than in, I say." The workman *did* say.

Mark blanked. If only the boys at his delightful modern secondary grammar had believed in that statement back when Mark had been in year ten and announcing to the world he was gay. Not that any of his peers had had any doubt before Mark had made his fabulous speech. But Mark presumed they would have preferred him to stay *in* on that day, considering many had received detention for the words of "encouragement" they had called out in a perfect display of teenage camaraderie.

"Well, I can do the tiles tomorra," the man carried on, oblivious to Mark's inner turmoil. "Fink about the rest of da roof, though. You don't want it cavin' in on ya."

Mark nodded, although, right then the thought of paying out five thousand pounds that he didn't have made him consider the alternative option.

"Righty-oh. Thank you very much for coming out on such short notice." Mark ushered him down the stairs.

"No probs. Give me card your granddad, then." The man handed over a bent business card, a mobile phone number scrawled on the back with black pen along with the words *The Man With The Van Who Can*. Mark pondered if there was anything that he couldn't? *Or wouldn't?*

"That would be rather futile. Grampy died quite some time ago."

"Oh." The man squinted, stepping out into the daylight and onto Mark's porch. "So *you* chose this?"

"Chose what?" Mark desperately tried not to furrow his brow.

The man waved his hand, indicating, Mark presumed, the entire house's internal decor.

"I like antiques." Could seventies decor be considered antique? He supposed it could.

"You get antique wallpaper these days then?"

Bastard. "Oh, indeed." Mark nodded. "Worth a fortune."

Mark slammed the door shut and rested his back against the wall, glancing around at the house he'd lived in coming along ten years now. It was falling apart and no redecoration had been done since probably the last time he'd been up in the loft. He sighed, slammed his mug down on the windowsill and decided now was the time for a decent cup of the good stuff.

Grabbing his black Barbour jacket from the coat hooks, he slipped his feet into the black loafers by the door then ventured out into the morning sun. And what a glorious day it was, perfect to be beside the seaside. And Mark was. He lived directly opposite the pebble beach of Marsby in the south east, a quaint little seaside town that homed more retirees than tourists. Not that Mark was retired. He could only wish for that, although he was leaning nearer to the end of his career than the start. Mid-career, perhaps? *Christ, maybe I should think about actually having a career rather than simply a job that barely pays the bills?*

Trying to forget that he had left a gaping hole in his roof—and now his ceiling having forgotten to shut the loft hatch—Mark rammed his hands into his jacket pockets and thanked whomever above for the abnormal radiant sun. And that was when the inevitable dark clouds glided overhead and droplets landed with splats on his cheeks. Such was Mark's luck. So he trotted that bit faster along the pathway beside the beach and into the main High Street, stopping at the welcoming sign of Macy's Ye Olde Style Tea Shoppe on the corner.

The bell above the door chimed as Mark hurried into his regular haunt. He'd been going there for quite a few years now, since his move back to his home town from the mean streets of London, and still hadn't figured out why Macy added the extra p and e to the shop. He shook his hair out like a wet dog and nodded at the umbrellas Macy always offered to customers on such regular occurrences as torrential rain, a quick downpour, scattered showers and that really fine light rain that has one believing they aren't getting wet until they get home and their clothes are sopping.

The shop was empty, which was rather odd. There was usually someone sipping on a decent cup of tea made from the loose leaves in a well-stewed pot. Macy made proper tea, using a strainer, and it tasted every bit of the aromatic leaves that it should. She was also a rather good baker and Mark was horrified that there were no buns, baps or any other derogatory term used for parts of the female anatomy displayed on the counter for Mark to scoff and instantly burn off the calories by breathing. He had a fast metabolism, which was both a dream and a curse.

As Mark slapped a hand down on the counter, he heard shuffling back in the kitchen area. Thank God Macy was there. He needed a chat. And a tea.

"Helloooo? Only me, love. Usual cuppa when you're ready."

Drumming his fingers on the counter, Mark swivelled a one-eighty. Vacant seats and no-one in the vicinity looking like they might want venture on in to grab a tea to go, which would be quite difficult as Macy only served tea in porcelain cups. And rightly so.

"So, Macy, love," Mark called out over his shoulder, thinking it was best to fill her in now or he might not have time to divulge all the details of his eventful morning before he had to head into work. "I've decided I'm better off if I just kill myself now."

He leaned forward over the counter, ensuring his voice would drift to the kitchen. "Turns out my roof might collapse on me anyway. And according to this rather annoyingly beefcaked member of the male species, the sight of whose perfectly rounded behind is now imprinted on me for many a future solo endeavour, and who graced me with a whole other English language making me feel every bit of my—*cough*—years, it's going to cost me rather more than my arm and my leg. And I'm sadly going to have to admit it, Macy love, that I'm not sure the fellow would accept an offer of my penis as monetary value. Not that I have a wealth of offers for that part of my anatomy these days anyway. Much like the pound to the euro, I swear it's shrinking in value."

He chuckled at his own joke, as he so often did, then spun around to face the seating area. A couple of joggers zoomed past the window, obviously on their beachside run rather than the mad dash for cakes and biscuits that he did.

"You okay, Mace? Need a hand?"

No reply. So Mark leafed through the selection of pre-packed biscuits crammed in the bowl by the till. Macy had one of those old-fashioned registers. No electronic buttons to press. No new-fangled tablet hooked up to the mains. It was basically a calculator with a drawer.

Choosing a packet of chocolate-dipped Viennese shortbread fingers, Mark cocked his head to peer through the open kitchen door. "I mean, Macy, what *is* the point in filing paperwork for a living just to earn enough money to fix a roof when I have no man to enjoy the comforts of my damp-free living space along with me? And by the time I find a willing participant to snuggle with me on my *antique* sofa looking at my *antique* wallpaper in my *antique* house, I'll be ready to pop my clogs anyway. So, death by sugar, please, Macy."

He slapped the counter to finalise his self-depreciative monologue, and nearly threw up the entire contents of his breakfast when a male vacated the back kitchen. Said man was wiping his hands on a rather beautifully stitched gingham tea towel. But that wasn't the only thing that was a delight for the eye. The man was shirtless—rippling muscles, a glowing sheen of glistening skin and white-wash jeans hanging low on his perfectly sculpted hips. Needless to say, that wasn't Macy.

"Hello," Mark said, because, it is the polite way to greet a man, regardless of the lack of shirt and the highly embarrassing fact that Mark had already told his life story, leaving out all, or indeed any, good bits.

"G'day," the man replied.

And Mark's head exploded. Or rather he wished that it would. "Where's Macy?" He mentally crossed his fingers in hope that she would soon poke out behind the tall hunk of an obviously Australian specimen and say that the man was deaf. Or at least hard of hearing. Or that he didn't understand English. Anything really.

"She had to shoot off, mate," the man replied. "Her mum."

Could Mark not cut a break these days?

"Oh dear. That's terrible. Is it serious?"

"Dunno, mate." The Aussie shrugged and slapped the tea towel onto the counter. "Something about her mum and the big C."

"Oh, dear God. What type of cancer?" Mark clutched a hand to his chest.

"No, the big *sea.* Ocean? She's off on some golden oldies cruise ship thing and Macy had to go with her as a carer or something."

Mark nodded. He had no words, after all.

"I said I'd mind the shop for her. I'm her cousin." Aussie stepped forward, wiped a hand down the back of his jeans then held it out to Mark. "Bradley. Brad."

Mark took the solid hand that had surprisingly smooth fingers and a firm grip. *Most definitely surfer hands.* Not that Mark had any idea what type of hands a surfer might own, other than slightly wrinkly owing to so much time in the water. But, he suspected, hands like this. Because all Australian men surfed. That was what both *Neighbours* and *Home and Away* had taught him in his youth.

Mark shook, not swaying his gaze from the light blue eyes of the man in front of him. *Brad. His name's Brad... Bradley, much better suited.* Specks of green flickered in Bradley's eyes, like mini frogs bouncing around in a swimming pool, sparkling against the piercing Aussie sun rays. A much better lido than Marsby's freezing fifty-metre monstrosity that was probably filled with more urine than chlorine. *Ha! I rhymed.*

It wasn't until the man—*Bradley, such a wonderful name*—attempted to free his hand that Mark realised he had just performed one of the rudest acts in the English realm.

"Mark," Mark suddenly blurted out. "Mark. I'm Mark." Because his name was Mark.

"Nice to meet ya, Mark." Bradley shot him a smile of perfectly aligned white teeth that Colgate would snap up in a second to be in their next commercial. "And I'm sorry to hear about your roof."

"Ah." Mark burned a lovely shade of crimson that matched the colour of his wallpaper. His *antique* wallpaper. "No bother. Nothing a cup of tea couldn't fix." Okay, that wasn't strictly true. If it was, he wouldn't have the problem in the first place.

"Righto, mate. I'm just getting to grips with everything, so bear with. I'll go grab a shirt. Was mighty hot behind there." Bradley jogged off back to the kitchen before Mark could blast out the proceeding lyrics to one of Nelly's finest...*So take off all your clothes...*

Bradley returned a few moments later, unfortunately having found suitable attire to wear, and handed Mark a mug. "On the house. First tea I've made here, so think of it as a trial run."

"Why, thank you very much."

"You take sugar?"

"No, no. Just milk," Mark assured him. "I'm sweet enough," he added because he was a complete idiot.

"Fair dos." Bradley held up a tiny jug of milk and began to pour it into Mark's mug. "Say when."

"When," Mark declared just before the desired amount of milk was in, suspecting that young Bradley might not have perfect reflexes to stop pouring at the exact right time and Mark wasn't a particularly milky tea drinker. He was more on the Midnight Savannah levels of tea colour, as referenced by Her Majesty's official colour chart.

Mark held up the cup in cheers, then took a sip. He closed his eyes to really savour it and swallowed down the delightful wake-up in a cup.

"Any good?"

"Perfect." Mark smiled.

Bradley returned the smile and raised it. It was the sweetest smile Mark had ever seen, full of pride and a feeling of a good job well done. It was only tea, but by God it was important.

"Well, sit down then." Brad waved a hand to a vacant table. "I thought I put the closed sign up but as you got in, might as well open up for good."

Mark whipped his head around. The *OPEN* sign hung on the *inside* of the door. Mark made a mental note to take the High Street chemist up on their offer of a free eye test with the purchase of any men's grooming product.

Taking a seat on one of the little square tables covered with a yellow and white checked plastic tablecloth, Mark sipped his tea. It seemed to be getting stronger with every taste, but Mark continued none the less. He didn't want to upset the dear Bradley, considering he was a complete novice. Mark started to wonder what else this man could be a novice in that Mark would be happy to play teacher in. Which instantly made him wince. He really should not be thinking along those lines.

Mark's life consisted of a series of disasters, followed by unfortunate mishaps, then brief but noteworthy embarrassing incidents, swiftly engulfed by immediate tragedy and swooping in on the left would be a spout of sheer disappointment. So, this guy would most certainly not be a novice and would be highly active on the heterosexual scene, no doubt.

"Hey, Mark?" Bradley's head popped up from the counter where he'd been crouching.

"Hmm?" Mark stilled the cup at his lips.

"You know if there are any decent gay bars in this town?"

And splat. A wet and sloppy tea bag fell from Mark's cup and landed on his nose with a squelch. Mark didn't move. There was no point. This wasn't an inconspicuous moment. This was yet another of those embarrassing incidents to add to his growing collection. There was no coming back from this. Mark plonked the cup on the table and peeled the tea bag from his face.

"That doesn't usually happen?" Bradley pointed to Mark's face.

Mark shook his head. "No." He wiped his nose with a napkin. "Usually one takes the tea bag out of the cup before serving."

Bradley covered his mouth with his hand, a look of sheer horror plastered on his face. "Oh, Jeez. Sorry, mate."

"No bother."

"Here." Bradley zipped over to the kettle. "Let me get you another one."

"No, no. That's quite all right." Mark stood. "Best be getting on anyway. Paperwork doesn't file itself." Which was rather fortunate, as Mark would be out of a job.

He sauntered toward the exit, slipping one of the extra-large umbrellas from the bucket Macy kept them in and attempted to wave a cheery, and nonchalant, goodbye. The umbrella popped open unannounced, one of the metal prods poking Mark in the eye, and he wrestled inside to slap it shut. Bradley whipped over the counter, sliding along it in true *Dukes of Hazzard* fashion, and grabbed the handle. They both found the sharp edge of the protruding button and Bradley slammed his thumb on top of Mark's to slap shut the umbrella, which swallowed both of their arms inside like a Venus fly trap.

"Sorry." Mark fumbled, desperately trying to open the thing up again. Their fingers were in danger of entwining and Mark closed his eyes at the sheer embarrassment, although he should have been used to the feeling after thirty-nine years of it.

"Here." Bradley gripped the pole, tugging it away. "Let me."

Mark slipped his arm out and Bradley handed the brolly back to him with a smile.

"Thanks." Mark took it, with caution.

"Looks like you're gonna need it." Bradley nodded at the window where huge raindrops splattered like water balloons. "Think it might rain here more than Sydney."

"It rains here more than a sodding rainforest. Least in a rainforest it's hot."

"Not at night, mate. Pretty cool then, I can tell ya."

"Really?" Mark's interest once again piqued.

"Yeah. You'll need a roof there too." Bradley winked. "Just in case you're considering a move."

"Perhaps not to somewhere wetter."

"Avoid Oz then." Bradley opened the door for Mark, the little bell tinkling and ending the conversation.

"Thanks for the tea." Mark stepped outside, opening his umbrella minus any personal injury.

"No probs, mate. Maybe once I get the hang of this place, I'll make you a decent one. Like my gran makes."

"That would be lovely. And do send Macy my love."

Bradley nodded and closed the door, switching the hanging sign to display *OPEN*. It swung against the other various posters stuck onto the window advertising the array of products that Macy sold in the shop, from real Cornish ice cream to hot chocolate. The sign caught on the corner of one of the leaflets, covering up most of the words, except for *available here*.

Bradley meandered away from the window, his hips swaying, then vaulted the counter in one swift athletic move. Mark pondered as to whether Bradley was *available here*. Probably not. This was Mark's life, after all.

Chapter Two

Nine to Five

Mark rushed through the glass door of his seafront office, his work phone ringing on arrival. Clambering through the desks, he mouthed his apology to Yvonne on the front reception for his bag whacking her in the face. He assumed it had, anyway, as she wore one of her more screwed-up grimaces, rather than the resting one she usually favoured.

He was a tad later than preferred in to work, thanks to the morning's escapades, and he slumped down on his rotating office chair that collapsed to the lowest rung on its axis. As per bloody usual. Mark could barely see over his desk, let alone dump his elbows on it. He fumbled for the lever underneath, adjusting the seat back to his preferred height settings, then grabbed the phone.

"Good morning." *Is it?* "Steinberg Accounts, Mark speaking, how may I help you?" His chipper tone was ten years in the making, and he could still achieve it whilst tucking the receiver between his chin and shoulder and wriggling free from his coat that had soaked through from the inevitable ten-minute downpour from his walk to the office from Macy's. Glorious sunshine gleamed outside his office window now though. *Go figure.*

"I hear you've met Brad." The female voice chuckled down the phone.

Mark slipped free of one side of his soggy Barbour outdoor wear jacket, making a mental note to contact their customer service department to complain that their *outdoor* range obviously didn't mean waterproof, then transferred the receiver to his other ear. The phone, disgruntled at being shoved around so early in the morning, protested by slapping down with a loud bang onto his desk.

"Bugger." Mark mouthed his apology over to Yvonne who had given him his second dose of eyeful that morning. She usually gave around fifteen per working day, so Mark was well-rehearsed on how to handle her after ten years on the job—by mouthing *sorry*, then mimicking holding a cup of tea up to his mouth. She nodded back, accepting his gift horse for what it was.

Mark fumbled with the receiver after several attempts of freeing his arm from his jacket sleeve and throwing it in a huff over the back of his seat. That extra bit of weight was all too much for the lowly workings of his vintage blue three-lever operating chair and it instantly slammed down to the bottom rung once more. Mark left it there, knowing when to admit defeat. He'd live to fight another day.

"Macy? Sorry, dropped the phone and had a fight with a chair."

"So tell me something new."

"Ha bloody ha." A milky cup of tea slammed down in front of him.

He offered up a grateful smile to Yvonne, who'd clearly taken pity on him for once, and wrapped his hands around the mug. Yvonne nodded, which was as affirmative as she usually was, and slumped off. Mark peered into the mug and managed to refrain from grimacing. The contents appeared more suited to a child's sippy cup than a wake-me-up for a thirty-something office worker. Still, one mustn't complain about how one received the gift of tea, no matter how vile it came.

"So, I just called the shop," Macy continued.

Mark twisted in his seat to look out of the full-length window that boasted the view of the seafront. Sipping from the mug, he grimaced. The full-fat milk that Yvonne had used to mask the taste of any actual tea curdled the roof of Mark's mouth. The stuff was off. He spat it out and the white dots swimming around in the liquid were like tadpoles, or little sperms. Mark shook his head. It had been a while since he'd seen any spunk that wasn't his own and it appeared he was now hallucinating about having it in his daily hot beverage. And whilst tea was his first and presently only love, he rather wanted it separate from any bodily excretions.

Setting the cup down, Mark glanced over his shoulder. Yvonne scratched her nails along a purple emery board, taking full opportunity of the boss's absence, so Mark threw the milky tea into the spider plant on the windowsill, the froth bubbling over the dried soil. He wasn't sure what out-of-date milk would do to the scarce foliage, but he wasn't particularly green-fingered, so wasn't too worried about creating some *Day of the Triffids* re-enactment in the otherwise boring seaside town. And even if it did, he'd get the day off work, so that was a bonus enough to attempt it.

"Yes?" Mark settled back into his chair, digging his cheek against the telephone receiver. He tapped a few keys on his PC keyboard in the hope that the thing wouldn't explode as he tried to log on for the day. The way his day was going, it wasn't to be unexpected.

"And Brad said he met a rather curious man who goes by the name of Mark."

"Well, yes, I did pop in." Mark tapped his password into the little box on the screen. An alert popped up, declaring it was wrong. It wasn't. Mark was one of those rather lackadaisical people who never feared the threat of invasion, cyber or otherwise, and had the same password for almost everything. Except his porn hub. He didn't want anyone *ever* getting into that. *Bank details? Pfft, have them.* Then HSBC might stop sending him threatening letters and he could pass them over to the geek who now had responsibility for his overdraft.

"He said the shop was closed but you managed to worm your way in." Macy chuckled. "I knew I should have just given you a spare set of keys. You're there more than me. Brad said he thought you might have worked there at first, what with you telling him your life story."

"You know, Macy…" Mark struck his fingertips down hard on his keyboard and rammed down the Enter button in the hope that his computer just wasn't convinced enough that Mark knew his own sodding password. "You can go off people."

The computer flashed up *password not valid* for the third time and Mark dropped his hand down on the keyboard, sending random letters flying into the little box on the screen. The computer returned another *password not valid* sign, which Mark delighted in flipping off.

"Mark?"

Mark swivelled in his seat, his knees tucked up to his chest. It seemed both his chair and computer were set to make his morning rather laborious.

"Mr Steinberg." And now his boss would no doubt be adding to the torment. "Good morning," he said, regardless of all the evidence to the contrary.

Mr Steinberg, CEO and owner of the accounting firm Mark worked at, raised his grey eyebrows. Relatively short and stout, with a completely bald head and a little pug nose that held black round-rimmed glasses, Mr Steinberg made up for his lack of height by his volume control. Mark noted the usual three pens stuck in his top lapel pocket, a red, a blue and a green. Mark had yet to discover what the green could be required for. Blue was used for the boss's signature and red for correcting Mark's work. The monthly stationery order from Staples always had a box of red biros waiting in the online cart.

"I see you are having problems there." Mr Steinberg nodded at Mark's computer screen.

Mark held a hand over the speaker part of the phone. "Yes. Have we had a password reset recently? IT making us all think this small accountancy firm in the idyllic town of Marsby is going to be hacked into by the CIA so we need to change our password every three bloody minutes?"

"No, Mark." Mr Steinberg leaned over Mark and clicked a button on his keyboard. "You had it on Caps Lock."

"Ah. Well, thank you." Mark twisted around in his seat. "I do hope the cyber bods aren't offended by my shouting this morning then." He chuckled, because one must laugh at one's own joke to ensure the intended audience are fully aware that it was meant to be funny.

"No problem." Mr Steinberg's reply was delivered in his standard stoicism, him clearly not catching on to Mark's verbal memo. "And when you've finished that call, I need to have a chat with you in my office, asap."

"Right-o." Mark nodded, then waggled the phone. "I'll just get rid of this bit of annoyance and be right with you."

Mr Steinberg's tiny round face raged a glorious shade of crimson-red. "I hope that's not a client!"

"Oh, no, no this is just a friend. Well, I say friend. It's a rather loose term at the moment. I'm still contemplating whether I need any more acquaintances in my life. I mean, I am rather tied up with my social commitments of doing the laundry and watching re-runs of *CSI* which weren't even that good the first time around."

"Mark?" Mr Steinberg interrupted.

"Mmm?"

"Come see me when you're finished here."

"Absolutely!" Mark replied, more chipper than the moment warranted and sighed as his boss stomped off into his private office. The door slammed, followed by the zapping shut of the window blinds. Slumping in his chair, Mark brought the phone mouthpiece back to his lips. "When your boss says 'come see me' that's a bad sign, right? I mean, if it was about work he would say 'I need to talk through the latest minutes of that meeting' or some equally informative way to help you prepare for what you were going in for."

"I don't know, Mark," Macy replied. "I've only ever worked for myself."

"Lucky you. I'm not sure I'd make a good employer for myself. I'd keep giving me the day off."

Macy laughed and Mark smiled at the feminine tone ringing down the telephone. Macy was possibly the only one in Mark's life who seemed to accept him for who he was. From the moment they'd met back when Macy was opening the tea shop and begging for customers, Mark had made it his mission to try every flavour of tea to help her out. She'd fallen into Mark's life as though she'd always been there. She laughed at his jokes—or more accurately laughed at him—plied him full of his daily tea fix and was as quirky as he was. She tended to favour oddly matched clothes and her shoes were always some ridiculous monstrosity pattern of some kind. She had frizzy red hair, often decorated with bows and ribbons that clashed with her shoes. She was a delight. How she could be related to the Australian Adonis was, to put quite frankly, a mind fuck.

"So, anyway, where are you and why did you not forewarn me of your absence from the shop and being replaced by my wet dream?" Another cup of tea sloshed down in front of Mark and he closed his eyes at the untimely intrusion and to avoid Yvonne's third eyeful coming his way.

"Milk was off." Yvonne stomped away to the reception area.

Mark *was* grateful for the second cup of tea, although it still bore resemblance to Skimmed Alive, but wished Yvonne wouldn't creep up on him the way she did, especially when his mouth liked to brain dump. Which, granted, happened more often than Mark would prefer. He took a sip of the drink and grimaced at the over-milky taste, but this one wasn't going to waste away in a pot of dried soil and green leaves emulating tarantula legs.

"Thought I'd give you a nice surprise," Macy sniggered. "Couldn't have you prepare for your first meeting with him now, could I? Where's the fun in that?"

"You never even told me you had a cousin from Australia. And one that looks like Thor the God of Sex."

"Thunder," Macy corrected.

"Hmm?" Mark managed to log on to the computer system and wished he hadn't when he scrolled through the list of demanding emails. "Oh, well, same thing in my case. Both loud, frightening and don't come around too often."

Macy laughed. "He's quite a bit younger than me. Dad's brother moved out to Sydney years ago, met his wife, had a kid. Brad. He's always just been a kid to me so never worth mentioning. He turned up on the doorstep this weekend and offered to mind the shop so I could take Mum on this cruise thing. Our gran ran a tearoom for years in London, so I figured he's got tea-making in his genes."

"Hmm." Mark didn't bother to correct her and kept to the more pressing matter at hand. "So, by quite a bit younger, what are we talking here?"

"He's in his twenties. *Early* twenties."

"A baby then. *Wonderful.*" Mark tutted. As if the age made any difference to the fact that Bradley resembled a demi-god and *he* resembled a shaggy dog. A really skinny shaggy dog. "And one that no doubt likes to frequent nightclubs and drink copious amounts of alcohol and does twitterers and book faces and chats with a snap."

Macy chuckled. "Actually he's more into extreme sports, travelling and survival stuff."

"I won't tell you the first thing that popped into my head when you said *extreme* sports." Mark winced though another sip of the horrid hot milk.

"Mark Johnson! That is my baby cousin!"

"Oh, give over. You hardly know the bloke. You can't be getting all protective." Mark clicked on an email that detailed the agenda for the afternoon's team meeting and groaned at his name displayed next to several of the items that he had forgotten he was meant to prepare for.

"Okay, true," Macy said. "And from what I've heard, he doesn't need any protecting by me, anyway."

"Oh yes? Why is that, my dear?" Mark clicked out of the email in an attempt to pretend he hadn't seen it and, therefore, unable to perform said tasks within it. Tapping the little button that would highlight the message back up as if it hadn't been read, he tugged over his daily mound of filing and paperwork. Flicking through that instead, he picked his mug back up and braced himself for further mouth torture. Seriously, how could someone make tea so terribly?

"He's also a stripper."

And for the second time that day, Mark had chosen the wrong moment to take a gulp of tea and proceeded to both spit out and snort in the liquid abomination at the same time.

"He's a what?" Mark wiped his hand across his nose. How much tea was it actually possible to snort in a day. A cup? A pot? An urn? Which was probably not what he should have been concerned with just then, considering his paperwork was now tainted with a lovely shade of Skimmed Alive. "Bugger."

"Thought that might have got your attention."

"You, Macy Summers, are a nasty woman."

"He's new in town. Doesn't know anyone. Why don't you go be his friend? Once you've got your mind out of the gutter, that is."

"Macy, I'm not sure I'm the type of friend young Bradley would like." Mark reached over his desk to hang a piece of the soaked paperwork along the radiator in the hope that the scolding metal that was always blasting hot during the summer and stone cold during the winter could help dry it off.

"He prefers Brad."

"And there, see, we wouldn't get on. Bradley is just so much more…decorous." Mark waved his hand.

"I have no idea what that means. But you call him what you want. Just go be his friend. For me. Please?"

"Oh, for heaven's sake." Mark huffed. "I'll pop by the café and say hi, but that's it. Not promising a long-lasting friendship. We clearly have nothing in common."

* * * *

Mark had to suck in a rather fierce breath before entering the tea shop for the second time that day. Work had dragged on, as it usually did, the only excitement being the meeting with Mr Steinberg had turned out to be regarding his boss's upcoming business trip and how he wanted Mark to run the office during his absence. Mark rather looked forward to being the one to tell Yvonne off for her glum reception expression and considered sending her on tea-making training.

Peering through the window, Mark set eyes on Bradley. The man was chit-chatting away, flashing his perfectly perfect smile to a couple of ladies at the counter. He was wearing a shirt, much to Mark's dismay and, quite probably, that of the ladies-who-didn't-lunch who currently occupied Bradley's personal space. The café was in quite some disarray, which meant there had been a steady influx of customers, and Mark hoped Bradley had improved his tea-making ability or Macy would be returning home to the real possibility of a new career.

He flattened out his shirt for no other reason than to delay his entry into the shop then pushed through the boundaries of reason and restraint by opening the blasted door. Bradley glanced up at the tinkling bell and his sickly-sweet smile increased.

"G'day, Mark."

"Hello." Mark closed the door behind him, the sign rattling on its metal chain. "Bradley." It was the unexpected snap of jealousy that had uttered Bradley's full name. Mark had wanted to ensure those young baby-bearers would know he had a history with their wanton sperm donor.

And there he went again, thinking about sperm. Perhaps it was a time-of-life thing? His sperm trying to nudge at him through his ball sac with their need to fertilise and fulfil their life destiny? *Well, sorry, my young fellows, there will be no egg fertilising of any sort for you little nippers. And you've had thirty-odd years to come to terms with the fact that your meals out come sans dessert.*

"Would you like a tea?" Bradley held up a yellow teapot.

"Is it bagless?" Mark approached the counter and smiled at the two girls, who returned theirs cautiously and trotted off to sit at one of the window tables and sip on the blood of a virgin. *Okay, so it's probably tea, but one shouldn't presume.*

"It is indeed." Bradley grinned, his blue eyes sparkling. "Took me a coupla goes but I got there in the end. Had to call on me gran, though. Just for checks."

"Well, then I feel I must certainly try the fruits of your, and her, labour," Mark replied a little too huskily and it sounded a lot like he was trying to flirt. So he added, "Super." Which would certainly go some way to rectifying any possible mistake that Mark was a man with the gift of the gab. *Has anyone actually uttered the word super since the release of the first Superman movie?* Which was in 1978, just around the time Mark was born into the world and some misalignment of the stars meant he would forever suffer the fact.

"Okay, mate." Bradley reached behind him with those gloriously beefy arms of his to grab a cup. "Go take a seat and I'll bring it over."

Mark bundled off to find the table the farthest away from the two girls who eyed him suspiciously. They must know who he was. Marsby was a very small town and his mother and father were well-known around the place. Plus Mark was the token minority. *That blasted speech and my sordid past will never leave me.*

"Here you go." Bradley slipped a cup and saucer onto the table in front of Mark. He hadn't added any milk and handed down a mini jug for Mark to add to his tea himself, which was absolutely the right thing to do. *One mustn't assume people want milk in their tea.* Mark smiled and nodded, adding the splash of milk into the cup.

"I didn't bring any sugar as I know you're sweet enough."

Mark smiled again, because it was all he had in his arsenal. Bradley stood over him and chewed his lip as Mark stirred the contents with the additional tea spoon and took a sip. "Perfect," he purred.

"You said that last time." Bradley waggled an accusing his finger.

"Ha. Yes, I did. I'm afraid I'm terribly British that way. I don't like to cause offence."

"Right, so does that mean this one is just as shit as the first?"

"Oh no, not at all. This one *is* perfect. The last perhaps needed a bit of work."

Bradley leaned forward to look Mark in the eye. "Now how do I ever believe a word you say?"

Mark smiled. "I guess you shouldn't ever trust me."

"Not with that smile, no." Bradley winked. He jogged back behind the counter, leaving Mark to ponder the actual meaning behind what the man had just said.

After a moment, the two ladies finished their teas and waved cheery goodbyes. Bradley flashed them a pearly white smile back and told them to please come again. Bring their friends. *Etcetera.* If any girls were to go missing from school and/or places of employment in the next few weeks, Mark would place a bet on where they would be found. *Wince. Touchy subject.*

"So I spoke to Macy," Mark called to him once he was certain that, this time, they were the only two in the shop.

"Yeah?" Bradley clanged down a handful of mugs onto the serving counter. "How's she doing?"

"Good. Good. I think." Mark furrowed his brow. "I actually didn't ask her."

"Oh, right."

"She just mentioned about you being new in town and you might want someone to show you around." Mark waved a hand. "Of course, I totally understand if you would prefer someone perhaps more your age to show you the delights of the very limited leisure services we have to offer such a young whippersnapper like yourself."

Did I really just say the word whippersnapper? Can one actually die of embarrassment?

Bradley laughed. "No, no, mate, that would be awesome." He smiled. "I've spent nights in rainforests and the outback, but here, England, I just don't get."

"What's not to get? We drive on the left and govern on the right."

"See." Bradley waggled his finger. "My guess is that was a joke but I still have no idea."

"No joke. All fact. And I would be more than happy to show you around."

"Excellent." Bradley flipped a tea towel over his broad shoulder. "When are you free?"

"The right question to ask is when am I *not* free." Mark stood and fished out a five-pound note from his leather wallet. He showed it up to Bradley and rained it onto the table. "Thanks for the tea. Looks like I can report to Macy all is in good hands."

"Yeah. Thanks. Although she'll think there's been no takings as I'm not touching that till."

"Don't blame you. I've left my number on the napkin. Just call if you need anything.".

"Sure will. Oh, and Mark?"

Mark raised his eyebrows, the bell tinkling as he opened the shop door.

"If you want, I could come look at your roof? I'm no expert, but I've fitted a few tiles in my time and I won't charge as much as the arse-crack dude. Just a tour of the town. Unless, that is, you were lying about not wanting to see any more of the man's arse? I never can tell with the British sense of humour."

Mark laughed. "No, I certainly wasn't lying."

Bradley smiled. "Well, if you're free then I can come by later this arvo, after I've shut this place. Take a look?"

Mark wondered if the stars were beginning to align back to their correct positions and the last thirty-nine years of bad luck was coming to an end. A hot, hunky Australian offering to fix his roof in exchange for a drink at the local? This was rather too good to be true. Which meant it would be and he wasn't to get his little sperms' hopes up that they might be gobbled down another man's throat for a change rather than caught in the palm of his own hand.

Still, the thought of young Bradley scaling up his loft ladder—and the possibility of giving Mark another backside view to add to his spank bank—did seem to provide him with more satisfaction than just the pros of affordable home improvement.

Chapter Three

Leap Frog

Mirrors lie. Or at least Mark's did. Throughout Mark's childhood he'd been taught by Walt bloody Disney that mirrors told you what you wanted. *Who's the fairest of them all?* Well, it certainly wasn't Mark sodding Johnson. His thick mound of dark hair, no matter what he did with it, just collapsed in defeat around his head as if it had given up on life some time ago. He had shaved it all off once like some mass-murder horror movie, thinking the new hair would be tamer under the threat of another invasion. It hadn't been. It had come back with a vengeance. Thicker, stronger, meaner. And it now grew out in all directions in a blatant disregard for style or fashion.

His reflection on the whole was something Mark tended to avoid. Mirrors reflected a skinny, ageing man with stubble that grew too quickly and wrinkles that lengthened and deepened with every glance. Once upon a time—like old Walt would say—he had considered himself a rather handsome fellow. He'd never had much trouble courting a man or two back in his teens and into his early twenties. But time, experience and life had gotten the better of him and he now stood in front of his full-length wardrobe mirror in the hope that it was actually his sixty-five-year-old father looking back at him. It wasn't. Which was a rather bitter pill to swallow, considering he had the epitome of Adam incarnate coming to his house in a few minutes.

Bugger it. Like I had a chance anyway.

He stroked his hair away from his forehead, trying to settle it into some sort of side brush-over. It, like everything else in his life, rebelled against anything he offered and slid back to fall around his face. So he gave up and worked on his clothes. He'd changed to a black shirt. *Less visible nipples.* But he'd sprayed deodorant before slipping it on and despite its branding claiming it wouldn't leave white marks or even a trace of those hideous yellow stains, it, of course, did. So Mark licked his fingers and wiped them down the side of his shirt to rub the flecks of white away. Funny how it was his armpits where the deodorant was sprayed yet no white marks were found there. No they were down at the front of his shirt where they couldn't be hidden underneath his sodding pits.

The white stuff just wouldn't shift through spittle alone. It never did, so Mark pondered as to why he tried to do it that way every single time. He huffed and trudged out of his bedroom across the landing to the bathroom. He did a quick check to ensure his loft hatch was still there, in case by some miracle it had been sealed shut, fixing both the leak and the need to sort out the mess left behind. It hadn't.

His bathroom, another bone of contention in his life. As he'd inherited the house from his grandparents, the place had been in quite some disarray, this room being the worst. It had been completely decked out in woodchip from floor to ceiling. Mark had gained splinters in places he would rather not divulge. So, on a rather impetuous whim one weekend, he had ripped the whole thing out, thinking he'd just need to add a bit of linoleum flooring, a few tiles over the sink and some paint around the rest. *Done.* But this was Mark. When was anything going to be such a smooth operation?

On ripping through the woodchip, he had soon realised why Grampy had chosen it to cover up the unlikely mess underneath. *Who decides to paint a bathroom deep purple anyway?* It had taken four large tubs of brilliant white paint to cover up the violaceous colouring, which had ended up looking decidedly a little off-grey. In the end, Mark had dug deep into his already shrunken pockets to pay someone to tile the whole bloody thing over, along with putting up plasterboard to hide the rest. Another hack job that meant every time Mark wandered into the bathroom to use the facilities—which should be a delightful sanctuary to the end of one's tiresome day—he found himself with a relenting urge to just blow the whole thing up.

Dabbing his grey flannel under the warm tap, he then wiped it along the white lines down his shirt and threw it into the sink with a slap. He looked back up to his reflection in the mirror, only to notice a few more lines. He picked up the flannel once more and wiped the other side. At this rate, he might as well just step into the shower and drench the whole thing off. Of course, he'd have to use more deodorant after that. *Perhaps that was what the company did to ensure he bought more of their product?*

The knock from the door rattled the mirror against the wall. He hadn't bothered to secure the thing properly—just one task too many in the bathroom of horrors—and so slapped a palm onto it to prevent the inevitable seven years bad luck. Spinning on his heel, he stalked out of the bathroom.

And forgot he was wearing the fluffy Christmas socks he'd received as a present from Macy last year and thus slipped on the second to last step, tumbling down on his arse.

"Bugger!"

"Mark? You okay, mate?" The Aussie accent was unmistakable.

"Yep, yes!" Mark crawled up and opened the front door.

Mark'd had no doubt that Bradley Summers was an attractive man. All muscles and smiles, with tan skin that bore no white lines anywhere. Well, Mark wasn't sure about *everywhere,* and he'd happily go find some, but the skin that he currently laid his eyes on showed no tan lines of T-shirt, socks, glasses or anything else that Mark would most certainly get if the sun decided to tan his skin instead of burning it red like it usually did.

Bradley's skin stretched youthfully over his tight physique and his blond-streaked hair floated in the gentle breeze, the way Mark imagined it would look when the man was surfing.

The pair of Bermuda-style shorts dangled two white strings from the elastic waistband and Mark fixated on them as they drifted to and fro in the light evening breeze. Mark's jaw dropped and he managed to guide his gaze upwards, as would be the norm when greeting guests to his home rather than focusing on their groin area. He then couldn't help but notice that the salmon-pink T-shirt Bradley wore could do with being a couple of sizes bigger on the fellow. *Surely that material prevents his lungs from expanding?*

"G'day." Bradley smiled.

Mark swooned, but shook himself out with a reminder he was a grown man. "Hello." *Why do I sound so bloody formal?* "Do come in." He really shouldn't let the man hang about on his doorstep. The neighbours would no doubt cop an eyeful and be over demanding to know how much Mark's new workman charged for anything that they *didn't* need doing in their houses.

"Thanks, mate." Brad stepped his pink Havaianas into Mark's antique house.

Mark became preoccupied by the feet in a pair of thongs, the like of which Mark's hadn't donned since the nineties. Bradley's feet were delightful—only a scattering of blondish hair over each wide and flat toe that spread out in perfect alignment with each other, with cut-down nails that looked as if the man enjoyed a pedicure or two. Bradley could be a foot model. The only modelling Mark's feet would be appropriate for were of a remake of *The Hobbit* or those adverts about nail fungal infection. The before shots.

Mark closed the door behind him and Bradley shot him a wide smile, flashing those white teeth. C*ould this man be any more perfect?* It almost made Mark want to slap him. He wouldn't though. Not only was that frightfully rude to do to a guest in his home, especially one that was coming to help fix his leaky roof, but also because Mark wasn't a very good hitter. So, instead, he gestured Bradley through the hallway and toward the back kitchen.

"How do you take your tea?" Mark clapped his hands together a little too overzealously after clicking the kettle on to boil.

"No, thanks, mate. Don't really drink tea."

That completely unnecessary sucker-punch to Mark's gut knocked the wind firmly from his sails and he couldn't even prevent the gurning from spreading across his face. How Macy could have believed these two would ever get along really was turning out to be quite some quandary.

"You're not one of those…" Mark trailed off, unable to form the words. "Coffee drinkers, are you?" His throat hacked out the most offensive c-word in his vocabulary along with a sizeable amount of phlegm.

Bradley chuckled, crossing his arms over his chest and perched his hip on the kitchen counter. "No. Don't really do hot drinks at all."

"Really?" Mark's voice elevated. "Well, that is… Quite something. Why on earth not?"

"Don't see the point in hot drinks." Bradley shrugged. "Drinks are supposed to refresh you, not make you sweat."

"Ha. Yes. I see." Mark really didn't.

The kettle clicked off, boiled. Mark still planned to partake in a hot beverage regardless of this new information regarding his guest's abhorrence to such things. *'Don't change for anyone,'* his mother had often said to him. Whilst changing her name, her domicile, her friendship group and her love of cats all so she could marry his father.

"So, what is it you do drink, say of a morning time?" Mark winced, realising what he'd said could be misconstrued somewhat. Hovering the kettle over his cup, he peered back to Bradley. "Not that I expect you to be here in the morning. I mean, that would be absurd." He waved the kettle around to accentuate his point, unsure how it did exactly. "I'm sure you don't take that long and, well…"

Mark ran fingers along his now perspiring forehead, unsure if it came from the steam billowing up from the kettle or him digging himself a massive hole. "Not, of course, that I imply that you give a rush job… Do a rush job. *Provide* a rush job." Mark shut his eyes and sighed. "I mean, I have no idea how long or short your jobs tend to be."

He blew out some air from his pursed lips and caught the leer of amusement from Bradley. "Work! Your work. Obviously. Not that I consider myself your work. Ha! That would be something. Or rather nothing, as most would say." He paused, urgently praying to someone, anyone, that the threatening roof were to just cave in on him and Bradley at that very moment. "Perhaps that isn't something I should say and just leave it to the others, eh?"

"OJ."

"I beg your pardon?" Mark furrowed his brow.

"Orange juice." Bradley stood straighter, his flip-flops slapping against the hard flooring. "What I drink in the morning? Freshly squeezed is best but as long as it's cool, wet and juicy, I'm game."

The tea bag on Mark's spoon splatted onto the floor rather than into the intended swing bin. Mark was stunned and did nothing but imagine what else Mr Australia might like cool, wet and juicy as of an a.m. He could help with two of those, of course. Cool was something he unfortunately lacked. *Perhaps I could put it in the fridge for a bit?*

Bradley nodded down to the floor. "Didn't think you did the tea bagging thing?"

Mark raised an eyebrow. "We all need to do a little tea bagging on occasion." Mark widened his eyes, mischief within them, and took a sip of the tea. He grimaced—no milk—and stuck his tongue out in disgust. No doubt ruining the delivery of the double entendre he had been brave enough to utter in the first place.

Bradley chuckled and handed Mark a bottle of milk from the fridge.

"Well." Mark poured in the milk. "I'm afraid I don't have orange juice. Closest thing here is a bit of blackcurrant squash left over from when I had some children here. Which was rather a long time ago, so the stuff is probably off, to be honest. No idea how long concentrated fruit juices last? Still looks purple. If that is the colour it is meant to be, of course? But there"—Mark slurped another gulp of the tea—"it's all yours if you want some refreshment."

"Tempting. But water is fine, thanks, mate."

"Water? Seems rather plain. I had you down as a more adventurous kind of fellow." Mark didn't know why he'd added the jazz-hand kind of wave. But he had. He filled a glass of water and handed it over.

Bradley gulped down a fair amount, then wiped his lips with the back of his hand. Small droplets of water smeared the man's fair hair on his forearms. Mark had a sudden urge to lick it off. To be honest, it wasn't a *sudden* urge. He had been imagining running his tongue over tan Australian skin for quite some time now. About twelve hours, to be exact.

"Well." Bradley plonked the glass down on the counter surface. "I'd ask for a Hellyers and Red Bull but I'm just about to climb up on your roof, so I guess that can wait till after."

"Ha, yes, wise."

"So I'll just go take a look." Bradley clapped his hands together and pointed past Mark to the back door. "Can I get out through there?"

Mark twisted around. "You can. But the leak is from up in the loft. Which is upstairs."

Bradley smiled, all teeth and gums. The man could make dental adverts at the same time as his feet ads and put an end to the stripping gigs. *No, I did not just start thinking about Bradley stripping. I. Did. Not.*

"But the leak is due to missing tiles, right?" Bradley scooted past him to get to the back door. "Which you can only replace on the *outside* of the roof."

"Ah." Mark plonked his cup down on the side and followed Bradley out to the back garden.

Bradley hurried halfway up the garden, which was mainly a small patio of crazy paving complete with a metal patio set consisting of two chairs and a round table. The rest was mowed to lawn, accentuated by a few of the plant pots his mother dropped around from time to time. Bradley faced the house, one hand on his hip, the other shielding his eyes from the setting sun, to glance up at the roof.

"Right-o. I'll just nip up there and take a closer look."

"Nip up there?" Mark said with a hesitant shock. "I'm terribly sorry, but I don't have a ladder."

"No worries, mate." Bradley's flip-flops slapped against the paving stones. "I can climb up."

"You can what now?"

Bradley didn't reply. Instead, he swung effortlessly up using the drainpipe on the side of the house and climbed onto the sliding roof of the kitchen lean-to. He then jumped farther, gripping at the windowsill of the first-floor bathroom, both his flip-flopped feet landing on their tiptoes. Mark gasped, awful visions of insurance claims and death by negligence accusations flickering before his eyes. But Bradley leaned back and propelled himself to jump another rung up the house and onto the tiled roof. He crawled on his hands and feet to the top of the slant, swinging his legs either side and sat, straddling the tip.

Mark gaped, speechless. There were no words for his reaction to what he saw. His groin had taken care of that.

"Right," Bradley called down to him. "You need two new clay tiles on the top here. That's no worries, mate. I can get them from the nearest builders' merch. Easy fix. No probs."

"Okay." Mark hesitated "Thank you. That's…wonderful." He added the lamest word in history because he obviously felt he hadn't embarrassed himself enough this very day.

Bradley didn't seem all too perturbed by the ridiculousness of the reply and nodded, smiled and lifted himself elegantly up to stand on the roof top, feet either side of the point. He then proceeded to slide one foot over the slope to run—*in flip-flops!*—down the slant to the gutter scurrying along the edge of the roof and jumped down to the ground with a graceful bend of the knees. A true gymnastic-style finish. He might as well have added a bow. Mark would have applauded if he could have gotten his tongue off the floor.

"Right." Bradley brushed down his board shorts. "So I'll get some tiles tomorrow and do it after I close up Macy's. Work for you?"

Mark swallowed, loosening his dry mouth.

"Mark?"

"Yes? I mean, yes, that's more than okay with me. Thank you."

"No probs."

"How much do you charge?" Mark pulled himself together. The thought of monetary transaction could do that.

"Oh right, well, I'll get the tiles and give you the bill for those. But as for my time –" Bradley shrugged. "How about I just get a little bit of yours?"

Mark coughed. "My what?" *Oh God, the man heard me back at Macy's talking about offering my penis as monetary exchange!*

"Your time. Maybe even down the pub? Saw one at the end of your street. Looks nice."

"Oh." Mark nodded. "Well, that pub, I'm afraid, is full of young bods. No one in there over the age of twenty-one. Wouldn't be doing any good in there."

Bradley raised his eyebrows.

"Ah. Of course, you probably would fit right in. How old are you anyway?"

"Just turned twenty-one."

Mark choked on his gulp of tea.

"Right, yes, well. I'm afraid I'll just cramp your style."

Bradley laughed and slipped Mark's tea from his cupped hands. "Come on, Mark. You're certainly not past it yet." He winked, then jogged back through into the house. "Don't worry, I won't keep you out late. You'll no doubt want your beauty sleep. And I can't stay till morning. You've got no OJ for a start."

Chapter Four

Drinkiepoos

The problem with Marsby, or perhaps not so much a problem as in unique selling point, was that it boasted more pubs per square mile than any other town in old Blighty. Mark wasn't sure what that said about the residents of his home town, but it went some way to explaining why the population of almost seven-thousand people, courtesy of the last national census, always turned up late for work. It was also a rather circumspect question to ask as to why each of those remarkable public houses, ranging from the ever-popular chains to the independent family-run ale houses, were always rammed full of people. Regardless of the day and the season.

Much like this day. A Monday. Whilst it was technically the summer months in England, it still wasn't exactly holiday season. So the Moon & Stars, on the corner set-up at the end of Mark's road that was bursting full of patrons, both inside and milling outside on the doorstep chugging on their death sticks, was both orthodox if rather cumbersome.

Mark didn't get on with crowds. He didn't get on with being alone much, either. He preferred a happier medium where he could mingle amongst the living whilst sipping a pint of Kent's real ale offerings and not have to stand whilst doing so. Nor tut furiously when people knocked his elbow, sloshing his pint each time someone passed him to pick up the packet of pork scratchings or scampi fries that they had forgotten to purchase during their first round.

Sweat formed on Mark's forehead as he pushed through the ye olde-style wooden swinging door entrance that bore some resemblance to the taverns of the American Midwest, Still, he did have a rather dishy Australian to look at whilst standing amongst the brutes at the bar to sip on his pint of Bishop's Finger. But that also made his social anxiety rise as he scouted around at the young bloods. They were mostly late-teens, sharing their first outing to a bar without the parents in tow to limit their intake of sickly-sweet alcopops or anything mixed with the deathly Red Bull. There were a few in their twenties who still considered themselves young enough to drink on a Monday, even if they did have to get up for work the next day. School wasn't an issue. One could do that on a hangover, but work was relentless with a headache. Mark had made that discovery time and time again. *Yet here I am…not learning.*

Mark spotted a couple at the back. The male counterpart sipping on a pint of the good stuff had enough of a receding hairline to suggest he could be an early-balding thirties gent, but Mark was still the oldest one in there. He knew that for sure. And it brought out his inner waffle.

"You drink that stuff?" Mark asked over the background noise that drowned out any coherent conversation. "You don't drink tea, but you'll drink something that looks and smells like the contents of my grandfather's colostomy bag?" Mark hovered his pint at his lips. "He's dead now, poor sod." He glanced heavenwards. "Or rather not actually. My grandmother was quite a difficult bee to live with. Think he popped his clogs first just to get a moment's peace to read the broadsheets upstairs, until she came up to join him and chitchat about all the WI scandals he'd missed out on."

Bradley breathed out an amused laugh. Mark curbed his flapping lips by curling them around the rim of his pint glass.

"Uh." Bradley held up the glass of whisky mixed with Red Bull and took a sip. "Yeah. Can you ever ask a simple question?"

"Yes." Mark swallowed, the rich and fruity bitterness of real ale sliding down his throat to rest nicely in his gut. "So, what brings you to old Blighty anyway?" He stopped. Bit his tongue. Dug his teeth in to the point that it actually hurt so as not to continue with an over-the-top waffle. Simple question.

Bradley didn't answer straight away. He took his sweet time. Swirling his drink, taking a relaxed mouthful and swishing the liquid nitrogen around in his mouth. His eyes sparked.

"Oh, for goodness sake." Mark rammed a hand into his jeans pocket. "I mean it's not like we can compete with the Great Barrier Reef over here or, what's that thing in the middle? Pictures make it look like a huge ant hill?"

Bradley snorted. "Uluru?"

"Bless you."

Bradley shook his head. "I can't believe you just compared one of the seven wonders of the world to an ant hill."

"Like I say, I've only seen the pictures. And that was on a card of Top Trumps I was forced to play with the small child who drinks blackcurrant cordial like it's going out of fashion." Mark slurped his pint, the froth catching his stubble and clinging on.

Bradley ran a thumb along Mark's top lip, wiping the white stuff away. Mark hadn't intended on leaving it there, so why Bradley had to go all 'mother with spit on a tissue' on him felt somewhat rather abstruse.

"Was it ever in fashion?" Bradley asked, swiping his thumb on his board shorts.

"What?" Mark was losing the trail of the conversation. It wouldn't have been the first time. Certainly not in a pub where the clientele needed a note to get out of PE the next morning.

"Blackcurrant." Bradley took a slurp from his tumbler glass of preposterous concoction. "Was blackcurrant ever *in* fashion?"

"Wouldn't know. Tea is my beverage of choice."

Bradley smiled and pointed at the pint of ale Mark held. He arched one eyebrow and Mark stared at it trailing up Bradley's forehead as if it had an argument with its neighbour the other side. Mark could never achieve that look with his own eyebrows. It was both or none.

"What's that you're drinking then?"

Mark held up the pint to his face, acknowledging the question with a clear display of mime.

"I have the distinct feeling you would have ridiculed me had I come in here and asked for a pot of tea for one."

"You're right about that, mate."

Bradley swiftly moved his gaze from Mark and along the other patrons in the bar. Some of them glanced their way, nodding in brief greeting or recognition. Probably not for Mark. Even though he was relatively well-known in the small town, it wasn't so much amongst this type of crowd. All the smiles were aimed at Bradley.

The guy did stand out some. Not only because of the bright pink, practically lycra T-shirt he wore and the garish shorts, with pink Havaianas on his perfect feet, but because he was such a flawless specimen of male. A teensy-tiny spark of pride fired over Mark that it was him, here, drinking with this man. His smug-mode was soon replaced by the more familiar insecurities questioning why that was. It would be what this tween crowd would be wondering anyway. Perhaps they thought Mark had paid him. Perhaps they thought this was some first-time internet dating hook-up and Mark must have put a different profile picture on his page to have bagged a man such as the god of all that is male.

Mark wriggled in his shirt as the sweats started up again. Mark knew what he looked like. He knew the picture of the two of them standing there together would look vastly like Mark was batting way out of his league. Possibly in a different sport altogether. He ran a finger inside the collar of his shirt and dragged it away from his perspiring neck. What he would give to throw that pint of Bishop's Finger down his shirt right now just to alleviate some of the hot sweats. He chose not to, though. That would only add fuel to the fire of those around who considered him old and, therefore, senile.

"Work." Bradley peered back to Mark in front of him.

"Pardon?"

"You asked why I'm here." Bradley waved his drink. "In old Blighty," he added in a ridiculous mocking British accent.

Mark pointed a finger from around his pint glass. "That won't get you any friends around here, you know."

Bradley laughed. "Maybe not. But I've got my tea-making to fall back on, right?"

"Ha! I hope you have other talents." Mark instantly regretted every single word. Not just because the conversation could lead to things he really didn't want to be wondering about whilst he was already in a hot and bothered stupor, but also because it made him blush. Which was quite the travesty as he couldn't hide his reddening cheeks when standing directly under the spotlight that illuminated the bar area.

He had chosen the spot because being in dimmed lighting tended to make him look gaunt. So being under a direct light, whilst showing up every blemish and wrinkle, didn't accentuate his too-thin cheekbones. He had spent a lot of time looking at himself in mirrors under various lights in order to know which one suited him more. He wasn't vain. More…paranoid perhaps. *With good reason.*

Bradley chuckled. Not a small, light laugh paying lip service to a tickling statement, but an extra-long, deep and belly-full one that made his eyes brighten and twinkle in the spotlights. A knowing chuckle. One that said, *I've noticed your blush and I raise it a sassy brazen titter and await your imminent squirm as you now backtrack your words*. And whilst that could be rather a lot to give away in one simple chortle, Mark knew that was what Bradley was thinking. After all, Bradley had no doubt seen himself in the mirror once or twice.

"Like roof fixing." Mark glugged his ale. The glass was nearing the dregs and Mark was getting agitated about it, as that would mean he either had to make his excuses to leave or do the dreaded *would you like another drink* question, only to be turned down in a humiliating act he was all-too-familiar with. "And climbing. You seem to be rather good at climbing."

"Yeah." Bradley nodded. "Did a bit of rock and wall climbing back home." He downed the rest of his fizzy caffeinated whisky, slamming the glass on to the bar towel with a sunken pop. He glanced down at his feet and waggled those beautiful toes. "Tend not to usually do it in thongs, though."

"Yes," Mark replied. "I can see why that might not be recommended."

"'Cause it gets right up your arse." Bradley grinned.

Mark narrowed his eyes, confusion spreading across his gaunt cheekbones.

"You guys call those bumless knickers girls wear thongs, right?"

"We could do," Mark replied. "If you mean we as in the British nation. But me, I'm rather debilitated when it comes to female undergarments. I'm afraid the last knickers I witnessed were the M&S cotton briefs my mother wore." Mark took his final glug of beer, slapping it on the bar next to the tumbler, then shot an embarrassed glance Bradley's way. "She probably still does wear them."

He added quickly, "M&S do a fantastic range these days and she always takes the trip into Dover for the bigger stores. And I'm pretty certain the dementia hasn't set in too much that she forgets her underwear." He ran a hand along his forehead. "Wouldn't want you thinking my mother goes commando."

"Wasn't thinking about your mother at all." Bradley winked. "Until now, that is." He chuckled. "I guess, then, I'm more interested in whether you and your mum share that interest."

"M&S underwear?"

"Going commando."

Mark snorted. His hands perspired ferociously along with the rest of his body. He went to open his mouth and dispute the fact with something probably even more embarrassing along the lines of, *my underwear is firmly under lock and key,* which was why it was a good thing young Bradley stepped forward and whispered in his shell-like.

"'Cause I do."

Mark coughed. He didn't need to. His throat was amply clear. His sinuses were all in good working order considering it was no longer flu season and the hay fever pollen count was particularly low. He just had no other response. If he'd had a watch, he might have glanced at that too. But he didn't. He made a note to go and buy one.

Bradley leaned against the bar, his hands clutching each arm folded across his chest and a smile forming.

"Well," Mark finally said. "I guess that must make it easier."

"For what?" Bradley nodded to the bartender over Mark's shoulder.

"For the stripping," Mark replied in the most stoic and deadpan way he could. He couldn't be entirely sure he'd pulled it off, but he darn well had a good go at showing the man that he knew what he did for a living and he wasn't in the least bit bothered by it. He tried to clear his mind of thinking about it. Because that would lead to something a bit more in your face. Or in Bradley's face. *Snort.*

"True." Bradley waved a finger above the two glasses.

The barman nodded, taking the empties and setting off to go get another round. Amazing how Bradley did that so effortlessly without even worrying about the whole asking and rejection thing. Mark might have wanted to go home.

"But." Bradley stood straighter. "The ladies do like a tease. So you have to be covered at some point, right? Otherwise it's not really stripping as in walking on stage in your undies."

Mark had to think about that. *Really hard.* He did so by nodding in agreement and doing his best to not allow his gaze to involuntarily trail down the body standing in front of him. He was pretty sure he pulled it off. He usually did.

"You're thinking about my undies." Bradley smirked and waggled his finger.

"I most certainly am not," Mark protested, loud and clear. He adjusted his shirt collar once again and ran a hand through his mound of thick dark hair. It stuck due to the increased humidity and sweat from his fingertips. "Anyway, didn't you just tell me that you forgo underwear?"

"Ah, yes."

A full pint of ale and another tumbler of whisky-slash-Red Bull concoction slammed down in front of them both. The barman hung his forearms over the draft handles and waved his palm. After rooting around in his pocket, Bradley handed over a scrunched-up twenty. The barman held it up to the light, grimacing, then had to accept the currency was legit and scuttled off to ram it into a till.

"So you're thinking about me *minus* my undies." Bradley smirked. "Tut, tut, Mark. Thought you were a gentleman."

"Well, I am afraid that if you say underwear and stripping in the same conversation, my mind is going to start wondering down under." Mark lifted the pint. "That's down there." He pointed to Bradley's groin. "And not down where Uhura is."

"Uluru."

"That's what I said."

"No, you said the name of that chick who has a thing for Spock."

Mark shut his eyes, savouring the fruity hops to calm his sudden irritation. Then huffed. He would just have to address it. "She does *not* have a thing for Spock."

"Lemme guess." Bradley chuckled. "No one can replace Shatner as the main man?"

"Well, obviously." Mark shook his head. "But truth be known, I'm not that old." That statement didn't have that much clout in these surroundings.

"No?" Bradley widened his eyes. "How old exactly then? I mean, are we talking *Next Generation* or *Deep Space Nine*?"

"You know your *Star Trek*," Mark noted. "That could be considered terribly geeky, you know."

Bradley laughed. Then, leaning forward, he brushed his lips to Mark's ear. "Just don't tell anyone."

The hairs on Mark's arms stood on end and, considering he had rather long dark hair, he was glad he had a shirt on to cover them up, or the other bar patrons might think Mark had just put his finger in some electric socket. The hair irritated the cotton sleeves of his shirt and Mark wriggled to calm the little fellows down. He was glad it was just his hair that had reacted in such an upright fashion, because he wasn't ready to go into his bank of ugly thoughts to calm any other parts of him down. He'd had enough of thinking about his mother's underwear already.

"A stripper who appreciates *Star Trek.*" Mark cleared his throat. "That's quite an unusual combination."

"Not really. Actually use it a bit in my act."

"Your act?" Mark coughed. "You have an act? Isn't it just stand on stage and slowly peel your clothes off to *I'm Sexy and I Know It?*"

"Right, so you can't be that old. You know LMFAO."

"Of course." Mark agreed. "That I do. Down with the kids. Exactly. Good band." *Please don't ask, please don't ask, please don't ask.*

Bradley raised that one darn eyebrow. *Maybe the other one is just lazy?*

"What does it stand for?"

He bloody asked.

Mark glazed over, swishing the contents in his pint glass. "Well, if it were an abbreviation for people my age, it's got to be *Let Me Find An Orderly.*"

Bradley laughed, his pectoral muscles wobbling through his painted-on top. Even the man's chuckles sounded Australian. He made such a racket that the rest of the bar seemed to stop to glance over at them.

"All right, all right." Mark tutted.

"Sorry, mate. I was just, you know, *laughing my fucking arse off.*"

"Glad I can be of amusement to you. It is my life's work to be of joy to others."

"No." Bradley smiled. "LMFAO. Laughing. My. Fucking. Arse. Off." He shrugged. "That's what it means."

"I see," Mark lied. He didn't see. "Clever."

"So how old are you then?"

"Too old."

"For what exactly."

"To hear about how you dress as a Star Fleet captain then rip it all off."

"Actually." Bradley's eyes sparkled. "I come on dressed as a nerd. You know, anorak, hair slicked down, broken glasses, buck teeth, Thermos."

"Sounds delightfully sexy," Mark mocked.

"Wait for it." Bradley waggled a finger. "Told you, the ladies like a tease. So I do these clumsy things around the stage. Try to open my tea flask but it spills over my top, have to take it off, don't I? Then I try to pick up something from the floor, trousers rip. Oops, they gotta go."

"This sounds awfully like most of my days." Mark shrugged. "Except people tend to tell me to keep the blasted things on."

"I doubt that." Bradley winked. "Anyway, I'm sure you're catching the drift. My glasses snap, so they come off. I get thrown some water from the stage which sorts the hair. Then—"

"Please don't say you soil yourself in order for the underwear to come off." Mark grimaced, holding up a hand to stave off whatever was going to tumble out of Bradley's mouth next.

"No." Bradley cocked his head in contemplation. "Although, that might work better."

"Better than what?"

"Setting them alight."

Mark spat his drink back into the pint glass, the fizzing spraying up from the sides. All gazes darted to him and he had a sudden urge to tell them all to get back to their textbooks before he gave them detention. He didn't, though. He was too focused on imagining Bradley's boxers on fire. "You what?"

"It's all safe." Bradley waved his glass. "Pyrotechnics. Stuff they use in the movies."

"Right, well," Mark stuttered. "That definitely sounds like it's worth a watch."

"You can if you like."

Mark hesitated, which was rather surprising considering the first thought that entered his head. He managed to not ask if Bradley had meant at a private showing. *Now.*

"I'm performing this weekend. Load of hen parties. Drag queen comedy then me and a couple other strippers. Come along."

Mark shook his head. "Now that, there, is most certainly something I am far too old for."

Bradley downed the rest of his drink and slammed it on the bar top. He wiped a hand over his lips and narrowed his eyes. Folding his arms across his chest, he sized Mark up. "Come on, tell me. How old?"

"Oh, goodness." Mark finished off the rest of his pint. "Thirty-nine."

Bradley gawked at Mark. "No way!" He slapped a palm to his chest. "I had no idea. Shit. We better get you home, granddad."

Mark cocked his head. "LMFAO."

Bradley grinned. Then ordered another round.

Chapter Five

NSFW

"Bugger!"

Mark fell from the edge of his bed and thumped down onto his bedroom floor. Thank heavens it was carpeted. He had wanted to rip the thing up and replace it with the most designer of sparkling wood flooring—like a disco floor—but had run out of money after the bathroom debacle and so had stuck with the garish red and orange shag pile that had been there when he'd inherited the place. Ironic, really, it being called a shag pile. Every day it openly mocked him that the floor would forever be shagged, but Mark sadly lacked that verb in his own life.

He wasn't quite sure how he had fallen out of his bed. He hadn't done that in, well, never. Clutching his head that banged to a beat out of sync with his heart rate, he rather wished he could have a sip of Bradley's Red Bull to give him the wings to get him up off the floor.

The Australian Adonis had clearly not been deterred by Mark's revelation of his age and had managed to persuade him that all Mark had needed to recapture his youth was a decent night out on the town. *On a bloody Monday.* He and Bradley had continued to drink, crawling the pubs that stretched along the seafront, until last orders were called. Why Mark had chosen to partake in one of Bradley's sickening concoctions of the lethal death energy liquid mixed with the strongest fire whisky would forever remain one of those mysteries and regrets in Mark's life. He could only assume that Bradley had flashed his white smile and Mark had had one too many ales by that point.

Rolling onto his front, noticing how dirty the carpet was and how it unfathomably smelt of stale smoke, he attempted to lift himself up. He retched, releasing a sickly-sweet tasting glob of putrid bile into his mouth. Grimacing, he swallowed it back down. Why, he wasn't sure. It wouldn't have made a difference to the carpet. If there was ever a moment that Mark wished he lived with someone to make him his morning cuppa, this was that very time. But, alas, he lived alone. Which, on further reflection, was probably a good thing, considering the state he was in.

He shook his head—another mistake as the pounding just got louder—and contemplated calling in sick. He was, technically, sick. But then remembered he was supposed to be in charge of the office today and that wouldn't be his best move as far as management went. Nope, he would just have to get up and get on with it. *Keep calm and carry on.*

Grunting, he stood, wobbled a bit on his toes and placed the heels of his palms to his temples to rid it of the *Stomp* re-enactment that was going on within his frontal lobe. The shower made far too much noise with its electric whirring, but Mark couldn't forgo the daily wash, what with smelling like a brewery mixed with the contents of a neglected lunch box. So he made light work of showering, every movement that of a new born foal. *Why do hangovers mess with balance?* He groaned all the way through dressing, opting for a lightweight shirt minus the tie as he wouldn't remember how to knot the thing at this point anyway.

Every step down the stair case was like tackling Everest. He didn't bother to make himself a tea. He planned to demand a cuppa from the bloke who had caused all this mess of a Tuesday morning, so shoved his keys in his pocket and bolted out into the fresh air.

Arriving at Macy's shop front, Mark cursed. A couple of old dears walking their dogs frowned, but he didn't have his usual immediate apologetic response. *Blasted Bradley and his laissez-faire attitude to self-employment.* The shoppe was closed. Whipping out his mobile phone from his pocket, he immediately hit Dial. No answer. *The bastard.*

With a firm press of the red button, he wished that mobile phones came with the ability to slam them down on the receiver like the good old days. It was simply impossible to end an angry phone call on a mobile. He slid his thumb along the screen and opened up a new message. Composing one with angry thumbs, he tapped so hard he thought he might add another few cracks to the screen. The whoosh indicated that the text hadn't just sat there in his Outbox like so many others—mostly to his mother. He shoved the phone back into his pocket and headed to work.

"Morning, Yvonne."

Yvonne glanced up from her computer screen, nodding in response, disapproval already sweeping across her face. Mark ignored it and went straight through the office to the end kitchenette. Flipping on the kettle, he groaned. His usual mug, all washed up on the side of the draining board, did manage to lift his mood a tad. He was a simple man after all. Black lettering wound around a silhouette face of Lionel Richie asking *Hello? Is It Tea You're Looking For?* Not only was it a great play on words, but it was also quite right.

He sighed, searching through the cupboards for where the cleaners had hidden his tea bags this time. His own-bought Twinings were nowhere to be found, so with a firm huff he added one of the dangling triangular bags into his cup. The water trickling into the porcelain gave Mark renewed energy, like an early morning hug would have, until he noted there was no milk. *Bugger!*

Mark slammed the fridge door with such force that it didn't actually shut. *Go figure.* Such was his life. Mark was now fairly certain the world was against him. It always had been. *Breathe, count to ten.* Before he reached five, his phone buzzed in his pocket. Yvonne entered and plonked her own mug down on the surface next to his with no accompanying words other than a tap of her pointy nail to the emblem. It emulated her personality too. *The work logo.*

"Sadly no milk, Yvonne." Mark attempted a combined pleading and pressuring look that suggested that she might want to pop out to the shop to go get some

She hummed then opted for a green tea. Mark held in the huff and waved his phone away from his face, squinting to decipher the message.

"Cute puppy." Yvonne peered over his shoulder, masking a chuckle. Something Mark wasn't ever sure he'd witnessed before.

On his phone display, for all to see, was Bradley's face, a huge pout with dog ears, nose and a slurpy tongue waggling with a written message sprawled across the middle, *Pouty Puppy Pologises.*

Mark fumbled with it for a moment then, deciding on black tea, trudged over to his desk and lowered carefully to sit. No movement, so he composed his reply.

I can see now why you didn't open the shop. Is this what happens when you drink after a certain time of night? Paw thing.

He chuckled, then logged in. His phone buzzed a returning text and Mark went to offer his apologetic expression over at Yvonne. She hadn't moved from her screen, clearly getting her fix of the online gossip pages now the boss wasn't in.

I need to rest to fix your woof

Several little images bounced in after the message, none of which Mark could fathom the meaning of. The art of conversation lost to yellow faces and primates. He stuck to the use of words for his next reply.

Macy will pound your arse

Clicking into his emails, he swiped through the various correspondence from clients and the one massive essay from his boss providing all the rules and procedures for whilst he was away and reminding him that the work experience kid due in that morning was the son of a personal friend. Mark wasn't sure why he needed to be reminded that the child must be treated with the utmost respect. His phone vibrated on the desk surface.

She'd be barking up the wrong tree. I prefer hounds on my arse

A smile curved on Mark's lips. Shaking himself out, he gave himself a stern talking to. Bradley was Macy's cousin. Mark was not meant to be engaging in flirtatious exchanges of text messages with the expat. Mark was several years Bradley's senior. *Old enough to be his father.* Was he? Mark was too hungover to do the maths on that one, so decided to accept that he was. Besides, Bradley was an Adonis. And Mark was not. This would only end one way, and Mark was not setting himself up for that sort of nonsense at his age. He shouldn't have done it at any age, to be honest. But that wasn't a story to dwell upon. He had work to do.

Sliding his chair under his desk, he clicked his mouse and fired up the *Guardian* online, then went to stalk a few old school "friends" on Facebook, along with checking if anyone had responded to his question of how to make a pivot table from a bunch of data in Excel on the online forum chat. No one had. Either no one knew or everyone thought he already should.

His phone buzzed again and his gaze trailed over to the lit-up screen. He dragged it in front of him, trying not to draw attention to the fact he was still texting whilst at work.

Do you have a personal email?

Mark furrowed his brow. Why would Bradley want his email? He shrugged and thought it was possibly to show him some roof tiles. He whooshed off his Hotmail address.

Cool. I sent you an email. It's NSFW. Need opinion.

Mark stared at the message, focusing on the four-letter word that contained no vowels. *Text speak, right?* Mentally putting various vowels in between the consonants like he was on a game of bloody *Countdown*, he came up stumped. He threw his phone on his desktop and typed into his Hotmail account. One bold email from a *BradSum1998* sat unopened at the top of the list of the usual junk mail. Mark shut his eyes. *199-bloody-8.* He bit down the revelation that he would have been eighteen the moment Bradley popped out into this world. Mark had been a grown man when Bradley had been in nappies. Ironically, that had also been the year that Mark had left Marsby, middle finger in the air and flicking his hair over his shoulder like some diva and announcing he would never return to this small seaside town. *Insert yellow embarrassed face, perhaps?*

Sighing, he clicked open the email and his eyes widened to the size of saucers. Not his grandmother's china saucers, but more likely the ones that Costa now offered with their ultra-sized mugs of tea in order to stamp out the pot-for-one option. Bradley, phone in hand as he had snapped an image of himself in front of a mirror, filled Mark's computer screen. Which, yes, Mark found odd. Why would one need to photograph oneself if standing in front of one's own reflection? But what was far more of a conundrum was why Bradley stood there stark-bollock naked. His meat and two veg were out on display for all and sundry, the meat draping a little to the left as it hung down over his ball sac.

Mark had to query this closer, quite possibly gaping open-mouthed, and he wouldn't have been surprised if a little drool didn't dribble from his salivating lips. And he completely forgot why he had been sent this image in the first place, or for what purpose. Until Mark leaned in toward his screen. *Involuntarily.*

Bradley lacked any hair on his body at all. Mark had been certain when laying eyes on the man's bare torso yesterday that Bradley had most definitely had hair scattered along his chest. And down his washboard stomach, trailing into the elastic band of his low-hung shorts and into what Mark had envisaged…imagined, no, assumed, *yes assumed,* would have led to an ample amount of hair on his pubic region.

Mark edged in closer to the screen, hand hovering over the mouse, and with an *accidental* swipe of his forefinger zoomed in on the most intimate part of Bradley's anatomy. Not a single hair follicle resided on those juicy balls. They looked like two perfectly rounded eggs, thick and full and ready to hatch. With some sort of kinetic energy, Mark leaned forward, his own hair rising from the static, and squinted. Cocking his head to the side, he licked his lips. Bradley had done a fantastic job of lathering himself up with oil to acquire the perfect sheen over his tight, stubble-free skin.

"Mark!"

Mark jumped in his seat and wiped a thumb along the corner of his mouth. Yvonne stood behind him, her eyes as wide as dinner plates but not quite as oval as those of the young lad next to her.

"Ah, Yvonne," Mark spluttered, desperately attempting to minimise the picture. Delete would be an utter travesty at this point. But with all the commotion, he slipped and zoomed in with his mouse. Bradley's naked and illustrious cock and balls now filled the entire twenty-five inches of Mark's computer screen.

Yvonne covered her eyes, then wrapped her arm around the young lad next to her and shoved her hand over his. Mark clicked, clicked again, clicked once more then decided it would be better to just turn the damn screen off.

"Hello. Yes?" Mark twisted in his seat, clenching his hands together in his lap, and raised his eyebrows. *Nonchalance. Works every time.*

Yvonne cleared her throat. "This is Robert. The work experience boy."

"Don't be silly." Mark waved a hand up at the boy. "He's barely out of nappies. Sure you've got the right kid?"

"I'm eighteen." The lad shuffled on his feet.

"Ah. Of course you are. Sorry, you get to my age and everyone looks young. When policeman and teachers look younger than you do, you know you've hit the downhill slide." Mark stood and held out a hand. "Welcome."

Robert took the hand and shook. Yvonne glared at Mark before stamping off to her place behind the reception desk. Mark sat, swiping his sweating palms down his legs.

"Right, well, first things first." Mark's phone buzzed and he trailed his gaze to the screen.

Well?

Switching the incriminating phone off, he decided a proper cup of tea would be golden right about now. With milk.

"Be a dear." Mark fished out a five-pound note from his pocket and handed it over to Robert, who stood there with a cross between amusement and disgust written over his face. "Run over to the shop and get some milk. Half a pint'll do. Green top. None of that red top rubbish. Blue top if they don't have the green. Then I'll get your desk sorted."

Mark breathed a sigh of relief as Robert sauntered out of the office. Rubbing a palm over his forehead, he slumped back in his seat that fell to the lowest rung. He left it there and rued the day he had ever met the Australian, who in twenty-four hours had wreaked havoc on Mark's normally mundane existence.

Why on earth would you send that to me AT WORK?

He composed the text with angry thumbs and whooshed it off.

Told you it wasn't safe for work. NSFW. Not.Safe.For.Work. Please don't tell me you opened that at the office?

Yes I bloody did. In front of a work experience kid.

The returning dozen or so laughing faces were all the conversation required.

Must remember to speak in sentences with you, Granddad. See you tonight.

Chapter Six

Like Riding a Bike

Mark kept his head down for the rest of the working day. Setting young Robert a few laborious and futile tasks such as stuffing envelopes and researching the company's competition bought Mark the time to get over his utter embarrassment and attempted to make him appear more of a professional. Mark rarely knew what he was meant to be doing himself most days, let alone tasking a new kid.

There had been no further texts, picture or otherwise, from Bradley and Mark found himself both relieved and disappointed in equal measures. He'd kept refreshing his emails, just in case another urgent message would fly through, but, alas, he received only the usual junk. His phone, which he kept at a convenient thumb's-length away, only displayed the photograph of the sun setting over the white cliffs of Dover that Mark had taken some years back.

So as the work day approached its bitter end, Mark had a slight spring to his step. This evening he would have a visitor. Anticipation rushed over him as he paced the pavement beside the pebble beach, much like the onslaught of early evening joggers from the Marsby Running Club who clearly had far too much energy for a Tuesday. Stupid thoughts kept poking at his mind, like wondering if Bradley might offer to show him the 4D version of his email. He rather hoped not. Mark didn't much fancy staring and drooling whilst Bradley was present to witness it. The image of Bradley's slick, firm and hairless body hadn't been one Mark could shake all day. He needed that image gone. Or at least a few moments alone with it.

Realising he should probably get a ladder if Bradley was to climb his roof again, as the last thing Mark needed was an insurance claim indicating that he allowed workmen to scale his house in a thong—*thongs!*—he popped next door to borrow the lovely Mr Cooper's stepladder. Mr Cooper didn't cause a fuss—he rarely did—and hardly left his house. He was a decent bloke, didn't get involved in any of the neighbourhood complaints and kept himself to himself. The perfect neighbour. On second reflections, wasn't that what people usually said about their neighbours when the news crew turned up to inform them that the police had uncovered several dead bodies under next door's patio? Mr Cooper did like to do a heck of a lot of gardening. So Mark carted the ladder through to his back garden and made a note to not cause himself any undue attention. *Like having an Australian hunk free-climb my house!*

His rickety shed at the end of his garden hadn't been opened in years either, but he fought his fear of spiders to check if there was anything within that might aid Bradley's roof-fixing mission. After two glances, he realised he had no idea what one would use to fix a roof, nor if said implement would reside in a shed. Plus he was fairly certain he hadn't ever bought such an apparatus, device and implement for such endeavours, anyway. Leaving the shed door open, he made his way back into the house and popped the kettle on. Not long into his after-work ritual of tea and a spot of local news on the telly, the doorbell rang.

Behind the front door, Bradley creased up laughing. It wasn't a casual laugh, either. Mark could tell the bloke had been having trouble keeping that snigger under wraps for the best part of the day. With setting eyes on Mark, Bradley was set free to erupt into a fit of childish giggles. Mark folded his arms and waited.

Sucking in a breath, Bradley at least attempted to regain some composure. But one look at Mark and the Aussie belted out a belly-laugh that reminded Mark of that old-style Drunken Sailor machine that used to be at the pier penny arcade.

Bradley swiped his eyes, tears trickling down his cheeks, and on clutching his stomach, the thin material of his RipCurl T-shirt inched up, revealing the smooth sheen of his washboard abdomen.

"Quite finished?" Mark tutted.

Bradley nodded. Then burst out laughing again.

"Oh, for goodness' sake." Mark slapped Bradley on the back of his arm. "Shut up. My neighbours'll complain about the noise pollution. And one of them is a serial killer, FYI."

"You know that abbreviation, then?" Bradley's smile even *looked* like it hurt his jaw.

"I am also aware of F, O and D," Mark deadpanned.

"That won't get your roof sorted." Bradley arched one delightful eyebrow. And Mark gave in to it and

Bradley's ability to save him two hundred *paaand* by ushering him into the hallway.

"Did you…" Bradley started up with the silent giggling again. "Did you really show some kid my picture?"

"Well, no." Mark flapped a hand. "I didn't *show* him, per se. I hadn't realised he was behind me whilst I opened your delightful correspondence that then zoomed in on your uncovered manhood."

Bradley snorted and Mark eyed him suspiciously. Not just because the man was like a giggling teenager, but mostly because of his ill-fitting attire. Ill-fitting as in not appropriate for manual labour and not that it didn't accentuate all Bradley's assets.

"Are you seriously going to scale a roof dressed like that?"

Bradley held his hands out in display, glancing down at his Lycra T-shirt, and pink running shorts that barely covered his arse cheeks. "What's wrong with it?"

"Shouldn't you be covered up more, in case of accidents? And steel-toe-capped shoes or something like that?" At least Bradley wasn't in flip-flops, but his well-worn mesh trainers didn't seem as though they would offer that much protection.

"It's two tiles, Mark. It'll take me ten minutes. No need to dress up for that." Bradley leaned in closer, lowering his voice to a quiver-making drawl. "Unless you're keen for a man in steel-toe-cap boots? I did hear your rave five-star review of the last dude you had up in your loft."

Mark's cheeks tinged, so he flapped his hand, ushering Bradley in again. "Are you coming in? If you stand there any longer Mrs Warley and Ms Richardson will have to start up their campaign again about how all the local jobs have been stolen by the immigrants."

Bradley arched an eyebrow.

"Which is absolutely fine with me, by the way," Mark stuttered on. "If us Brits can't be bothered, then why not have others take on the tasks? You're all cheaper for a start."

"I'm doing this for free."

"There you go. Case in point."

Bradley laughed. And still just hovered on his doorstep.

"You're letting all the cold air in." Mark could almost hear that in his mother's voice.

"You got a back entrance I can use?" Bradley asked, once his laughter had subdued.

"I beg your pardon?"

Bradley waggled a finger. "Tut, tut, Mark. You've got a right dirty mind, old man."

"Less of the old, please. I do not need to be constantly reminded. My mirrors do that for the both of us."

"Your mirrors need smashing."

"To add yet another few years' bad luck? I'd rather just allow the image."

Bradley shook his head, his features softening from the cheeky chappy he'd been before. He sighed before starting up again. "I got some things to bring around the back. Rather not traipse it through your antique house. So if you got an alley, I can go that way?"

"Ah, right, of course. I'll unlock the gate for you. Just to the right of the house. And fuck you about the *antique* comment."

Bradley chuckled.

Mark ran out to the back, fiddled with the rusty lock on his gate under the pretence that he hadn't lost the key some years back and had broken the thing to ensure access, then ushered Bradley in. Bradley plonked his tool box on the floor, rubbed his hands together and squinted up at the house.

"I got you a ladder." Mark waved to the tiny stepladder resting up against the back wall.

Bradley bit his bottom lip, curtailing yet another laugh. "Not sure that'll get me far, but cheers."

"I see you have your own tools, but feel free to have a rummage in the shed for anything that might be of use." Mark waved a hand. "Not sure there will be, though. DIY really isn't my forte."

"Everyone should learn how to do it themselves, mate." Bradley winked, then ambled up to the shed.

Bradley poking his head through made his backside stick out of the door frame. Mark cocked his head, copping a load of those pink-cotton-covered buttocks, the material so thin that Mark could tell Bradley had forgone wearing anything underneath. It was just the criss-cross pattern of the white mesh inside that was visible through the pink. Slapping a hand either side of the door frame, Bradley leaned farther in and his calf muscles flexed, bulging from his hairless legs that looked delightful enough to lick. Mark had an abundance of hair, everywhere, and had never really been a fan of the swimmer look, but right then, his tongue tingled to taste flesh with no fluff.

"You ride, Mark?"

Mark shook himself out. "What? *Pardon*?"

Bradley peered back out and chuckled. "Bikes?" He nudged a thumb into the shed "There's a bike in there. Do you ride it?"

"Oh." Mark blew out a puff of air. "No, not really. That bike's rather old. Could not tell you the last time I rode that thing." He could, but it wasn't a particularly pleasing story, so he didn't bother.

"Looks in pretty good nick." Bradley rejoined Mark at the front of the house. "I hired one from the place down the seafront. After I fix your roof, we'll go for a ride."

Bradley didn't wait for any type of response, affirmative or negative, and set up the stepladder against the back wall. It hadn't been much of a question anyway, more of a statement, and Mark was once again astounded by the confidence in the young man. No fear at all. Of rejection or heights, it would seem.

"Um," Mark stuttered, watching Bradley scale his house, holding his tool box and the tiles. "I'm not sure about the bike ride."

"What you not sure of?" Bradley knelt on the roof, his back to Mark. "We'll just cycle to the next town, have a beer, cycle back."

"So now you want me to drink and ride?"

"One beer, Mark."

Mark wiped his brow, squinting up at the roof. The scraping and clanging sounded like the noises one would expect.

"I'm sure they'll serve tea," Bradley called down. "And I promise not to laugh if you order it."

"That's very cordial of you." Mark folded his arms.

Bradley chuckled and continued with his rooftop task. Mark, undecided whether to leave the man to it or stand there as some safety net should Bradley slip and fall, shuffled on the spot. Not that Mark fancied his chances at catching the bloke. He couldn't even catch a cold to get him out of work for a few days.

"So was it Riker or Wesley you were keen on?" Bradley's voice drifted down.

"Excuse me?"

"I worked out from your age that you must have been a *Next Generation*er. Probably teens, right? So you must have watched it for the tight onesie uniforms." Bradley peered down at Mark. "So, which one? The smouldering number one, or the young handsome genius?"

"Why couldn't it have been Captain Picard? Bald guys can be extremely sexy, especially when a figure of authority."

"So, you have a thing for hairless men? Good to know." Bradley winked. "And, I dunno, mate, I prefer something to tug, y'know?"

Mark snorted, drifting a hand through his thick hair. "Why did you shave all your hair off, anyway? And why couldn't you have sent that to friends back home? Surely they would be better for opinions on that sort of thing?"

"Time difference, mate. You were online. And I got told I needed it all off for the stripping job this Saturday. The new place wants us all streamlined."

"Streamlined?" Mark echoed, elongating the word.

"You know, *smooth*."

"Well, that you are."

Bradley chuckled. "So, come on, out with it. Riker or Wesley?"

Mark sighed. "I have to admit that when I first started watching, Riker did exude a certain charm, and I will never understand why he and Dianna never lasted."

Bradley laughed, standing on the roof and wiping his hands down his shorts. "That's all fixed for ya, mate." With that, he skidded down the slants on his backside, the tool box in his lap and jumped down to ground level.

Mark stood mouth agape as Bradley popped up in front of him.

"Won't hold forever—you'll need to replace the whole thing. But at least that'll keep you dry whilst you snuggle on the sofa, right?"

Mark narrowed his eyes. "Did you hear the whole thing?"

"Yep." Bradley tapped Mark's shoulder, then picked up his tool box. "I'll go run this back home, grab my bike, and we'll go for a ride. You might want to change, though." Bradley waved his free hand at Mark's work attire. "Cycling in shirt and trousers can't be good. See you in a sec."

Mark uttered a noise from his throat, but nothing that Bradley could hear nor decipher as he sped down his alleyway and out of view. *Why the blasted hell did I open that damn shed?*

* * * *

A few minutes later, Bradley turned up at Mark's on his mountain bike, looking every inch a man who cycled the Tour De France, whereas Mark had had to dig really deep in his drawers to find something that would pass for work-out gear. He'd settled on a pair of jogging bottoms that still bore a few splodges of paint from the bathroom debacle, and an old university sweatshirt. His bike also hadn't seen the light of day in a fair few years and was as rusty as Mark was at riding it.

Bradley bit his bottom lip. "Nice trackie-dacks. Last one to the pub buys the first round."

"*First* round? I thought we were just having the—" Mark stopped talking for two reasons. One, Bradley had cycled off and therefore wouldn't have heard him anyway, and two, Bradley had cycled off standing from the bicycle seat and his pert arse cheeks waggled in the air with those floaty shorts fluttering in the breeze.

"Going for a ride, Mark?" Mr Cooper dumped a black bin bag at the edge of his front garden.

Mark stared at the bag, then up at Mr Cooper's friendly smile. Wiping his hands down his dirty jeans, Mr Cooper raised his eyebrows at the continued silence and Mark had never ridden away so fast. Because he didn't want to get the first round in, that was all.

Reaching the path along the beach, Mark cycled behind, with Bradley out front. Mark didn't have a bicycle helmet, and the sea breeze wafted his hair into his face, destroying the delightful view up ahead. But he pounded on, passing the derelict fishing boat that the kids used as a playground, the huts selling pink rock and cheap flip-flops and past the sandy area where the old folk scouted for cockles and winkles. He started to relax and enjoy it. He hadn't done this in a really long time, and considering he lived in such an idyllic area, he couldn't fathom why. Since returning to his seaside home town, Mark had closed himself off to all this.

Bradley waved his arm ahead in some circling motion, which Mark took to mean he was going to be taking the turn that would have him leaving the beachside to cycle the enclosed cliffside route instead. Mark was a little wary of that. Whilst he hadn't ventured along the footpath that led along the sheer chalk cliff edge into the next village for some time, he doubted global warming erosion would have reduced the lethal three-hundred-and-fifty-feet fall into the English Channel. The view was breathtaking enough as it was.

The footpath wasn't designed for cycling, and whilst Bradley might have been a daredevil in off-road mountain biking, Mark was not. The cobbled cliff edge made his rusty bike shake and Mark's heart rate elevated to newfound levels. The only thing keeping him going was the thought of the tea shop that he knew resided along the track. Sod Bradley and his search for the pub. This was a quaint seaside town where tea shops were as plentiful as tatty gift shops and sticks of rainbow rock. He could almost taste the tea through the scent of the sea air and the seagull squawks. He found his legs pumping harder—he even attempted standing-up cycling to catch up to Bradley. He'd have delight in whizzing past and showing him what skinny legs could achieve. But then his foot slipped off the pedal, followed by a clanking of the chain being ripped from the spokes and the bike waggled to one side, smashing into the ridiculously flimsy wired fencing.

"Bugger!" Mark wiped his forehead, glancing up ahead where Bradley was now a mere dot on the horizon. Whilst it had been easy enough to remember how to *ride* a bike, fixing a chain wasn't going to come so easy. Nor did Mark really want to have to get his hands oily. Plus the flimsy fence wouldn't even hold the damn bike up, and the cliffside footpath was void of anything else that Mark could use to rest the bike up against. So he jumped off, huffed and kicked the tyre.

"You all right, mate?" Bradley's tyres skidded on the chalk surface, spitting up the grit onto Mark's black trousers.

"Could you hold the bike? I need to fix the chain."

Bradley straddled his bike and held Mark's handlebars. Mark crouched, grimacing as he curled his fingers around the oily chain and attempted to lock it back into the spokes. A gust of wind blew from the left, crashing the sea waves against the rocks below and reminding Mark of how close he was to certain death, and also ruffling his wild and carefree hair. Mark shook his head, spluttering out the locks that had somehow gotten into his mouth, and swiped the fringe from his eyes.

"That's some hair." Bradley smirked.

"Thanks." Chain now reattached, Mark stood and set one foot on the pedal. "I grew it all myself."

Bradley laughed, swiping a hand through his blond streaks. "Mine doesn't grow out. Not in any style anyway."

Mark climbed on the bike. "This isn't a chosen style, if that's what you think? This is what happens when I can't be bothered to go the barber's for a few weeks. It grows faster than mould on economy sliced bread."

"Lucky you." Bradley smiled. "I'll bet that hair feels great to grip between your fingers."

Mark held Bradley's brash gaze, then cocked his head and contemplated the meaning behind the statement. Eventually, Bradley laughed. So Mark, realising he was the butt of some joke, shoved his foot down on the pedal to cycle off. Not more than a few seconds later, Bradley raced past him, his rounded arse bopping from side to side over the seat. *Forget it, Mark, he's doing it on purpose, he's a tease. He said as much.*

"Come on, Mark," Bradley called over his shoulder. "First one there gets the round in, so if you want tea, you gotta beat me!"

He's also an arsehole.

* * * *

Two pints of beer plonked down on the wooden bench in front of Mark. Bradley grinned, slipped into the picnic table's opposite seat and downed a quarter of his pint. Mark sighed. Not only had he not beaten Bradley, but both tea shops that resided on the clifftop walk had closed for the evening, leaving the pub-restaurant at the end the only option after all. It was a pretty decent place, at least. Set up against the cliff edge, it boasted a decent fencing around its beer garden, which was a good thing as otherwise the kids' play area might cost quite a bit in public liability insurance.

Mark gazed out at the view. The sun set into the blue of the English Channel and the ferries docked in Dover port up ahead. Rather quaint, rather English and rather tranquil, as Mark suspected not many people went for an early evening pint on a Tuesday. He'd all but forgotten how picturesque his home town could be. It was as though his eyes had been opened to the beauty.

"Perfect."

Mark whipped his head forward. Bradley smiled, then drifted his gaze out to sea.

"Yes." Mark breathed it all in. "It is rather beautiful. I'd forgotten."

"You don't come out here much then?"

"Not anymore. I guess when you live atop somewhere, you stop seeing it."

Bradley took a gulp of beer and nodded, wiping the froth from his top lip.

"Must be like that for you in Sydney?" Mark slurped from his glass, the beer actually a welcome relief.

"Yeah. I guess." Bradley shrugged. "It's a cool place. Has its beauty, I suppose. The beaches. Good surf. Good nightlife."

"Why did you leave?"

"I like to travel. See the world. Hate being stuck in one place. So I've done a few outback treks, rainforest stays. Testing my limits."

So the bloke's a flighty one. Good to know.

"Macy said you're into extreme sports and survival. What brought you to England? Here of all places." Mark waved his hand at the idyllic, yet still, surroundings. "It's quite possibly the dullest place on Earth. Most you'll need to survive against here are the pressures of Brexit."

Bradley laughed, his eyes shining, and gripped his pint. "I needed out of my last place, y'know? I'd been full-on for a while, travelling, job after job since I left school at sixteen." He hung his head. "I was told I'd find something in my last stop. But, well, I didn't."

"Told?"

Bradley shrugged, sipping from his pint glass and his cheeks tinged. *Interesting.*

"Where was your last stop?"

"London. Stayed with my gran for a bit."

"And what on earth were you told you'd find in the big smoke?" Perhaps there was a little bias in Mark's scoffed-out query. London didn't hold that many a good memory for him. He'd run from it, not to it. Okay, so he'd run to it first, then swivelled around and come back home, tail between his legs.

Bradley's chest rose. "Something." He shrugged. "I was mistaken. So after another reading, my gran suggested I head out this way, to meet my cousin. Figured I'd come see what this place has to offer and still keep the occasional stripping gig in London."

"Reading?"

"Yeah. Like, fortune? Gran kinda does it too."

"Like, crystal ball, palm reading, tarot card nonsense?" He should have kept the last word out of that question as, on witnessing the shrinking shoulders of the man before him, Mark had a stab of remorse at his mockery. Bradley looked much better being broad than being hunched.

"Gran's into tasseography. But I prefer the astrology method. Makes more sense that it's written in the stars, y'know?"

Mark didn't bother asking what the stuffing of dead animals had to do with reading fortune and instead stuck to the easier question. "That what is?"

"What's coming to you." Bradley shook his head. "Your turn to laugh at me, now."

Mark didn't laugh. Instead, he stared into Bradley's blue-green eyes as if he was seeing him for the first time, and was oddly fascinated by the man. So young, so confident, so brazen, yet there was something there. Something that maybe Bradley was running from. *Or to?*

"You believe in that stuff?"

"Yeah. A little. I believe the world gives you what you want when you really need it. Maybe not right away, but eventually. All you need to do is ask and trust the stars know what they're doing. And to not think too much about what's thrown at you."

"That's..."

"Stupid. Juvenile. I know, I've been told." Bradley knocked back the rest of his beer.

"No, not stupid." Mark waved his own glass, before attempting to follow suit and down the lot. He didn't get far and had to hold in the belch from the gassy contents. "Nor so much juvenile. A touch optimistic, perhaps."

"Yeah. People tell me that. But what's the alternative?"

"The alternative to what?"

"Fate. If you don't believe that you have a destiny, a plan, a reason to be here and a matched lover in wait, then, well, life's a bit scary otherwise."

Mark pondered all that for a moment whilst gazing past Bradley at the squawking gulls circling overhead.

"So why not experience all the world has to offer you?" Bradley continued, his blue eyes sparking so the green flecks danced within. "Ride the waves, jump the cliffs, travel the land. If being static hasn't brought you your fortune, then you need to go out there, search for the signs and find it."

"Huh. Interesting." Mark had been that optimistic too once. "Trouble is, when you get to my age, things like money and responsibility prevent all that."

"Only if you let it. That's putting your fate in the hands of the economists. You need to ask the stars, or the leaves, what your next move should be. As otherwise, you're ignoring fate. And that's a pretty sad existence, if you ask me."

"But you need money to travel."

"You can earn money wherever you travel."

"And a roof over your head?"

Bradley arched that impressive eyebrow. "You should know all about how a roof doesn't last forever."

Mark couldn't think of a single response. None that Bradley would want to hear anyway. It'd only dull the man's sanguine outlook.

"Better drink up, Mark." Bradley pointed to Mark's near-full pint. "Don't wanna be riding back in the dark. The stars can lead, but not light up a clifftop path."

In one, possibly two gulps, Mark finished his drink and stood. He allowed Bradley to go first, simply because he was faster and not because Mark enjoyed the view from behind. *Honest*. Bradley waved him off and within a few minutes he was back on the coastal path and riding with his hands behind his back and not on the handlebars. Smug bastard. There was no way Mark would be attempting that.

A short way in and Mark's foot slipped from the pedal, a sharp clunk and rattle indicating the chain had cycled its last round. Mark feared for his life as his bike once again threw him toward the minimal fencing. *Is this what is written in the stars for me? Death by cliff edge?* The bike chain rattled against the wheel, dangling from having been snapped in two, and caught in the spokes, sending the tyres skidding in the chalk and Mark crashing to the ground in a heap.

"Don't have much luck you, do you, mate?" Bradley screeched to a halt in front, then looped around and held out a hand.

"Understatement." Mark took the offered hand and Bradley yanked him up.

Hands on hips, Mark inspected the bike. Broken. Unfixable. Even *he* knew that.

"How far is it back to yours?"

Mark sighed. "Three, possibly four miles."

Bradley nodded and slapped a foot on his pedal.

"You're going to leave me here to walk?" Mark's voice elevated.

Bradley tapped the bike frame. "No. You're gonna park your arse on that and I'll ride us both home."

"I really hope you are kidding."

Bradley shook his head and tapped the frame again.

"Absolutely not." Mark folded his arms in finality.

"Mark, don't be a wuss. You can't walk four miles in the dark next to a bloody cliff. And I'm not leaving you here. Leave the bike and jump the fuck on."

Mark huffed, running a hand across his furrowed brow. This, he knew, was not a good idea. But what other options did he have?

"I've never ridden seatie before." Mark stepped up to Bradley's bike.

"Bet you say that to all the boys." Bradley clucked his tongue with a wink.

Mark chose to ignore that and lifted onto Bradley's bike frame. The bike wobbled. Even Mark's waif-like physique couldn't prevent it, but Bradley stamped his feet onto the ground and steadied it. Wrapping his fingers around the pole, Mark gripped on for dear life. With a chuckle, Bradley pushed down on the pedal and the bike swerved toward the cliff edge.

"Oh, fuck balls!" Mark saw his crappy life flash before his eyes. *I should never have come back to Marsby!*

"Hold on." Bradley managed to stabilise the bike, and with a firm push down on the pedals, soared along the cliff edge.

Bradley's knees hit Mark's on each upward cycle, and Mark shuffled up toward the handlebars, his grip on the pole making his knuckles turn as white as the cliffs of Dover. Picking up the pace, Bradley pumped faster and Mark's hair blew out of control.

"Take it back about the hair, mate." Bradley tried to peer around Mark. "You might have to tell me if there's something coming."

"Just keep going. Quickly, please."

"Do you say that to all the boys, too?"

Mark tightened his grip and closed his eyes as Bradley regained momentum and lifted up to pedal, his arse no doubt waving in the air for someone else to cop an eyeful. Relaxing a little and trusting that Bradley might know what he was doing—*or would that be like trusting the stars*—he opened his eyes.

"Bugger!" Mark pointed up ahead. "Careful. Gulls!"

"What?" Bradley swung the handlebars to the left, skidding the bike up the grassy bank and the tyres slid in the dry mud, sending them both toppling to the ground. Mark landed on his back, the bike and one of Bradley's legs digging into his stomach, and Bradley collapsed alongside.

Mark grunted. Bradley chuckled, his face a mere breath away from Mark's. Mark could smell the fermented lager.

"Bradley," Mark squeezed out of his crushed larynx.

"We're this close now, Mark. Call me Brad."

"I can't."

"Because I'm crushing you?"

"Because Bradley is better."

Bradley breathed out a smile. He made no effort to move and was close enough that Mark could taste the fermented beer on each exhalation. At least Bradley *could* exhale. Mark was having a teensy bit of trouble at that.

"Mark?"

"Yes?"

"Remember that stuff I said back at the pub? About my gran?"

Mark nodded as much as he could with a bike and Bradley's bulk on top of him, which wasn't much at all. But Bradley seemed to take that as encouragement enough to continue his idle chitchat and suffocation methods.

"Do you want to know what she told me? What my leaves said?"

"Bradley, we might have to discuss life's greater purpose some other time? Over tea, perhaps? No offence, I'm sure it's important to you, but I'm in danger of suffocating here."

"Sorry, mate." Bradley hefted up from the ground, then grabbed the bike's handles and yanked it up.

Coughing, Mark scrambled up and wiped down his joggers. He ruffled out his hair that he was sure contained many a dirt, rock and whatever else resides on a clifftop edge that wouldn't be taken for a highlight or two. When he glanced up, Bradley smiled.

"What?"

"Nothing. Just…" Bradley shook his head then leaned over the bike and pressed his lips to Mark's.

Mark was more than a little stunned. He just stood there. Not reacting, not moving, not understanding. Bradley pulled back, holding the bike, and shrugged, a slight tinge to his fresh-faced cheeks.

"What the hell was that?" It came out higher-pitched than Mark had intended.

"They call it a kiss these days." Bradley smiled.

"Really?" The rest of Mark's vocabulary got stuck in his throat. So without the use of words, he twisted on his heel and stormed away along the footpath.

"Mark?"

Mark didn't stop. He stomped harder, tripping over a few stray rocks, but levelled out and shot a look of disdain over his shoulder. "Contrary to popular belief, Bradley Summers, I am not the only gay in the village for your Summers' fling!"

Chapter Seven

Hairtred

Having walked the remainder of the way home, Mark now stared at his reflection in the bathroom mirror, his electric toothbrush buzzing across his teeth so furiously he might just spit blood as well as feathers. He sighed, the foamy mint splattering against the mirror and making it look like a decorator's radio. He wiped it off, smearing white smudges across the glass and hampering the view. It needn't matter. He hated what he saw anyway.

Bradley hadn't followed him. Hadn't called him. Hadn't sent any messages, face-filled or otherwise. And Mark couldn't blame him. Bradley most certainly wasn't the sort of bloke who would rush after a middle-aged man having a middle-aged crisis. He probably had a wealth of offers from other men, women or gender non-specific. He'd probably done a couple swipes on his phone and called one up, cycling to the hook-up point in those tiny pink shorts.

Mark spared no more thoughts about the shorts, nor the man, and slumped into an early grave. Well, it was his bed, but it might as well have been his final resting place.

The next morning brought no more messages, and with one look into his smudged mirror, he faced the inevitable. He needed a haircut. He always hated Wednesdays, too. Throwing open his wardrobe, he rummaged around for something to lift his dreary mood and chose a shirt that he hadn't worn a zillion times before—a nice floral-patterned one that Damian had bought for him one birthday. *'Can't be miserable wearing a top that resembles a countryside meadow on a bright summer's morning.'* That was what Damian had insisted anyhow. Mark wasn't too sure he should be following his flouncy theatrical friend's fashion advice, but he slipped his arms into it anyway and checked himself in the mirror. It would have to do.

Slipping his phone into his back pocket and trying not to be disappointed that Bradley had made no effort to check Mark had arrived home safe, he trundled down the stairs. Perhaps Australia wasn't aware of the need for three rings? Or more likely, Mark had made it abundantly clear that he was not in the market for friends with a care package. Head down, he stepped out of his house and slammed his door shut.

"Morning, Mark."

Mark, startled, jumped nearly three feet away from Mr Cooper leering over the separating bush. "Morning. Lovely day."

"It is, isn't it?" Mr Cooper glanced up to the sky. "Might I trouble you for the stepladder back? I'll be needing that today to get up into my loft."

"Of course. The gate is open, help yourself." *Am I an accomplice to murder by being so agreeable? Better than being murdered,* he supposed, and hurried off on the walk to work.

He upped the pace on reaching Macy's Tea Shoppe but he couldn't prevent the flicker of his gaze through the window. It was open. Bradley, behind the counter, was serving tea to an elderly couple, their dog waggling its tail beside them. Bradley knelt down, ruffled the Labradoodle's ears and offered a bowl of water. He appeared in rather a chipper mood. *Last night's hook-up must have been a good one.* Peering over the dog's head, Bradley locked onto Mark's gaze through the glass. Mark's stomach lurched into his throat, so he bundled across the road and right into the tourist train tooting its horn heading toward the seafront.

"Watch out, Mark!" Charlie, the driver, had attended Mark's old grammar school in Dover. They'd both been top of the class at one point. Clearly it had worked out well for them both. Charlie not only drove the mini-train, but also owned the pop-up ticket booth for the tourist boat trips. And Mark filed paperwork. At least Charlie always had a smile. Even for locals who didn't pay his wages. "You keen to get to work for once?"

"Ha! Always." With a wave, Mark ran over to his office and passed Yvonne on the front desk. "I'm going to pop out at lunch today, Yvonne."

Yvonne hummed in response. Either she didn't hear or, more likely, didn't care. Mark went through the rigmarole of chair battling, but the chair obviously felt the Wednesday Woes as much as Mark and wasn't as determined to beat him. Which was a shame—Mark would have to start working on time for once.

Yvonne had opened the office window, blowing in the sea breeze that ruffled the unfiled paperwork on his desk and his mound of hair in to his eyes. Maybe there was something to this 'in the stars' nonsense, as the weather was clearly making Mark aware of the two tasks he had been putting off for months now.

"What should I do today?"

Mark flicked his hair. Robert, the work experience kid, glanced anywhere but where Mark resided.

"Ah, yes, right." Office management would take his mind off uncompleted tasks and unwanted Australian advances. "I've got some feedback forms from clients that need inputting so I can create this pivot table malarkey for the boss." Mark rooted through his in-tray and tugged out a plastic folder, handing it over to Robert. "There's a template on the shared drive under feedback, so just use that. I trust you know how to input data?"

Robert glanced down at the plastic wallet bulging of papers as if it was the sole culprit for murdering his grandmother, then set his disdainful expression on Mark, realising that there were two involved in her untimely death.

"Can't you use SurveyMonkey?"

"I know people may say data input is something that a chimp can do, but I can assure you trained monkeys are rather lacking in these neck of the woods, and this will give some insight into the workings of our business." Mark sighed. *Kids these days. They think they can go straight to management pay grade without passing go but still collecting the two hundred paaand.*

"No." Robert rolled his eyes. "SurveyMonkey is an online software program. You can create surveys and stuff and it does all the working out for you. No need for pivot tables."

Mark swivelled his chair from side to side, contemplating what the tiny child before him had said. He took it all in. It was good, solid information. Perhaps could be worth looking into. But Mark was the professional, here. Something he needed to maintain at least some pretence of. Tapping a biro to his lips, he hummed.

"Had problems with it before." Mark twisted back to face his computer and waved a hand. "Handwritten forms are so much more reliable."

"What if I can't read their writing?"

"Make it up." Mark clicked on the internet browser on his PC. "But be sure that it says 'Mark, office manager, was delightful and helpful, the best customer service liaison we've ever encountered, ten out of ten.'" Mark winked.

"Huh." Robert lifted the paperwork to read over the first one through the clear plastic wallet. "Guess your pivot charts show a slight favourable leaning, then."

"My pivot tables are none of your business."

"Bet they're that fella's though." Robert raised his eyebrows and nodded to Mark's computer screen.

Said screen was void of anything other than the bouncing logo that Google favoured this week.

"That's not even a correct euphemism," Mark snapped. "Nor a double entendre. You can work on your office banter while you type out 'yes' or 'no' into a box a hundred times over." Mark gave off a rather serene smile then twisted back around in his seat. The chair broke its mid-week slump by springing into action and flopping down to the last rung. Mark's hair fell back into his eyes with the rapid drop. He blew it away.

Fuck Wednesdays. Fuck work experience children. Fuck pivot fucking tables.

He peered over his shoulder, ensuring Robert was seated behind his desk and couldn't see, then typed *SurveyMonkey* into the search box. He face-palmed and added another thing that could fuck off on a Wednesday. Or any day for that matter.

* * * *

Lunch time couldn't come quick enough and on the stroke of twelve, Mark locked his computer in case of prying eyes and made his way from the office to the High Street. Shoving in a ham sandwich from the supermarket, he grimaced. The bread was wet and the ham dry. He was pretty certain it was meant to be the other way around, but he didn't ponder further as cheap sarnies were never worth stressing over.

There were only two places along the main High Street where he could get his hair cut. The Marsby Barbers, owned by a rather friendly Turkish gent called Zeke, that boasted glossy images of different styles and celebrity hair trends pasted on the bare walls. Although that would indicate Zeke could achieve the latest look, Mark had noticed that most clients came out with the exact same short back and sides, even the girls who ventured in on a whim. The only other option was the uber-trendy hair and beauty salon, Shimmer, owned by Janice, his mother's best friend. Anyone who could make Mark's elderly mother still rock the glam-gran look—not that she was a gran as Mark hadn't procreated and she always made a point of mentioning that fact at every family gathering—was worth their weight in Marsby pink rock.

"Marky Mark! You come in?" Zeke poked his head out of the box-shaped barbers and ushered with both hands. "I do special today. I make you look bloody gorgeous!"

"Mark! How lovely to see you!" Janice clonked her heels onto the pavement and gave Zeke a glare. "We have a promotion on highlights."

Mark glanced from one to the other. All he wanted was a bloody trim. Without giving Mark the time to reply to either, Janice curled her slender fingers around his arm and dragged him into the brightly lit Shimmer. He at least offered an apologetic shrug Zeke's way. Janice was the lesser of two evils. The last thing he needed was it to get back to his mother that he'd snubbed her best pal. And at least in Shimmer he was able to listen to all the old dears chatting about the state of the High Street since Woolies had closed down—all whilst he enjoyed a head massage. Zeke didn't offer those services—relaxing scalp scraping or placating his mother.

Janice shoved him with the nearest junior stylist, wrapping him in the black cape to feel every bit the goth when juxtaposed against his pale skin, and not-too-elegantly dipped him back to the wash basin. He braced himself for the forthcoming questions of upcoming holiday, work achievements and the inevitable love life details. *Pre-prepared answers on a postcard please, one that displayed the fetching seaside marina, perhaps?* Luckily, nothing came. He started to enjoy the moment of silence.

Once in the styling booth, he accepted the cup of tea offered that he had no desire to drink, what with it looking like it had been made yesterday, Janice returned and ran her fingers through his hair, her grimace evident in the mirror reflection.

"It's been a while, hasn't it, Mark?" she asked, taking out her scissors.

Mark had to pause. Had his mother been moaning about Mark's lack of sexual relations during her weekly visits here? Realising Janice was probably referring to his last visit to the salon, he shrugged. The answer would still be the same to either question.

"I suppose it has." *Too long.*

"So I see. Do you want me to go a bit shorter this time?" She combed through the back of his hair that curled up every time she flattened it down. "Unless you're trying to grow it long, of course?"

"No, not trying to grow it long." Mark sighed. "Not trying to grow it at all, actually."

Snippety scissors rushed through his hair and Mark shut his eyes, hoping he could just get a few moments of solitude.

"Your mother was in here yesterday."

Great.

"Yes?"

"She said you're now managing that little office of yours."

How on earth would she know that? Oh, she wouldn't. She was doing her usual "my son is doing soooo well" speech to save face that her darling boy wasn't just flying by the seat of his pants.

"Just keeping an eye on things whilst the boss is away."

"Oh." *Snip, snip, snip.* "And she mentioned that you're back on the dating scene. Y'know, after…"

Short back and sides were becoming more appealing by the second.

"I guess there aren't many like you here, though?"

"I'm sorry?" Mark saw the lines on his forehead through the mirror.

"Bet it was easier in London. Bloody homosexuals on every street corner there. Here, you just get what you can, right?"

Mark hung his head, only for it to be scraped back up by pointy nails.

"Makes people wonder why you did come back." She snipped away at his fringe. "Well, your mother wonders, anyhow. I told her, though, I told her that London isn't for everyone and maybe you want a quiet life. Some people prefer that, don't they? Boring job, boring life. Not everyone wants high-flying careers, travels to far-flung destinations and whatnot. No, best you just stay here." She tapped his shoulder to really drum in the point. "Take care of your mother. 'Cause your dad won't be around forever for her."

Mark didn't mention that his mother also wouldn't be around forever, although he was beginning to think that that might not be the case after all.

"Indeed," was all Mark found his mouth would mutter.

Janice rattled on more about her fabulous brood, most of whom had flown the nest and now either travelling the world, married with sprogs and one who had landed a coveted position in the Navy. Mark now knew why his mother had wanted to compete with all that. Must be hard for her to have to admit her son, who had been top of the class at one point and voted most likely to achieve, now took orders to file paperwork and had no love life of which to speak of. *No life to speak of.*

"Don't leave it so long next time." Janice tapped his shoulders and swerved off to the front desk. Not even her close friendship with his mother would allow for any mates-rates here, either.

After handing over the last of his month's wages, Mark stepped out of the salon and breathed in the gust of air. Zeke leaned against the open doorway of his barbers, arms folded and gave Mark's hair the once over.

"Bloody gorgeous." He stepped back inside and slammed the door.

With no further musings, Mark ruffled a hand through his hair, twisted on his heel and slammed face first into a brick wall.

Okay, so it wasn't quite a brick wall. But it felt just as solid. Trouble was, this one smelled much more desirable and Mark breathed in, the musky scent tickling his tongue.

"G'day."

Mark forced himself to take a step backwards. "Bradley." The name rolled off his tongue in a seductive whisper. He rectified that with a cough, one meant to be a clearing of his throat but that ended up catching on some stray piece of soggy bread from the awful sandwich and came out sounding like his grandmother after having smoked twenty Rothmans. "You know, I always thought 'g'day' was one of those stereotypical greetings we believe of you Aussie's."

"It is."

"But yet you say it."

"I play on it." Bradley smiled. "When I know it'll make people swoon."

"Bradley—" Mark tried again to get out what he needed to say.

"Call me Brad, Mark."

"Brad." Mark paused at the 'd', his tongue sticking to the roof of his mouth.

Bradley smiled, blowing out an amused puff of air from his nostrils, and glanced away. It gave Mark a moment to study the man. Not for the tight-fitting lemon-coloured T-shirt clinging to his defined chest, nor for the pair of multicoloured board shorts as bright as Mark's shirt, or for the row of beads clutching Bradley's throat on a leather band and appearing to choke the poor fellow. Not even for the take-out coffee cup he held in his meaty hand, but for the lack of sparkle in his demeanour. *Shit. Did I do that to him? One bike ride with Mark Johnson and everyone turns grey.*

"You've had your hair cut," Bradley broke the silence.

"Uh. Yes." Mark avoided showing him exactly where. He hadn't moved two inches from the outside of either salon.

"It looks good."

Mark waited for the insult. It didn't come. And Bradley shrugged.

"Less to grip hold of, but still enough to run fingers through." Bradley's spark returned for that delivery, but was soon replaced by the entering sombreness as he shuffled his flip-flops along the pavement.

"Bradley—"

"Mark—" They uttered each other's names in unison.

Bradley laughed. "You go first."

"No, no." Mark shook his head, his hair not as wildly billowing but floating effortlessly along with the impact nonetheless. "We all know my problem with opening my mouth too much."

Bradley arched one eyebrow with a sly smile. "Or not enough." He smirked. "Sorry, mate, couldn't resist. Poor taste."

"Much like that drink you're holding?" Mark nodded to the cup. "Thought you didn't drink coffee."

Bradley glanced down to the cup as if he hadn't realised he had been holding it, then held it up and handed it over to Mark.

"Oh, right, no, this is for you. Tea, no sugar." He lowered his head to peer up at Mark and fluttered his eyelashes. "'Cause you're sweet enough. And just the right shade of caramel brown."

"I'm just the right shade of caramel brown?"

Bradley bellowed out a laugh. "No, mate. The tea is."

"You brought me tea?" Mark cautiously reached out to take the cup, feeling a lot like a junkie getting his sordid street corner fix.

"Well, yeah." Bradley shrugged. "You didn't come by the shop this morning, and I know how much you live for tea. Don't know how you got through the morning without it." He scraped his flip-flop against the stony gravel once more, shoving his hands into the pockets of his shorts. "It's sort of a peace offering. Was coming by your office to give it to you, when I saw you come out of there."

Sipping the tea through the little plastic hole, Mark felt the invigorating rush run over him like an enveloping hot blanket. Needless to say, it was a rather decent cup of tea. Certainly the best one he'd had all day. And, remarkably, still hot.

"Thank you." Mark held the cup in cheers. "Although, I'm glad you didn't come by the office. There are a few staff members who have probably seen enough of you already."

"Nah, they wouldn't have been focusing on my face."

Mark spluttered his tea, cursing that he couldn't get through a beverage around Bradley without personal injury.

"Listen, Mark," Bradley shuffled closer and swiped his fingers over the Mark's clutching the cup. "I wanted to say sorry. About the kiss? I shouldn't have done that yesterday."

"Right." Mark licked his lips, unsure what to reply next. And still unsure what Bradley's, and his, reactions had been all about.

"I dunno, I just…spur of the moment. Your lips were there and your hair was all over the place." He shrugged. "You looked…cute."

Mark coughed again, choosing to keep his lips firmly on the hole of the cup.

"And, well, the stars said…" Bradley shook his head. "Doesn't matter. And you've chopped all your hair off now, so—"

"So it was just my hair you wanted?"

"Well, no." Bradley exhaled sharply. "Like I say, you were there. And you had that look about you."

"What look is that, may I ask? Helplessly squashed to death by a rusty bike?"

Bradley laughed. "Pretty much."

Mark raised both eyebrows, having still not mastered just the one arch.

"Look, okay, I have a confession to make." Bradley licked his lips. "Two, actually."

"Oh, yes?" Mark tried to appear nonchalant but his breaking and elevating voice put a stop to that.

"Macy," Bradley said. "She, uh, she told me about you."

"I see." Mark wasn't sure if what he was seeing was in focus or not. Perhaps an eye test would be tomorrow's lunch time endeavour.

"Yeah," Bradley continued. "She talked a lot about you. Said we might get on. Told me to try, y'know, get you out a bit. Said you'd been alone for a while."

Mark flickered his eyes closed. "Oh, God," he muttered into the cup. "I'm a pity companion."

"No, no!" Bradley rushed out. "Honestly, I had no idea what you'd be like and said I'd give it a go for her. But, seriously, mate, I don't tolerate that many people for long. Especially if it's not going how I was told it would. Why I move around so much. So I figured I'd just come fix your roof and be done. But, I don't know." Bradley ruffled his blond tassels. "It was like how my gran said it would be. The bike, the cliff. And you make me laugh." He smiled. "Mostly I'm laughing at you, but, whatever, you're funny."

"I'm not sure if that warrants a thank you or not."

"I'm sorry I took it too far. I get you're not interested. My gran must've got it wrong." Bradley dipped his head. "Maybe she's getting too old." Straightening out, he pasted on his engaging smile. "Let's just start over. I'd like to be your friend, while I'm in town." He held out his hand.

Mark took the cup away from his lips, sighed then shook Bradley's hand, the softness of his fingertips indenting into Mark's skin.

"I'd like that too," Mark finally said. "And I'm sorry, I don't normally go storming off like that when someone kisses me." He cocked his head. "Not that it happens too often, mind. I'm just not in the market for—"

Bradley signalled him to stop. "I got it, I got it. Duly noted." He cut him off, which perhaps was a good thing as Mark wasn't sure what he *was* in the market for. "One more thing, I got you in on Saturday."

"Saturday?"

"Yeah." Bradley smiled. "The stripping gig. You said you'd like to come see? So I cleared it with the boss. You can come. I'm choreographing the team dance, my choice and that, so be nice for some support."

"Ah." Mark wished he wasn't so terribly British at this point as one can never say no to a person's face.

"See you Saturday, Mark." Bradley winked, twisted on his flip-flops and bounded up the High Street. He glanced back over his shoulder before crossing the road. "Love the shirt. It's like a summer meadow just threw up—"

"Don't finish that sentence."

Mark shuddered at the thought that he now had to fit bloody clothes shopping into his already busy weekly schedule.

Chapter Eight

Chin Wag

Thursday and Friday flew by. It was as if they were in some kind of hurry to just get on with things. Unlike Mark. He rather hoped for the usual slog to the end of the working week so he could rid himself of the butterflies vomiting in his stomach. Nothing particularly noteworthy happened and Mark was feeling a false sense of security. Senses of security were always false in his life. And it came on Saturday morning when rooting around in his wardrobe for something that could pass as going-out clothes. With a slam of the door, he came to the realisation he had to call in reinforcements.

"Marky, Marky, Marky. I have soooo missed your sweet serenade."

Mark shut his eyes as he clutched his mobile phone in his hand. Calling Damian always managed to bring out the exasperation. Still, the guy was a fashionista and constantly complained about Mark's attire, often buying him floral shirts in mockery, so Mark had no choice if he wanted to show up at a London night haunt looking less like an antique, or carpet, or wallpaper for that matter.

"I missed you at my last show," Damian rattled on and Mark could *hear* the pout. "No bother. I was a hoot. And, might I add, absolutely stole the show." Damian was into Am-Dram. Although the way he went on about it, anyone would think he was treading the boards in the West End and not at the pop-up stage in the community centre.

"Apologies, I was otherwise engaged," Mark lied.

"I doubt that very much. In both senses of the word. So, what can I do for you this fine Saturday morning, dahling." He also managed to pronounce the silent 'h'.

"Are you free for a spot of shopping?"

"Grocery?" The elevation in Damian's reply helped Mark to envisage the grimace that would have accompanied it.

"Clothes."

"Pick me up and take me to Canterbury. One hour. No later or I'll buy it all myself and send you the bill."

The click and whirr ensued, and Mark pinched the bridge of his nose. He most certainly needed tea to get through the next few hours of city shopping. So he took the mug along for the forty-minute drive to where Damian lived in Canterbury and after picking him up, toward the shopping precinct.

Mark had met Damian a few years back after his return to Marsby and when he had thought that he had needed to get on with some sort of social life. A brief spell of amateur dramatics later, where Mark's acting wasn't as hot as the free beverages served during rehearsals, Mark had knocked that idea firmly on the head. But he had met Damian and they'd become quite closely acquainted over the years. Sort of. They'd tried it once, possibly twice. But neither occasion had been as worthy of a standing ovation, a five-star review or a repeated run, much like any of Damian's amateur productions. They'd stuck to just being friends. With mutual benefits—Mark got the occasional advice on fashion and Damian had the occasional audience at his reworkings of Shakespeare.

"What are we looking for, dahling?" Damian asked as they parked up in the multi-storey and headed straight into the one and only department store Mark was going to be allowing. Damian was professionally kitted out, black chinos hugging his slender frame, a tan shirt tucked in with just a few buttons undone at the top to reveal a few stray hairs poking out and a long trench coat that wafted as though he was in a re-enactment of the *Matrix*. Oh, and with tiny round dark glasses and slicked-back hair all adding to the dramatic ensemble. *I would like the blue pill, please. Or whatever one it is that will take me back home.*

"I don't know, just something that won't make me stick out like a sore thumb."

"Marky, sweet-pea, you'll stick out like a sore thumb whatever you wear," Damian offered in his best solidarity voice. Which was none.

"Thank you, Damie." Mark looked around. They'd entered the lingerie section, frilled brassieres and several types of knickers hanging on display in all their glory. Even Mark with his limited knowledge of garments knew he shouldn't waste any time browsing this part.

"Oh, don't be like that." Damian linked his arm in with Mark's and marched him through the point of no return toward the escalators. He breathed in excitedly on reaching the men's department and even gave a brief triple clap of his hands whilst bouncing on his tippy-toes. Not for the clothes on the rails, but for the multitude of *unclothed* mannequins that for some reason gave Mark odd flashbacks of a certain email debacle. "You know what I mean. It's not a *gay* strip club, is it?"

Mark shook his head, wishing he hadn't filled Damian in on the drive over as to where he was actually going that evening and why he would need Damian's advice.

"Hen parties and divorcees. *Gurls.*" Damian shuddered. "You will be the only male there not getting your kit off. You might as well dress your thumb up in a tutu and have it sing *Y.M.C.A.*"

"Wonderful." Mark stuck his hands into his jacket pocket and his fingers curled around his mobile phone. "Perhaps I should just call this off? I have no idea why I'm going in the first place. Other than to prove I am some dreary old loner."

"Oh, give over." Damian slapped his arm. "You'll be like the bleeding Pied Piper."

"Sorry?"

"They'll swarm around you. Women love gay men, sweetie." Damian sniffed and rummaged along a rail of leather coats that Mark hoped wouldn't be for him. "Just look completely out of place and scared shitless by the whole thing and they'll flock to you like flies around a shit heap." Damian grinned. "They'll forget that you've probably sucked more cock than all the women in there put together."

"Damo, stop. I beg of you," Mark pleaded, roaming his gaze around the store in the hope no one had been in earshot. "Besides, that's not strictly true for me, is it? You, on the other hand..."

"What can I say, lovie." Damian waved his hand in the air. "You need to fuck a few frogs before you get your Tom Hardy."

"Tom Hardy?" Mark scanned through a few shirts on hangers just to make it look like he was getting into all this shopping malarkey.

"Oh, yes." Damian cocked his head at Mark. "Sorry, is he too British for you now? Are you solely into Australian expats?"

"I'm not into Australian expats. I'm doing this purely as a friend," Mark lied, keeping his eyes firmly on a shirt he knew would make him look like a lampshade.

"Of course you are, dahhhllllling," Damian replied, elongating the extra h's and trilling the l's with his tongue flapping against the root of his mouth. Ripping the awful shirt from Mark's hands, he tutted then shoved it forcefully back on the rail. "What the hell are you doing?"

"Shopping."

"Oh, dear Lord God, and every divine being of the universe." Damian slammed his palms dramatically on his hips. Damian did everything dramatically. So use of the word meant it was really rather *overly* dramatic. Like his acting. "You must really have it bad. You haven't even asked for tea first."

"Ah." Mark angled his head. "Let's go get a tea, then."

"Good, I need a decent Capu to get me in the zone for kitting you out." Damian waved his hand over Mark's frame and screwed his nose up at the plain jeans and long-sleeve woollen jumper Mark had rushed on at home. "Funny how you've never let me dress you before." Damian waggled his eyebrows. "Undress, maybe. But dress—"

"Tea?" Mark stormed off toward the department store cafe.

Filled with mostly old dears, the café served tea in one of those little silver pots that supposedly keeps it hot. It didn't much. But it did redeem itself by holding enough for about three cups of the stuff. After locating a table for two at the back, Mark settled down to his brew—something he would always have an avid opinion on, anyhow.

"So." Damian hefted down into the seat opposite and added a few sachets of sugar to his frothy cappuccino. The swirl of a heart on top told Mark that Damian had worked his charm on the lad serving behind the counter. Just yet another one of those bash-over-the-head moments reminding Mark why it had never worked out between the two of them. Sometimes Mark needed those *aide memoires* of why he was choosing—yes, *choosing*—to remain single even though there was a perfectly good bloke opposite him who would gladly take Mark to bed. He just wouldn't stay there. Not like in some *Misery*-kidnap chained-to-the-posts sort of way. Just in a "I'm popping out and will accidentally shove my dick in someone else's gob whilst I'm there" sort of way.

Mark sighed.

"I want to hear all about this Australian hunk who you're venturing back into the big smoke for." Slurping from his mug, Damian over-dramatised the shivers. "He'd have to be quite something to get you going back there, amirite?"

"He's Macy's cousin." Mark left that there.

"Gay?"

"Yes. I believe so."

"Mmm-hmm, I don't doubt you'd be going through all this rigmarole for a straight man. Or even a switch hitter."

Mark pinched the bridge of his nose. Metaphorically. Physically, he drank tea.

"I'm simply going because he asked me to. He hasn't got many friends here yet and I'm too polite to say no."

"That last one is most definitely correct. But." Damian took a sip of cappuccino and swallowed it down, leaving the froth on his top lip. "I don't believe the other two are just simple statements."

Mark dabbed a finger on his own lips, indicating that Damian might wish to do the same. Damian stared at him, then glanced around. Settling back on Mark, Damian shrugged and gulped down another load of froth that piled up on his lip. The lad from the counter shimmied over and Damian took that chance to swipe his tongue over the lot and swallow it down with a flutter of his eyelashes. The lad smiled, handing over a napkin. As Damian unfolded it, he grinned at the number written on with blotted marker pen. Mark rolled his eyes to the point he could see his skull.

"Anyway." Damian slapped the table between them. "Don't change the subject."

"I wasn't aware that I did."

"How did Mr Australia manage to coerce our Marky Mark, our poor old bachelor forever-for-reasons-undivulged, out to the male-of-the-night haunt?"

"That sounds ominously like I'm a gigolo. Or that he is."

"You say potato."

"Huh?"

"Stripping is just the front gig." Damian lowered his head, peering over nonexistent spectacles. "It's what goes on behind that earns the money."

Mark's cup handle slipped from his fingers, but he managed to prevent the whole thing from falling to the table, just lose a little of its contents that sloshed onto the surface. That hadn't been something he'd thought about. Of course, it made sense. And Damon would know. Not because he'd stripped in his lifetime, but he roamed in circles that occasionally did that sort of thing.

"Hang on." Mark wiped up the spillage with the napkin that bore the server's number. Damian didn't seem to notice. "Don't all actors get tarnished with that same old brush? Wouldn't it be prudent to assume all strippers are also prostitutes?"

Damon shrugged. "I'd sell my body for a lead in *Les Mis*."

"That's you, though, Damo. You'd sell your body for walk-on part in *Doctors*."

Damon gasped, then clapped. "I so would. I could be the dashing young stranger, back from an elite SAS mission and suffering from PTSD and all I need is the right probe to whip me out of depression."

"A walk-on part, Damo. No speaking. Just blend into the background."

"I could never blend into the background."

"That's an understatement."

"Everyone needs a backstory, my friend. Even the extras." Damon finished his cappuccino, settled back in the chair and rubbed his chin. "So what is Mr Australia's backstory? Why come to England? To Marsby, for that matter?" He scrunched up his face. "And why strip? Apart from the obvious, 'I got the body, I get to flaunt it'? And why—" Damian leaned forward, those invisible specs getting another slide down his nose. " —has he chosen you as his prey?"

"I'm hardly his prey." Mark brushed off the memory of Bradley's bulk squashing him, then using the opportune moment to kiss him. He still found it hard to believe it had happened at all. And it also led onto all those questions that Damian had just pointed out. Why would the hunk of all that is male be interested in Mark—friendship or otherwise?

"Tell me why you think this is all nonsense," Damian said. "I do so love to hear your downtrodden, self-loathing speeches. It gives me a sense of enormous well-being."

Mark stuck his finger up. "One. He's too young."

"Age?"

"Twenty-one."

Damon gasped, palm slapped to his chest, and all the old dears stopped chomping on their carrot cakes to glance over. "That's like jailbait." He pointed at Mark and elevated his 'drama' voice. "Arrest him, officer! Now!"

"Shhh!"

Damian laughed. "Oh, no, wait. He's not jailbait. He's an adult. Legal. Next one."

"He's Macy's cousin."

Damian gasped yet again. "Incest! I can't stand to look at you any longer." He covered his eyes, then peeked through his fingers. "Oh, wait, it's not."

"Fine." Mark hoped this next one might bring some clout as to why Bradley Summers and Mark Johnson were not to be shipped—*that is what it's called, right? Meaning shipped away on some desert island together, where Bradley would use all his Bear Grylls skills. Huh, I could write poetry...* "He's devilishly handsome. Fit, toned, athletic, adventurous, sexy, charismatic..." *Okay, that's more a shopping list.*

Damian propped his elbow on the table, rested his head into his hand and fluttered his long eyelashes. "Sounds positively dreamy."

"Oh, bugger off." Mark glared for all of a millisecond before chuckling at Damian's wistful expression.

Damian slapped his hand down on the tabletop, the china cups and tin tea pot jumping into the air and landing with a clang and a tinkle.

"Mark Johnson," Damian bellowed in his best Brian Blessed impersonation. Which was rather odd coming from the svelte and effeminate character in front of Mark. "Have you never heard of opposites attract? Isn't that why we didn't work out?"

"I'm not just talking about being the same way, Damian." Mark replied in a hushed voice. "It's more like what the hell would an Adonis like Bradley Summers want with a man like me? I offer nothing. I am an old has-been, or rather never was, content on putting on my fluffy slippers of a night-time to watch *Gogglebox* rather than scale mountains and do acrobatics." Mark shrugged. "I am greying, apparently. I am skinny. I am wrinkly. This whole thing is absurd. I am a pity invite as Macy told him I needed to get out. So get out, I will. But I will not be anyone's pity shag, either."

"A shag's a shag, darling." Damian folded his arms across his chest and leaned back in the chair. After a moment of glaring, he waved a flippant hand. "You offer him *experience*." Damian's playfulness dissipated into an unorthodox seriousness.

"I can assure you, Bradley has experience," Mark replied, slurping his tea. "I doubt I can offer anything new."

"Whatever." Damian shot him a pitying glance. "You haven't changed a bit."

"How do you mean?"

"You thought you were old the day you turned twenty-five."

"You didn't know me at twenty-five. I still lived in London."

"That's just statistics."

Mark furrowed his brow and opened his mouth to correct the statement, but Damian cut him off with a violent prod of his finger over the table.

"You need to realise you are not old. You are not even middle-aged…*yet*. And, anyway, silver foxes are so on-trend at the moment. It's living in that death town that's made you think that way. Everything moves at a snail's pace, and so do you. You, Mark, are one sexy beast. No, you are not all rippling muscles under that God-*awful* jumper that I will enjoy ripping off you later, but it's not what you got, it's what you do with it that counts. And, well, no complaints here on that front."

"Um, Damo?" Mark interrupted. "You never let me put it near you. In my book, that's a pretty damning complaint."

"Well, yes, I suppose so, but that's not to do with you," Damian replied. "Just, y'know, I'm saving that for Tom Hardy."

"What's to say that Bradley isn't waiting for a Tom Hardy, too?" Mark said, slumping back in his seat. He tucked his hand into his trouser pocket and tugged out his phone, twisting it in his hands.

"He didn't invite Tom Hardy," Damian replied. "He invited you. Mark Johnson. Urg, even your name is bland."

"Thanks. And Tom Hardy probably isn't on his speed dial."

Damian leered forward. "If Mark Johnson is on Australian Adonis's speed dial, then I would say that's a firm contender that he might be hoping that you put it in him. At the gay bar…at the g-a-y bar!"

"Oh, for goodness sake, please shut up."

Damian bellowed a laugh and slapped Mark's arm on the table. Mark shook him off and was just about to say something else to quell any idea that Bradley's invitation to watch him get mauled by women was anything other than an attempt to show Mark how fantastic he was and how completely inept Mark was, when his phone buzzed in his hand. The vibrations shocked him enough to drop the thing on the table top and Damian grabbed it. Mark tried to protest but knew there was no point. It would only be a text message reminding him of his upcoming appointment for a health check. Or his mother reminding him of the same.

"Well, well, well," Damian's eyebrows waggled amusedly.

"What?"

"'Mark, can't wait for you to cum in my back passage.'" Damian bit his bottom lip and widened his eyes. "I'd say that's an in. An easy, delightful slide of an in."

Mark snatched the phone from Damian and read the incoming message. He huffed, flopping the phone into his lap.

"It says to use the back entrance to the club," Mark stated. "Bastard."

Damian chuckled, waving a nonchalant hand. "I paraphrased. The little emoji at the end there says to read between the lines."

"What's an emoji?"

"Mark, dahhhling," Damian tutted. "Get with the programme. If you're going to have a teenage boyfriend, you need to get with the emoticons. Words are of no use to those not out of nappies yet."

"Could we just go get me some clothes, please?"

"Oh, finally!" Damian scrabbled out of his seat, swished his oversized scarf around his neck and clicked his fingers.

I'm going to regret this.

* * * *

It took well over the hour that Mark had set aside for Damian to convince him to buy the really expensive pair of jeans from the designer side of the store, along with a nice slim-fitted black shirt that had shimmering silver stars dotted over it, and a pair of dark brown boots. Nothing too out there, and nothing too obviously purchased that day. He must remember to take the tags off when changing into them at the train station loos.

It was the short leather jacket, sans collar, where the argument really got started. Mark hadn't ever gone for leathers. In or out of the bedroom. He felt like he would be trying too hard if ever he purchased a leather jacket. And his mother always pertained that the very ownership of one would be advertising his sexuality to the holidaymakers. Which Mark never understood. Leather, to him, belonged on the regular weekend Harley riders that zoomed across the seafront blaring out *Born to be Bad*. Most of them worked in accounts and finance during the week, and there were a couple of teachers, and one chemist. So they weren't really bad to the core. More weekend bothersome.

Damian bought the thing with his own money, declaring it was a gift and that Mark could not turn up to his date with Bradley in an old golfing Barbour jacket that still had the tear on it from when he got caught in the barbed wire that time. *Huh, that'll be why it isn't now waterproof.* That was yet another anecdote that Damian was forbidden from ever recounting. To anyone. And he threatened to, so Mark accepted the gift graciously and hoped he wouldn't be mauled by feral animals in the street. Or mugged.

Now he stood in the station loo cubicle, hopping on one foot to pull his clothes off in an area that wasn't big enough to swing a cat let alone change an entire outfit. He'd bought new boxer shorts too. He had no idea why. They were on sale, and whilst he didn't envisage anyone ever seeing them, they had looked rather good on the male model on the cover. Perhaps after this contortion efforts, he'd have miraculously gained a few pounds in muscle bulk and formed a six-pack. Thankfully, there was no mirror on this inside of the door. He'd only be disappointed.

Vacating the stall, he met Damian perching on the row of sinks, biting his thumbnail. He stared at Mark, expression blank and apathetic.

"Oh, forget it!" Mark threw his hands in the air and twisted back to the cubicle.

Damian grabbed his shoulders and spun him around. He wolf-whistled. "Look at you." He shoved him forward, putting Mark firmly in front of the thing he avoided most days—his reflection.

Mark ruffled a hand through his hair, swishing it about to give it more, or less, bounce, then ran the hand over his stubble that he still refused to shave. "I look like I've tried too hard."

"Nonsense!" Damian dropped his hands on Mark's shoulders from behind, adding a grounding weight, and peered over to meet his gaze through the glass. "You look divine." His husky voice dripped into Mark's ear and made him shiver. It had just been too long since anyone had been that up close and personal with him.

"This isn't me."

"No." Damian nodded in agreement. "It's better."

"Fancy just coming home to watch *Gogglebox* with me? I can blow off this stupid idea." Mark widened hopeful eyes at the mirror.

Damian kissed Mark's cheek. "No can do, my friend. This one here has a hot date too, you know."

"You never said." Mark spun to face him. "Who with?"

"Well, I say hot, but more tepid. Remember Pete?"

"Oh, God, Damo. Why are you going there again?"

"Because I have needs." Grabbing Mark's face, he yanked him forward and slapped a kiss onto his lips. "Not all of us get hunky Australian men raining down on us." Damian backed away and grinned. "You are going to get truly bored of *It's Raining Men* tonight."

Mark hung his head, pinching the bridge of his nose. "Oh, dear, God."

"I'm almost tempted to come along and watch you. It'll be better than watching Pete trying to seduce me with his silk scarf again."

"If you don't like him, why do you say yes to every date?"

Damian shrugged. "If you don't like Adonis, why have you said yes to watching him get his kit off?"

"Totally different."

Damian tapped Mark's cheek. "Sure it is, sweetheart."

Mark shook his head then handed over his bag of old clothes. "Can you take these? I'll come pick them up after. Last train to Canterbury is half-eleven. So I'll get that and come straight to you. Leave the key out. I won't knock on your bedroom door if you've got Placid Pete staying."

"Keep them." Damian shoved them back with a wry smile. "You can use them in the morning when you get up from a hotel bed next to one hunky specimen."

"Damo," Mark urged, ruffling the plastic bag that had cost him an extra five bloody pence to purchase even after the three hundred pounds he had forked out for one sodding outfit.

Damian snatched the bag. "Fine." He prodded Mark's nose. "It's better for you to do the walk of shame anyway."

"Never gonna happen."

Chapter Nine

Dragged Up

Arriving at the venue, Mark had a sudden wish that he smoked, or at least could tolerate other people's smoke in order to stand outside rather than venturing into the dingy basement bar. A long line of cackling ladies of all shapes and sizes, and in varied costumes detailing their unique association with their hen, stood outside waiting to be let into the corner entrance of the Adonis Cabaret night club situated between London's Old Street and the more trendy Shoreditch evening haunts.

Mark took a deep breath, attempting to shove his hands into his jacket pocket. *Bugger.* They were still stitched together. He thought about ripping them open, but decided better of it. He still hoped he would be able to return the thing unscathed first thing in the morning. So he tapped his hands against his legs, peered up at the huge zap banner display outside the entrance and exhaled fiercely. Bradley's photo, in all his shirtless glory, mingled with four other Adonis males that surrounded a drag queen, detailing this was not a night to be missed. *Sadly.*

Mark's phone vibrated in his jeans pocket, masking his grumble. He fished it out and checked the display.

Just go in, you tart.

Damian. Was Mark's camera accidentally switched on and whizzing photos of his whereabout to Damian? Well, no, that'd just be showing pictures of his arse. Nope, Damian just knew him too well. He would know that Mark had been standing outside the venue for quite some time and had made several attempts to venture back to the station and board the returning train. Perhaps he should just do that? Bradley couldn't really be expecting him to turn up. He wouldn't even notice—

Mark's phone rang with Bradley's name popping up. Was the world watching him today?

"Hello," he answered. *So formal, so polite.* "Hi." *Better.* "What's up?" *Too far, Mark, too far.*

"G'day, mate, where are ya?"

"Oh, um, right, sorry, yes, I'm—" Mark paused, looking back at his phone, double checking once again that no photo app, dog snap or otherwise, was on.

He could say the train was cancelled. Or perhaps that his friend needed him. Or he wasn't feeling too well. Anything, really. Bradley hadn't seen him. He could then toddle off to the closest coffee shop and ask for a tea, only to be stared at like he'd spoken a foreign language. London wasn't known for its tea shops so much as Marsby was. They drank coffee here to give themselves the caffeine fix needed to meet the pace of life. He'd never managed that even when living in the city. Coffee, that was. The faster pace was inevitable. Much like his rapid aging.

"Mark?"

Mark hadn't realised his inner thoughts had taken that long to process. It was the tea. He'd been imagining what type of tea he would like…

"Sorry, yes, I'm afraid the train's delayed." Mark closed his eyes to utter the blatant lie.

"Mark?"

"Yes?"

"You're a lousy liar." Bradley chuckled. "I can hear women's screeches behind you, mate. And whilst I don't doubt you have that effect on females, I do doubt they'll all be in Marsby scouting you out. Now get your arse in here."

Mark sighed. "Bradley?" He dug his thumb into his eye.

"Brad."

"Oh, for goodness sake." Mark slapped his hand against his thigh. "Bradley is far better suited to you. You want to be friends, get used to it, okay?"

"You've got a bit of a mean streak in you. I like it."

"Give over." Mark rolled his eyes. "Why on earth do you want me here, anyway? That bit I can't work out."

"Really?" Bradley's voice elevated. "Guess you'll have to come in and find out then."

Another huff and Mark came to the conclusion he should just get this thing over and done with. "Fine, fine. Where do I go?"

"I'll come get ya." The whir indicated Bradley had hung up.

Mark sighed, shoving his phone in his jeans pocket, and once again tried to tuck his hands in his jacket. He cursed when one of the stitches broke. Now he couldn't take the blasted thing back! He shuffled on the spot, feeling as out of place as, well, he always did in any given social situation. Crowds were not his thing. Drinking was not his thing. Strippers were not his thing. Surrounded by hen parties was not his thing.

Mark pondered what it could be that *was* his thing? Could it really only be tea? How had it come to that?

A sudden squeal of high-pitched screams jolted him from his life-choice musings and Mark glanced up to see who or what had caused such a commotion. A pop star, a cute puppy—*what makes these women squeal?*

Turned out, Bradley Summers did.

The man himself appeared from the crowd, laughed at the wolf-whistling and stumbled passed the hordes that had formed a tight circle around him. Hands were everywhere, scrabbling to touch the meaty flesh on display. He wasn't naked exactly, but the oversized yellow fireman's trousers strapped on by braces did nothing to cover his bare, hairless chest. And if Mark didn't know better, which he didn't, that body was slicked up in a sparkling, glistening oil that radiated from his smooth skin and wafted a spicy aroma as he dragged himself ever closer to Mark.

Mark was aware he was salivating. Far more than any of those decked out in figure-hugging T-shirts that claimed *Lisa's Lovelie's Were Let Loose*. His basic functions had gone out the window, along with poor Lisa's grammar.

Bradley smiled, then chuckled and proceeded to wipe Mark's mouth for him with his thumb. *Utter mortification.*

"Nice jacket." Bradley wiped his fingers down his bright yellow plastic trousers.

Mark looked him in the eye. He did. He was sure of it. Until Bradley cupped a hand under his chin and dragged it up. *Ah, yes, there's the blue-green.*

"Oh, this old thing?" Mark finally stuttered out and ruffled the squeaking new leather over his shoulders. "Had it years."

Bradley chuckled. "Yeah?" He stepped in so close that warm, sweet-tasting breath trickled onto Mark's tongue.

He grunted as Bradley yanked something from the jacket, a slicing pop and crack breaking through Mark's pretence. When Bradley held up the shop-tag, he grinned then screwed it up in a balled fist.

"Well, I obviously never wore it all that much." Mark might as well dig his own grave.

"Perhaps you should have." Bradley winked. "Looks good on you."

"Ha," Mark laughed. "I'd love to return the compliment, but..." He waved down at Bradley's attire. "Sans jacket. I'm sure you'd get third-degree burns were you to rush into a burning building like that. Or do you specialise in rescuing cats up a tree? Because I'm sure you'd also get a scratch or two for the effort."

"Would you?"

"Huh?" Mark furrowed his brow.

"Scratch me for the effort of this rescue?"

"I'm very close to it."

Bradley laughed. "Well, it does get mighty hot in there." He nodded toward the basement bar. "You might even have to take *that* jacket off."

"Or perhaps I could just stand out here and admire the delightful sights." Mark glanced around the bustling High Street consisting of drunk women, homeless men, littered pavements and graffiti-ridden walls.

"You'll have much better sights in there, believe me," Bradley replied, wrapping a greasy arm around Mark's shoulders and steering him toward the queue.

Mark wiped a hand over his brow and dipped his head. It wasn't shame—it was avoiding the death glares from Lisa's Lovelie's and Rachel's Roquette's. The ones who weren't whistling were demanding to be given the same VIP treatment as Mark because it was Cheryl's last night for a tongue kiss.

"Sorry, ladies," Bradley called over, ducking himself and Mark away from prying hands. "This one's all mine."

"Oh, God," Mark grumbled.

Now he was being used as an openly mocking spectacle. Why on earth had he thought this was a good idea? Apart from having a strong, muscular and rather peculiar sweet-smelling arm around his shoulders and a sudden urge to sink his teeth into the pert nipples only mildly covered by a set of black braces, Mark struggled for rational reason to have strayed from the norm.

Too late now. Bradley steered him through the darkened entrance and down the carpeted steps where the place opened out into a basement nightclub. At the bottom, in front of a curving screen of Adonis men, they were greeted by a six-foot platinum blonde, squeezed into a glittering red mini dress and sparkling red stilettos. Whilst it did bear some resemblance to his mother in her early days, the dark beard gave some indication that this one wouldn't have been welcome at his mother's Women's Institute meetings.

"Well, hello, there, handsome." The deep, husky voice rattled the walls and the grin that followed smeared lipstick onto the edges of coarse beard hair. "You must be Aussie's guest of honour for this evening?"

"Mark." Unsure whether to hold out a hand, bow or, possibly, curtsey—maybe a kiss was in order?—Mark stumbled through his name. *How the fuck does one greet a drag queen? And is it tragic that I don't know the answer to that?*

The queen decided to take that concern away from Mark and stepped forward to plant a kiss to his cheek and squeeze a beefy handful of his arse. Bradley slipped his arm from Mark's shoulders and cleared his throat.

"You are adorable!" Drag queen clapped her hands in delight, then pinched Mark's cheek.

"Leave it, Juana." Bradley chuckled, but his voice was firm along with the hand he slipped on the small of Mark's back.

"Juana?" Mark pointed the question at Bradley.

"Juana Bang," Bradley replied, deadpan.

"And I so *do*!" Juana winked. "Do you *whanna*? Either of you two will do. Or maybe I'll just watch you both?"

"Ah," Mark said. "It's going to be like that all night, is it?"

Bradley leaned forward and held his lips mere inches from Mark's ear. That breath, that sweet, warm breath landed on Mark's cheeks once more and he blushed. Thank heavens for dark stubble.

"Don't tell me you don't go for a man in drag?" Bradley whispered.

"Why, do you?" Mark twisted so his lips were a breath away from Bradley's. Plump, smooth, kissable pink lips that curved into an endearing smile.

"I've been known to step into my inner fem." Bradley winked. "But tonight, I'm playing all man."

"Right. Good. I suppose." He held Bradley's gaze, ignoring the tingles that swished around his whole body, reinvigorating those stiff old limbs to life.

"Christ on a bike, you two!" Juana flapped her hands in front of her fluttering fake eyelashes. "It's like watching *Love, Simon* here. With a middle-aged lead."

"Shut up, Juana." Bradley pushed Mark on the back.

Was that embarrassment? Was Bradley *blushing*? Mark wouldn't like to comment, so he allowed the grappling manhandling all the way through to the adjacent bar. It was all darkness and glitter balls, with rows upon rows of chairs facing the stage. The circular bar area was manned by a tender dressed in nothing but a dickie bow and tight shorts.

Mark swallowed. Maybe he had died and this was limbo?

"Drinks are on the house for you, mate." Bradley smiled, his eyes relaxing. "Order what you want. I gotta go back out there. For the pictures."

"Can I have tea?" Mark asked. He was deadly serious.

"Sure." Bradley nodded at the barman with a smirk. "He'll have a Long Island Iced Tea, extra-strong."

"Sure thing, Brad." The way the barmen breathed out Bradley's name prickled Mark's skin and it burned ever more when Bradley returned a wink, a wide sparkling smile, and scurried off toward the double doors.

"I'm pretty sure you know I usually go for English Breakfast," Mark called after him, because he couldn't bear for the man to leave him stranded. Or just leave him. Where was their banter, their back and forth, their…them? *Give over, Mark. You're delusional with early-onset dementia.*

Bradley spun, backing through the swinging doors. "The only brekkie on the cards is an Aussie one." The flapping doors after Bradley's exit filtered the odd flash of light from the cameras into the darkened bar. Mark was alone, except for the near-naked man serving him. In this situation, Mark wasn't surprised to find himself wondering what food was served at an Aussie breakfast.

A goblet filled with mini pink umbrellas, a plastic penis shaped ornament and a straw was plonked down in front of him. "Get a bit of Long Island in you before you switch to continental."

Mark wrapped a hand around the glass. "Excuse me?"

"Brad." The barman nodded. "He's continental, ain't he?"

"Oh, no, Australia is in Oceania. Continental would be European."

"Oh. So what would it be then? Before you…"

"Go down under?"

"Bet you would, mate." The barman winked, then scurried off to serve the first horde who had cackled through the door and looked like they'd already consumed a vast amount of alcohol prior to the stuff they now ordered by the bucketload.

Mark sniffed his drink, avoiding eye contact, and stirred the yellow liquid with the bright pink plastic cock. There was something he hoped never to have in his tea. Still, at least this would taste a little of tea. It was in the title, after all.

It didn't. But by three of them, Mark tended not to care so much.

The rows of seats had filled up by the time Mark ordered his fourth Long Island Iced whilst propped up at the bar. Or more like the bar was propping him up by that point. Considering the drinks were flowing free, Mark thought he might as well enjoy the novel experience of not having to fork out an entire year's wages for a drink.

The noisy chatter died down and Ms Juana Bang marched her way onto the stage. Juana Bang was actually quite funny and Mark found himself chuckling along with the lewd jokes and banter that she sparked up with a few of the brasher bridesmaid brigades, when the first Adonis act was upon them all.

What is the plural of Adonis? Add the s or take it away and randomly add an i like a cactus? Well, the Adonis cabaret performers do provide a fair amount of prick. Hee hee. Okay, far too much alcohol for you, Mark.

Holding Out for a Hero blasted out from the speakers and four men leapt onto the stage in identical inappropriate fireman's uniforms to the one Bradley had donned. Bradley was there, too. Mark couldn't miss him, mainly because he chose to only focus on his performance. Bradley was a better dancer, that was all, and Mark appreciated skill. Bradley had a far more energetic and gymnastic style, even launching through a couple of splits and handstands to the audience's utter, squealing, delight. Mark could see the appeal but chose to keep his lips firmly around his straw that now had a cock stuck to that too, instead of sticking his fingers in his mouth and whistling. He also resisted the urge to join in with the, "Off, off, off." *Just.*

Sadly, no trousers came off. Apparently, there was more to come, and Mark wondered how far this cabaret act actually went, considering he knew how thorough Bradley had been with his personal preparations. So did most of Mark's office, come to that. Was this really the *Full Monty*? He slurped up the remains in his glass and prepared for the possibility he'd be seeing that sheen-like body once more. Along with all of Lisa's Lovelie's. As in, her friends. Not that he expected Lisa to be baring all her assets as part of the Adonis act. Although, the way things were going so far, Mark wasn't going to be ruling anything out.

The lights switched off, rendering the basement pitch-black. At least Mark hoped that it had been intentional and he hadn't passed out from too much cock—*ha*—tail. It was confirmed that he was still upright and in full control of his capabilities when strobe lighting flickered across the audience in waves.

"Do we have a treat for you ladies tonight!" Juana's deep voice boomed over the bass thumping through the walls. "And gentleman, of course. Hi, Mark! Everyone say hi to Mark!"

Two hundred women twisted in their seats as the spotlight dropped on Mark. They waved, whistled and said "hi". Mark held up a hand and was just about to spin it around and leave the middle finger waving skyward when the light swivelled away from him.

"Please welcome to the stage, and to the country, all the way from Down Under, and don't we know how far we want him to go down, eh, ladies! And gentleman."

How far could he realistically launch this glass? The chances of it not reaching the stage and landing on one of Lisa's Lovelie's prevented him from finding out.

"You've seen him on YouTube, I know you all have, you dirty pervs!" Juana chuckled into her microphone, the deep droning tone vibrating the floor beneath Mark's feet.

YouTube? Bradley was, like, *famous*? *Nice of him to mention that.*

"And now, please, give a warm welcome to Geek God, currently known as our Aussie Adonis, *Brad*!"

An eruption of cheers, followed by a bouncing intro of electrified music started up. The strobe lights stretched from the stage and out to the audience, flashing over each row of girls. Mark straightened, to get a proper look, and his heart beat a little faster too, as if it was clapping along with the pounding bass line and stamping stilettos, waiting for Bradley to appear.

And emerge he did, leaping out from behind the ruffled curtains. Gone was the fire outfit, though. And, possibly, some of his dignity, as he wriggled his hips and thrust his groin, that was not leaving anything for the imagination to conjure up, within an all-in-one Star Fleet uniform. So tight was the outfit that every sordid curvature and every delightful outline of Bradley's perfectly sculpted body was captured within soft, inviting fibres.

Holy fuckballs. The empty cocktail glass dropped from Mark's loosened fingers and fell to the floor with a clatter. Turned out, it was made of plastic. Rather fortuitous for such moments. Not that Mark could tear his gaze from the stage to care all that much. Bradley was roaming the boards with such ease and elegance, and a presence Mark had been unaware the man possessed. He was so unassuming, normally. Attractive, yes, a looker that turned heads, but not full of himself, or conceited and brash, like he appeared to be when teasing the audience, and Mark counted himself in that, and firing his "phaser".

He was all tongue waggles and suggestive winks and salacious swishes of his hips. But none of it was detrimental to being in sync with the music—even the mischievous tearing of the zip from his collar to his sternum was in time. Bradley had choregraphed this act to a T.

What Mark would give for a real tea, right then. He had, however, found something that was also his thing. Men dressed up as a *Star Trek* captain. Maybe not men, per se. *Bradley*. Beautiful, perfect, Bradley. Had he done this on purpose? It was only a couple of days ago they'd had their conversation about his love for the old series. Could Bradley really have conjured all this up in a couple of days and that this act, this strip tease, was why he had been so bloody insistent that Mark be here? But why? *Why* would he do that? For him? For *Mark*? Could Mark have got this all wrong? Could Bradley be trying to say something with all this? A declaration? Or was this that darned old fate that Bradley banged on about?

And how much Long Island Ice Tea have I actually consumed?

All thoughts were ripped from Mark when the lyrical part of the accompanying music shattered his trance. Bradley peered out to the crowd, caught Mark's gaze, smirked and mimed the blasted words, 'I'd do things to you, if you were born in the eighties, the eighties."

Mark's toe dipping into the realms of romantic possibilities froze. *This is a joke.*

He watched Bradley slip one shoulder out from his costume and realised there wasn't enough Long Island Iced Tea to numb this moment. Releasing one slicked up and muscle-bound arm to more squeals of delight from the audience, Bradley danced off to another part of the stage and regaled those in that area of the audience with more of his flesh and energetic groin thrusts.

He went back into character mode and shot from his phaser into the crowd, who all demanded that more of Bradley's attire should fall to the wayside. Which didn't seem to be far off from an inappropriate ask, as an "alien" crashed onto the stage, aiding those demands along by tackling Bradley to the floor. Uniform well and truly ripped. That would never have made it passed the test stages at Star Fleet Academy.

Still, no one seemed to mind as Bradley's gleaming torso was now on display for all and sundry. And what a torso it was. Mark had been in awe of every ridge when he'd zoomed in on the picture sent to his email, and through the tightness of the lycra he wore, but up there, Mark's appetite for rolling his tongue along every inch had just tripled in magnitude.

What is this? I have never drooled over gym queens, ever! Bradley was hardly a gym queen. Honed to perfection, yes. But there was so much more to—

The alien scurried off the stage and Bradley grappled up, tearing himself free from the rest of that darn hindering uniform, leaving Mark staring, mouth agape, wondering what it was he was arguing with himself about. Bradley was left in nothing but a pair of tight Union Jack briefs, the red letters *GEEK BOY* spread across his pert arse cheeks, which he then proceeded to clench and flex in time with the music.

Mark hated himself for licking his lips.

Chuckling, Bradley turned back to the audience and indicated for the seats to part the way through the middle. The other Adonis all darted out of nowhere to help form an aisle, manicured nails all scrabbling to wrap themselves around bumped biceps and thick thighs. Mark cocked his head.

Bradley jumped down from the stage, then launched into a running flip and tuck through the separated chairs, landing on his feet in front of Mark at the back of the bar.

"Oh." Mark widened his eyes. "Hello."

Bradley winked and mouthed "Hi," before pirouetting back up to the stage and ending his delightful performance by holding his phaser in front of his groin and ripping off the briefs. How, Mark couldn't fathom. He tended to hop around the bedroom to rip off his own and mostly ended up falling down to kick the rest off. That from Bradley had been one slick tear that had Mark dizzy. Grinning, Bradley threw the garment in to the audience as a beam of light shot out from his phaser-slash-groin, making it impossible to get a real look at Bradley's handful, and all the lights suddenly turned off, pitching the place into darkness.

The crowd erupted. And Mark was a little concerned that he might have, too.

"Wasn't he just great, ladies!" A spotlight illuminated Juana on the stage to a chorus of whistles and screams. "Fancy your chances at serenading our young men?"

Three chairs were plonked down on stage by three of the Adonises—Bradley being one and now back in a new pair of boxer briefs. They all stood beside Juana, awaiting further instruction, but Mark caught Bradley's gaze fluttering out to the crowd. He slinked away into the shadows. He was sure he was still blushing. He'd had quite enough of that for tonight.

"So, go forth, my young men." Juana flapped her oversized nails at the audience. "Find me the one you want to watch dance for you!"

Three ripped men jumped down into the fray and scanned the girls who had flung their arms wildly into the air and waved with a frantic "choose me, choose me" desperation. Two of the Adonises chose quickly, dragging up giggling hens, but Bradley roamed toward the back.

Oh, hell no. Mark shook his head.

Bradley grinned and pointed. To Mark.

Mark shook his head, more fiercely that time with less of the amusement and more of the utter horror and confirmation of his blatant refusal. No amount of Long Island Ice Tea was going to get him up there. Bradley, unperturbed, curled a finger out in front of his face and beckoned with a sure-fire *come-hither* look in his eye.

"Dance for me, Mark," Bradley called over the loud squeals and whoops from the audience.

"I'd really rather not, if it's all the same to you." Perhaps *fuck off* might have been better received, as Bradley didn't seem to get the hint, instead grabbing Mark's hand and tugging him forward.

"Too late." Bradley did not release his firm grip until Mark was up on that stage, squinting out to the heckling crowd.

I've had finer moments.

"Well, hello, there," Juana drawled into the microphone. "We meet again. Everybody, this is Mark! He's gay."

The crowd roared, and Mark would have liked to have said the feeling he received was like that of a popstar, but sadly, he just felt like a right utter wanker. The moment was up there with the memory of his school speech, when the entire school had applauded his bravery, only for him to be met with cackles, fists and leftover contents of lunchboxes on his way home.

"I'm sure I'm not the only one," Mark called out through gritted teeth, gaze firmly fixed on Bradley who sank into one of the seats on stage.

"Now, now, Mark." Juana covered her mouth to speak away from the microphone this time. "No spoiling the illusion."

The best thing Mark could think to do right then was to pull camaraderie with the other two women who had been dragged up on stage, form a bond through the humiliation. He glanced to his right. Of course they would be pure goddesses, equipped in the art of lap dance seduction.

It was Mark that was here for the comic relief. *Wonderful. This is what Bradley had planned all along!*

"Okay, ladies!" Juana bellowed back into the microphone, snapping Mark from his homicidal thoughts. "And, gent."

She winked at Mark, but he ignored it in favour of offering the deadliest of death stares to Bradley, seated in front of him with his face at Mark's groin level. Bradley, the utter bastard, laughed.

"In order to win the ultimate prize, you must dance, strut your stuff and seduce as best you can. The audience will decide our winner via the applaudometer." Juana held up a contraption that had clearly been made by Blue Peter in the sixties. Mark was dubious about its authenticity. "Cue the music, boys!"

"What's the prize?" Mark hollered over at Juana.

She pretended not to hear him and the loud boom from the music's bass line ricocheted off the walls and banged into Mark's temple. Was he hungover already?

The two girls either side of Mark were overly keen and thrust their ample cleavages forward into the faces of their own personal Adonis. Mark was rooted to the spot. What could he do? His idea of dancing was step to the side and back again. Hardly what one would call seductive.

"Come on, Mark!" Bradley urged, beckoning with two hands and offering his lap for Mark to utilise for his enjoyment. In public. No, not just in public. On stage. On show.

Kill me now.

"I will get you for this." Mark replied through gritted teeth. How? He'd figure that out another time.

Bradley chuckled.

The four Long Island Iced Teas decided then was the time to work their magic and Mark stepped forward in an attempt to prove he wasn't one to run away from a challenge. Clearing his throat, he ruffled back his hair and step, shuffle, stepped toward Bradley. The other two ladies were giving the moment their best, straddling their Adonises or grinding their behinds. No bother, Mark could work what he had in his arsenal.

Unzipping his leather jacket, Mark threw his head back and put his mound of thick hair to full use by flicking his head back and forth. He got into it, letting the music wash over his resolve and cavorted in closer to Bradley. He could almost forget a couple of hundred people were watching him. It wasn't as if he'd ever have to watch it himself.

"Off, off, off!" The words of encouragement from the audience rung in his ears.

"You heard them." Bradley winked and gripped his fingers tightly on his bare thighs.

Was that because the Adonises weren't allowed to touch? The others certainly hadn't handled their dancers. Did Bradley want to touch him? The very thought urged Mark onwards. He slipped off his new leather jacket, curled a finger through the loop and twirled it around his head.

It would have been a good move, but rather overzealous in his whirling, Mark whacked the dancing girl next to him with it. She squealed, clutching her eye and fell into the lap of her Adonis.

Oh bugger, the zip!

Mark held up his hands. "Sorry. Oh, bugger, I'm so sorry."

The music screeched to a halt, the first aiders launched onto the stage and Mark rubbed soothing circles along the girl's back.

Bradley pissed his tiny, tight pants.

* * * *

"I don't think she'll sue, so you're all right." Bradley clamped his lips shut, his shoulders wobbling through fighting back the urge to laugh.

"Wonderful." Mark pushed away from the wall of the smokers' corner outside, where he had been hiding for the remainder of the evening.

He had been offered a number of cigarettes from the ladies who'd taken pity on him, but had declined graciously. If he even attempted to start smoking now he would only hack up a lung, or set the entire nightclub alight, such was the way his day, and entire existence, was unfolding.

Bradley had finished his stripping stint and changed back into more appropriate attire for the outside weather and the club was turning back into the full-on night haunt.

"I would like to say, thanks for inviting me, but, well..."

"You had fun, right?" Bradley had an almost hopeful hint of elevation to his question.

"No," Mark lied.

He had actually had rather a lot of fun, minus the near-gouging-out-of-eyeball experience. But the Lisa Lovely had won her prize, which was a date with her Adonis, so Mark realised that was a win/win. Win for her, obviously, and a win for him having not to have actually won. Because a date with Bradley? That was never going to happen. Not now Mark had proven himself to be a klutz, a safety hazard and in no way a magnetic force in the art of seduction.

"I'm going to slink back home now and never venture into London again until every person who may have been here has aged significantly that they either die, or the memory dies with them. Either, or, it'll be a while."

"You know they film that, right?"

"Oh, hell, no." Mark pinched the bridge of his nose. Now he was going to rival Bradley's YouTube success but in a whole different ball game.

Bradley chuckled. "Maybe you're better suited to slow dancing?"

"Must be your accent there," Mark replied, "because I'm sure you meant to pronounce that *no* dancing."

"I dunno, mate. I think you'd look good in a ballroom. Bow tie, elegant. Right up your street."

"My mother and father used to make me go watch them ballroom dancing," Mark admitted. "It's not something I look on with fondness."

"All right." Bradley shivered, a cold breeze blowing.

"You need more clothes on." Mark indicated the vest and tight jeans that Bradley was wearing in minus temperatures.

"Yes, Daddy."

"Oi! None of that, thank you. I am not old enough to be your daddy."

"Just my sugar one." Bradley winked.

Mark had no idea what to say to that. It dredged up a bunch of things that Mark had chosen to long forget.

"Anyway, you gotta appreciate the song I chose, right?" Bradley's wide-eyed gaze was full of boyish charm.

"Ah, yes." Mark nodded. "Nice."

"'Cause you were born in the eighties, right?" Bradley grinned.

"No," Mark deadpanned. "Nope, not the eighties. Sadly."

"You're thirty-nine?" Bradley furrowed his brow. "I'm sure I worked that out right."

"I was born in seventy-nine. December seventy-nine. The cusp of the eighties, so if you were trying to insinuate something with that song, I'm afraid it sorely missed."

What a way to kill a moment. Not that this was a moment, mind. Mark had made sure of that with his lap dance gone wrong. And he couldn't shake his sullen mood.

"You're a Sagittarius?" Bradley asked.

"I believe so, yes."

"Huh." Bradley bit his lip with a faraway look in his eye. "A fire sign. The Archer. And a traveller."

"See, the stars can be wrong."

"Come on." Bradley slapped Mark on the back. "Let's go get a train back home, then, yeah? Stick to the seaside for you."

Mark nodded. It was probably for the best. He'd left London some time back and now at least he knew he'd outgrown the nighttime frolicking. It was a good thing. Like closure on the place. And on him, and any hope that he could recapture his lost youth by hanging around with someone far younger. This had all been a mistake. A big mistake. Back to slippers and damp living spaces. It was fine.

Mark fished his phone out of his back pocket and checked the time. "Bugger. We've missed the train."

Bradley shrugged. "No worries. Hotel it is." He smiled, holding out his arm and whistling for the black cab passing to stop. "Come on, Mark. I'm knackered!"

Mark didn't have much of a choice. The next train wasn't for, like, another thirty minutes.

Chapter Ten

Beddie Byes

"Name?"

"Mr and Mrs Smith." Bradley grinned at the hotel receptionist and shot a wink over his shoulder at Mark.

"Who's the miss?" the receptionist asked with a sly smile.

"Yet to find that out." Bradley waggled his eyebrows.

Mark could have gone home. Should have gone home. There had been another train. Instead, he'd decided to allow Bradley to halt the taxi outside the Holiday Inn in Shoreditch and usher him into the reception area without much protest. Mark had no idea why. He thought he'd been quite clear to himself that this charade needed to end. And now Bradley was offering all sorts of jibes. What was this? What was going on?

"For goodness' sake." Mark stepped forward, pulling his wallet out from his back pocket and slapping a credit card down on the counter. "Please book a twin room under the name Mark Johnson."

Bradley gasped, slapping a hand to his chest. "Darling, you said you'd take my name!"

The receptionist did her best to not to laugh whilst swiping Mark's card. He couldn't blame her. They did look an odd pair. There was Bradley—all muscle and glistening from the oil spread over his face, down his neck line to his sternum. Not that Mark had been staring at the droplets sparkling Bradley's skin. It was just the man's inadequate deep V-line vest top showed far too much flesh not to notice. Then there was him. Leather jacket firmly zipped up to the top and face pale through sheer embarrassment.

"You can always get your own room," Mark challenged.

"At these prices?" Bradley elevated his voice. "That's all my tips gone."

"I suppose tonight's performance means you were probably down in the tips?"

The earlier drinks were now wearing off, leaving in their wake a haze of guilt. Mark could remember *what* he'd done but not exactly *why* he'd done it. Such as most of his life minus alcohol.

"Nah, mate." Bradley tapped the counter. "Made double what I usually do. Think people felt sorry for me that I didn't get a proper lap dance." He pouted.

"Oh, right, well." Mark pocketed his returning card. "Your fault there."

"How's that?"

"You chose the wrong partner." Mark drummed his nails on the counter while the receptionist tapped her nails along the new-fangled tablet.

"I don't know about that, Mark." Bradley glanced up to the receptionist who returned his dashing smile.

Traitor.

"I'm sorry, sir," the receptionist finally said. "There are no twin rooms available. We only have the superior double."

Mark went to open his mouth and decline, deciding it was probably better to either find somewhere else or maybe there was still time to catch that last train? This had all been a mistake anyway. But Bradley slapped his hand down on the counter.

"Sold." He winked.

The receptionist gave a polite nod and booked them in, handing over the key card. "Breakfast is served until ten on Sundays. Would you like a wakeup call?"

"No," Mark blurted. "No, thank you."

"We sleep in on Sundays." Bradley grinned.

Mark made a mental note to get Damien to stencil on his forehead that he should only drink tea made with the use of a kettle and not an array of alcoholic spirits from now on.

The room was on the fifth floor, and Mark let them both into the large suite that boasted a corridor leading from the door past a set of dark wooden double wardrobes and into the main area complete with sofa, desk and a huge king-size bed. There was enough space to home a family of four.

"So, are you a lefty or a righty?" Bradley asked, hands on hips, standing at the foot of the ridiculously large bed.

Mark tore his gaze from having been marvelling at the east London skyline. "I'm sorry?" Political viewpoints weren't exactly high on Mark's bedtime musings.

"Do you sleep on the left or the right?" Brad asked, pointing at each side of the bed covered in mounds of pillows and scatter cushions.

"Oh, I see." Mark gazed down on the bed with tense concentration, even adding a scrape of his chiny chin chin. It had been so long since he'd actually shared a bed to know which side of it he preferred. He usually just got in, wrapped himself up and got on with it. Sleeping, that was. Because nothing else here was on the cards. Nothing. At. All.

"It's okay, Mark." Bradley launched onto the bed and threw all the cushions to the floor. "I usually sleep in the middle, too."

"Of course you do." Mark scanned the room and breathed a sigh of relief at the kettle and mugs perched on the dressing table. Such a sight for sore eyes. He immediately went over and did the inevitable.

"You're having tea?" Bradley twisted on the bed, lying flat with his arms behind his head.

"Of course." Mark stomped through to the bathroom and filled the kettle, which for some unfathomable reason did not fit under the tiny sink without contorting it at an angle, ultimately making most of the water spurt from the spout. Good job Bradley didn't like tea—there wouldn't be enough to make two cups.

In the main room, Mark avoided looking at Bradley relaxed on the bed and set the kettle to boil. He stood, arms folded, waiting. It seemed the saying 'a watched kettle never boils' was especially true on this occasion, as nothing stirred to life. After a moment, Bradley jumped up from the bed, leaning a hair's breadth from Mark, and reached behind him to flick the electric switch. The kettle sparked to life and Bradley didn't remove his person from invading Mark's personal space.

"I turned you on." Bradley's sweet breath trickled onto Mark's face. What was it that made Bradley's breath so damn sweet?

"Thank you." *Christ, my sexy banter is atrocious.*

"You're welcome." Bradley stepped away and raked his gaze over Mark. "And, Mark? That really is a nice jacket, but you can take it off inside." He sank to perch on the edge of the bed. "I mean, if I sit over here, I'm far enough away for you not to cause me personal injury. Still extract the thing carefully, mind. I've got a job where having one less eye might cause me to lose earnings."

"Ha, bloody, ha. I doubt your stripping clientele would mind though. I don't think they were looking at your face."

"True." Bradley nodded. "But I'm also running a café at the moment. Serving hot drinks. Might make it difficult having stilted vision for that sorta thing."

"I could make tea with one eye." Mark pointed a finger at Bradley. "I could make tea blind." God knew why he said that in a boastful tone. Although, he was pretty sure he could. In his own house, perhaps. Knowing where everything was. But still, it wasn't exactly something that was up there in the skills department on his curriculum vitae. Nor something to brag about to a gymnastic-bending Australian Adonis in an attempt to make himself appear more, well, appealing.

Bradley stood, stepped forward and took hold of the zip clasp on Mark's jacket. Without breaking eye contact, Bradley dragged the zip down. Each toothy grip cracked as he glided it all the way to the bottom. Tugging at the end made the jacket fall apart, and

Bradley tucked his thumbs into either side, sliding it off Mark's shoulders.

Now that is how to remove a jacket with pure seduction.

Mark held his breath. And it was only because he was aware of the leftover remnants of Long Island Iced Tea and didn't want to waft stale alcohol breath onto Bradley's face. He also couldn't be sure that he wouldn't snot over him should he choose to ever exhale again. At this point, Mark was in danger of passing out. It didn't help that Bradley's mere lingering presence had Mark on a knife's edge and that every hair on his body tingled with anticipation. His lips were telling him to launch forward, to seize the moment, to be able to taste what it was that made Bradley's breath smell so sweet.

But his rational mind told him not to be so bloody daft.

Bradley slipped his hands on Mark's shoulders, spun him around so Mark's back was to him then covered Mark's eyes with warm, freshly scented fingers. Mark breathed in. Again. Asphyxiation was a real possibility.

"Go on then, Mark," Bradley rasped into his ear. "Show me your talent."

Delightfully warm breath trickled down Mark's neck and danced along his spine, reigniting all those senses that had lain dormant. It had been so long. So bloody long. Why shouldn't he? Why *couldn't* he? Why couldn't he just take this moment, act on instinct and leave it all behind in this room? There were sparks, Mark could see that even with Bradley's hands clamped over his eyes. He could feel the energy bubbling between them, could even taste the hot, sizzling air—

The kettle clicked off. Boiled. *Ah.*

"Make me a cuppa," Bradley whispered, voice so seductively low it was a wonder Mark didn't climax along with the water. "I'll try some of your hot stuff if you can handle that jug in the dark."

Mark swallowed. *Shit, Bradley will feel that in his calloused surfer hands. He can sense my nerves. He'll be feeding on it forever.*

So he tried to not move any facial muscles—a lot harder than he'd first thought. Everything itched. And was hot. He was sure it wasn't Bradley's hands over his eyes that were suddenly clammy. *Do eyes sweat?*

"It's all about trust, Mark." Bradley's voice sounded like it was coming from far away and not right by his ear. Perhaps it was the change in tone. The teasing had gone and a seriousness had surfaced.

"Can you trust me not to let you get hurt?"

Mark exhaled sharply. His pulse quickened and he was sure Bradley would feel the pounding through Mark's temple. *Trust? What a word.*

Mark had lost trust in most things some time back.

But Bradley was new. *Shiny* new.

Take a bleedin' chance, Marky Mark! Mark shook his head. *Shut up, Damian. Not now.*

Oh, God, I'm batshit crazy!

"I'm thirsty, Mark."

"All right, all right." Mark scrabbled for the mugs he knew were on the tray to left of the kettle. Within them was a tea bag encased in its square packet. Easy, tear it and chuck it in. Achieved.

"Well done." Bradley's appraisal made Mark beam a little churlishly.

"Thank you. I have done this before."

"Really? With your eyes closed?"

"Well, not exactly like this. But I have scrabbled around in the dark to make tea when there's been a power cut."

"How'd you boil the water with no electricity?"

"I used the tap."

"Cold cuppa?" Bradley exclaimed, edging back.

"I didn't say it was a particularly good one."

Mark curled his hand around the kettle handle and lifted it from the holster. Bradley's fingers loosened over his eyes, making way for some vision, albeit a little blurred.

"Careful, Mark. Your mugs are a little too close to your groin."

"I wouldn't worry. That area was numbed some time ago."

"Really? That's a real shame." Bradley didn't sound teasing, or annoyed, more sympathetic and it unnerved Mark somewhat.

"It is." Feeling around for the mugs, Mark focused on the task and not what had made him utter those words so carelessly.

"You know, Mark, you reveal a lot more about yourself when you can't see me."

"Perhaps it's because I don't have to witness your mocking reaction to my woes."

"I'm not that mean. You've got a past, that's obvious. I don't mock that stuff. In fact, I'd like to hear more. I'd like to get to know you. Get to understand what makes Mark so afraid to open up."

Whilst Bradley had been speaking, Mark had manged to trickle the water into one mug, but the more he listened, he inched the kettle along to where he thought the next mug was.

Ripping his hands away, Bradley launched back. "Far out, Mark!"

Mark heard the dribble and sizzle of boiling water onto carpet fibres before his eyes adjusted and saw the burst of steam from the floor. Slapping the kettle down onto the table, he twisted. Bradley sat on the edge of the bed, holding on to his bare foot and blowing onto it.

"Oh, God, did I get you?" Mark asked.

"Yeah. No worries, mate. My fault." He wiped over his big toe. His perfect big toe! "I'll just go run it under the cold tap." He stood and stretched. "Actually, I'll go wash off all this oil. Not really a good thing between the sheets. Drink your tea, Mark."

Mark watched as Bradley ripped off his vest, tore off his jeans and glided into the bathroom like a cat. A bulky, perfectly formed cat. Should he be referring to Bradley as something feminine? Possibly not, because from where Mark stood, with a perfect view into the frosted shower cubicle as Bradley hadn't bothered closing the bathroom door, Bradley was all male.

Shaking himself free from any over blatant ogling, Mark finished making his tea and sat on the edge of the bed to drink it. And to give himself a stern talking-to. But before he'd got as far as calling himself a muppet, the shower stream switched off and Bradley emerged back into the bedroom, towel wrapped low around his hips.

Bradley smiled. Not smirked, or grinned, just smiled. Sweetly. And if Mark didn't know better, a little bashfully.

Mark found himself smiling back.

Then averted his eyes when Bradley ripped the towel from his waist, scrubbed it through his hair and launched it over the soft couch. Mark took a swig of tea.

It went down the wrong way and he had to cough into a balled fist.

"Careful, Mark. You'll have me thinking you're a spitter." Bradley scraped back the duvet and climbed into the bed. Naked.

Mark wasn't sure why he was so surprised. It wasn't as if either of them had any luggage in order to change into pyjamas. And Bradley certainly didn't look like the average pyjama-wearing type. But it was still a rather bold move.

"Do you snore, Mark?" Bradley lay on his front, ruffled the pillows around him, and draped the duvet over his pert backside.

"Not that I'm aware of," Mark replied. "But, then, I only sleep with myself."

"Really?" Bradley widened intrigued eyes.

"As in, I sleep alone," Mark corrected. He wasn't admitting that he relied on his masturbation efforts as sleeping accompaniment. Even if it was true. "Damian told me I did once, but we'd had quite a lot to drink that night and I'd been standing outside waiting for his bloody performance to end, so I was sure I had a cold. Still, not a nice thing for one to say to someone dying of influenza."

"Who's Damian?" Bradley twisted onto his side and propped himself up on his arm.

"Oh, a friend," Mark replied. "Lovely man. Funny. Annoying. Thinks a little too much of himself sometimes, and other times not quite enough."

"Sounds like someone I know."

Mark met Bradley's gaze across the bed and Bradley returned a smile. Another genuine one. Not the playful ones he'd been brandishing around for so long. It warmed Mark a little, seeing Bradley when he was out of his persona, like when he'd first met him in the cafe. Like when he'd apologised about the kiss. Actually, Bradley hadn't been anything but genuine. *Hasn't he?*

"Do *you* snore?" Mark discarded the now empty mug onto the desk.

"No one's ever told me," Bradley replied. "I, too, sleep alone."

"Pfft." Mark flapped his hand. "Don't give me that. You mean to say you don't go home with someone after every one of those gigs of yours?" He remained perched on the edge of the bed but curled one leg under his backside to get comfy. He hadn't quite worked up the courage to lie down yet and wondered how he ever would. "Or a hotel?"

Bradley leaned up. "No, Mark. For one, most of those gigs are heaving with Sheilas. And I'm not sure if I have made this clear or not, but I don't really go for pink bits."

"And the other strippers?" Mark asked, raising his eyebrows.

"Most of them do." Bradley shrugged. "Some aren't fussy either way for the right price, if you know what I mean."

"You ever been tempted to do that?" Mark's voice shook. He wasn't sure if it was the question he was asking, or the fear of the answer, or just that it suddenly got that much colder in the room now the steam from the shower had all dissipated.

"No." Bradley's voice was stern with conviction. "I get offers, sure. We all do. Cash pushed into our hands, meet me outside, phone numbers with promises written on napkins. I'm not interested. You think I'd be working at Macy's tea shop if I was? Those boys earn a ton of dollar for that sort of thing."

Mark bit his lip, hanging his head in shame for having even asked the question, let alone thinking that the answer might be the affirmative. The fluffy duvet wrapped around the Aussie looked ever so comfy, and rather inviting. But Mark still hadn't inched any closer, or thought how he was going to take his clothes off in front of the perfect specimen of all male.

"Bradley?" Mark croaked out the name.

"Brad."

"Bradley." Mark glanced up and met Bradley's gaze.

"Mark." Bradley slapped the bed beside him. "Take your damn clothes off and get under this bed. I'm tired. You're tired. Whatever you want to ask, ask it under the warmth of duck feathers."

Mark widened his eyes. Then, with an exasperated huff, Bradley flipped around on his front and covered his head with the pillow. "There, not looking."

Well, that was what Mark thought he'd said, but considering his face was sunk into soft down feathers, it had come out muffled. But as Bradley didn't move, Mark thought it rather cruel to let the poor fellow suffocate whilst he contemplated whether Bradley would, indeed, have a sneak peek. So, he stood, checked Bradley still wasn't moving and peeled off his clothes, discarding most to the hotel room floor. He left on his new boxers, just, well, *because*...and snuck in under the covers. Bradley didn't stir and Mark feared that he'd taken too long and Bradley had passed out. Two near fatalities in one evening would be all too much for Mark to bear.

"Are you okay?" Mark whispered.

Bradley lifted his head from the pillow, sucking in a gasp of air.

"All good, mate." Bradley grinned.

Mark didn't tear his gaze from Bradley across the pillows. He was entranced by him. Bradley's hair was fuzzy from air drying after the shower and his blue-green eyes sparkled in the moonlight dripping in from the open curtains. He appeared a hell of a lot more youthful than Mark had noticed before. Boyish, perhaps. With the duvet hiding his bulky, perfectly sculpted body, he looked every bit his twenty-one years. He looked innocent. And that made Mark slightly concerned.

"How on earth did you get into stripping?"

Bradley scooted himself up the bed and tucked his arms under the pillow, like getting comfy to tell a story.

"I was fixing this roof, back in Sydney. Been labouring for a few months to get money to travel. Was gonna take me forever, but I was determined to pay for the trip myself. Turned out, the house we're fixing up belongs to a club owner. One day it was, like, forty degrees out, so most of us had stripped to bottoms only. The owner said I could make a hell of a lot more dollar if I took my clothes off at his club for one night compared to the three months' pay I would get for fixing his house."

Bradley ruffled his forehead on the pillow in what Mark would assume was slight embarrassment of the admittance to what happened. It warmed Mark more than the duck feathers. And tea.

"So I said I'd go try it out. First night I made over two thousand dollars. Some of that was the flat wage. The rest in tips. After that, well, it's a no-brainer, right? I could pay for my trip in no time. The bloke set me up on YouTube, posted my videos, and I got a following. Offers poured in from around the globe to dance at various nightclubs. It meant I could travel and work."

"Do you like it?"

"Sure." Bradley shrugged. "I like dancing. I like having fun. One day I won't have this body, so why not use it while I can, right?"

"Ha," Mark replied. "I wouldn't really know about that. I've never had that body."

Bradley winked. "You can have it if you want."

"That would take years of solid hard training and probably a complete change in diet, not to mention DNA."

Bradley slipped closer and whispered in Mark's ear. "I didn't mean it like that."

Mark swallowed, hard. Bradley noticed and so slipped away across the bed to his own side, leaving Mark cold.

"Can I tell you something without you getting cranky?"

"Yes," Mark croaked out. "Of course, there is no guarantee. I have no idea what you are about to say. I mean, I cannot completely say for sure that my inner toddler might not burst free if you were to tell me that you've, say, decided to turn Macy's into a drop-in stripping workshop. That might cause a little unexpected outburst on my part."

"I won't be changing Macy's into a stripper workshop."

"Good," Mark replied with a firm nod. "That would seriously downgrade the town and I'm just not sure that the old dears who come in for their daily cuppa would appreciate your hairless balls replacing their sponge fingers—"

"You're beautiful," Bradley cut in, face serious, as he smiled through Mark's babble.

"What?"

Mark was pretty sure he'd heard and was in no way fishing to hear it again. The question just left his mouth before he could think better of it. Maybe a little confirmation to ensure he had heard *correctly* wouldn't go amiss, but he didn't want to appear ungrateful. Or, worse, deaf.

"You." Bradley edged closer and Mark breathed in deeply, trying to get a grip on his hammering heart and his bodily functions. "Are." He rubbed his nose across Mark's, trickling that sweet breath on his skin. "Beautiful."

Mark knew he couldn't say *"what"* again. So he settled for something far more worthy of his two-pound payment for the thesaurus app on his iPhone.

"Pffffft."

Chapter Eleven

A Helping Hand

Sleep evaded Mark. It didn't help that he hadn't shut his eyes yet. Bradley, however, had fluttered his eyes to a close after Mark's frantically ridiculous reply to his beautiful comment, and settled in for the night. Mark couldn't blame him. It wasn't like he had offered anything in the way of pillow talk.

For once in his life, Mark had been rendered speechless. No one had ever called him beautiful before. That phrase was more fitting to icons like Audrey Hepburn or Keira Knightley. At a push, if he had to call a male member of the species beautiful, he would consider, well, probably Bradley. Especially now he was all tucked up in bed, duvet wrapped up to his chin as he faced Mark, eyes closed so his thick lashes blended together in perfect harmony, and snored.

Huh, so Bradley does snore. That was certainly something Mark would have delight in confirming to him in the morning.

Damian would be slapping Mark about now if he were here. But then again, if Damian were there, it would have ruined the moment somewhat anyway. And no doubt Damian would have elbowed Mark out of the way and nabbed Bradley for himself using his tried and tested flirting techniques. Damian was no wallflower. Damian would have given Bradley the lap dance of his life. Damian would have followed Bradley to the shower cubicle, sunk to his knees and sucked that gorgeous cock until Bradley couldn't stand upright. Then they'd have formed the two-backed beast here in this bed until dawn. Humping each other until the chafing got all too much.

Mark nearly threw up at the thought.

But the point still stood. Mark had utterly, catastrophically missed his chance at pursuing something more than friendship with his wet dream—a sex God, a perfect specimen of male, a model, no less. A *stripper*, for God's sake!

But more than any of that…a Bradley.

Sure, Bradley was easy on the eye. Mark could understand why he was picked off a roof and shoved into performance art. *Is that the polite way of referring to taking your clothes off for money?* He had that all-Australian surfer bod with sun-kissed skin, bright white smile and luscious pink, kissable lips. His hair shone as golden as the sand from Bondi Beach—according to the pictures Mark had seen in the brochures—and his eyes were as blue as the Pacific Ocean. He was perfect. Like the Great Barrier Reef, he was a wonder of Mark's insignificant and boring world.

But he was also, well, just Bradley. Fun-loving, sweet, kind. He wasn't as face-value as Mark had maybe been expecting.

It's always the good-looking ones that rip out your heart, squeeze it between treacherous fingers and stamp on it during their hasty retreat, though.

Sighing, Mark stared up to the ceiling. The bedside lamp was still on, shimmering a mild orange glow around the room. He would turn it off, but that meant either leaning over Bradley and risk waking him up, or getting out of bed to walk around to his side and turn it off, which meant a walk back in the dark and Mark had already proved that he couldn't be trusted without his eyesight.

Why couldn't he just be more like Damian? Or George?

Oh, God, George. This was all his fault.

Mark shut his eyes, attempting to quell the rush of memories. For the first time in a long time, it did. Except, instead of memories, it was fantasies that came to the forefront. Beautiful, lustful, excitable fantasies. Of Bradley. Of Mark kissing him. Touching him. Licking him. Of Mark exploring that perfectly sculpted body and learning every inch of it using his tongue alone. Of Mark discovering what it was that makes Bradley squirm, that turned him to a blubbering wreck, of what made Bradley shiver, and squeal and—

Bugger!

Mark now had a raging stiffy.

He needed to think about something else. Which was a darn sight harder than it normally would have been when the source of his furious hard-on was lying in the bed next to him. *Naked, for goodness sake!*

Why the hell did Bradley have to be naked?

Mark whimpered. There was no reasonable way he could defuse this situation. If he even tried to think of something else, Bradley would move, snore, breathe even, and Mark would be back to square one, and he was in danger of making a tent out of the duvet with how hard his dick was right then. There was no two ways about it. He needed a wank.

As carefully as he could, he slid out from under the duvet and rolled away, falling in a heap onto the floor. Then, just because it wasn't enough of a predicament to be found in, Mark crawled over to the bathroom. He stood and pushed the door to. He didn't shut it completely because that might stir Bradley awake and it also let in a haze of dusky light for Mark to see what he was doing. Not that he couldn't wank in the dark, but he was expecting this was going to hit volcanic eruption levels and he wanted to ensure he caught all remnants. The last thing he needed was a *There's Something About Mary* moment.

Glancing around the bathroom, he had to decide how to do this. Get in the bath? Over the sink? Sit on the toilet? Or just stand in front of the mirror? He could feel his erection wavering the more he thought about it.

Now there was irony he could get on board with.

Right, over the sink it was. Even if he had to look himself in the mirror and be a witness to his own sex-face. Which would be a buzz killer. Still, he could just close his eyes and think about Bradley. In the next room. Naked. In bed.

The pure fucking irony!

Once free of his boxers, his dick bounced up eagerly like a puppy at the pet store that had been walked past one too many times. And like a puppy, Mark intended to stroke it to make it feel better. Wrapping his hands around the engorged flesh, he was even a little startled and how bloated his balls were. *Christ, bit of back-up here, old fellow.*

He stroked, *easy does it*, up and down. The tingles of pleasure rippled through his veins, urging him that bit faster. *As soon as this is all done we can go get in bed beside an Australian hunk.*

Mark grunted, gliding his hand up and down, imagining Bradley beneath him with a sheen of smooth, tight skin. This wasn't going to take as long as he first thought. He might even have time for another brew after.

Oh, yeah, that's it. Mmmmm…

"Mark?" Bradley's muffled voice interrupted Mark's rapid flow.

Mark froze. Or rather he thought he did. Unfortunately, his hand was too far gone into the moment and his dick wasn't letting him forget about it. Resuming his harried slides, he believed the best response was that of a true Brit—*Keep Calm and Carry On.*

"Mark, are you okay?"

Mark heard the rustling of a duvet being scraped over a finely tuned body and perfect feet sliding along the soft fibres of a carpet but nothing could have forced him to quit what he'd started. *Just get it over with!*

"Are you sick?" Bradley's voice, full of endearing concern, filtered through the gap in the door. "I can hear whimpering."

"No, no." Mark grunted. "Just going to the loo." Was that a better or worse response than the truth? His boisterous grunt would only lead to Bradley assuming he had a dicky tummy.

"Oh, right." Bradley paused at the door, not moving.

Mark could sense him. Like he was always able to tell when his mother roamed behind his bedroom door in his teenage years, making it impossible to bash one out.

He swore it was why she had done it. Raised a good old Catholic girl, she didn't believe in self-pleasure. *Poor woman.*

Although, this was hardly pleasure at the moment. Torture, more like.

Listening for Bradley's footsteps, Mark held his breath. Bradley didn't move. *What sort of person stands behind the door of someone going to the toilet? Oh Christ, he doesn't believe me.*

There was only one thing for it. To actually go to the toilet.

Ha! More fool you, Bradley Summers!

It was debateable who the real fool here was. Mark knew that.

Staggering over to the toilet, he willed his penis to be on his side for once. But it was firmly stuck up. Just like his mother.

Would you stop thinking about Mummy at this point!

That did it. His dick deflated in his hand.

"Mark?" Bradley tapped the door and Mark's heart leapt into his throat.

Jesus wept! He probably would, watching this comedy of errors.

"You okay, mate?" The door pushed open and in stepped Bradley.

Mark covered his meat and two veg in the palm of one hand. "Yes, fine, thank you." His quivering voice suggested otherwise but Mark was too far gone to care.

"Right." Bradley folded his arms. And Mark did his best not to roam his gaze southwards.

"It's terribly off-putting having someone watch you take a piss, y'know?" Mark's clipped tone made Bradley back off.

Mark flushed the toilet, for effect only. Then, still covering his manhood, he sauntered past Bradley and back toward the bed, all the while his face burned scarlet.

"Mark?"

Mark spun. "Yes?"

"Next time." Bradley took one step forward and leaned into Mark's ear. "Just ask for a helping hand." Then, without any prior warning or written consent, Bradley pressed a kiss to the tip of Mark's nose, slid back onto the bed and pulled the duvet around his streamlined figure. He wriggled to get comfy amongst the fluffy down and Mark stood frozen. Should he? Could he?

He'd been given the okay… It didn't have to mean anything. Or maybe it would? It could?

He opened his mouth.

"'M'tired, Mark," Bradley mumbled into the pillow. "So if you do want a hand, can you ask me in the morning?"

Bradley peeped one eye open, and offered a sleepy, but most definitely sassy, smile.

"You do snore," Mark retaliated.

Bradley chucked a pillow at him.

Chapter Twelve

Breakfast Bap

The next morning sent a ray of bright sunlight across the room and woke Mark up. Not that he'd gotten much sleep. Whenever he'd made himself vaguely comfortable in the bed, Bradley had kicked out a foot or a hand and ended up touching him, which was just all too much for Mark.

It seemed Mark had woken first, or at least he thought he had. Bradley's head was buried deep under the pillows, his breathing soft and even. Not that Mark had been watching him. That would be creepy. But Mark was convinced enough from his thorough assessment—*yes, that's a better word*—that he'd be able to slip from the bed without being detected.

He held his breath while doing it anyway and rootled around the floor for his clothes. Finding his jeans first, he stepped one foot into them and realised he would be joining Bradley in going commando this morning as surely that was better than wearing last night's boxers?

"Where are you going?"

Mid-way in pulling up his jeans, Mark spun to face Bradley emerging from under the pillow. Startled, he hopped on one leg and attempted to free his foot from being strangled by the hem. *Blasted skinny variety of denim! I should've stuck to the boot-cut!* Slipping on something nondescript, he fell with a crash the floor, his arse flailing into the air like a moon to rival the early sun.

Could I really have expected the morning to go any differently?

"Far out!" Bradley pushed up on his arms, peering over the side of the bed. "You all right?"

"Perfect, thank you."

"Yeah." Bradley licked his lips. "You really are."

Mark collapsed, twisted and resumed squirming into his jeans as if nothing abnormal had happened.

With all things considered, it hadn't.

"You in a hurry to get somewhere?" Bradley sat up, the duvet sliding down his torso to rest at his…

Oh, God, that bulge! Mark averted his eyes and searched for his shirt instead, reminding himself that it had been hard enough to get his jeans on without adding anything extra into the immovable denim.

"Breakfast." Mark ripped his shirt from the back of the desk chair and slid each arm into it. "It's included in the extortionate room fee, and is of the buffet variety, so I plan to get my money's worth."

"I see." Bradley scooted to the end of the bed, duvet still covering his midsection, and clasped his hands on his lap. He peered up to Mark with an abashed look. One that said he wasn't up for being a spectacle this early in the morning.

"Right, I'll just, er…" Mark didn't finish his sentence and trundled off into the bathroom, giving them both room to breathe. Or, more accurately, allowing Mark to take a few calming breaths.

He nearly hyperventilated until Bradley's beckoning call cut him off.

"Are we giving this buffet a run for its money or what?"

Mark gave the affirmative by opening the door.

They traipsed through the hotel in relative silence, making their way down the creaking stairs to reach the breakfast dining hall. It was loud and busy, and if it wasn't for the real fear of no morning cuppa, Mark would have quite liked to have left. The other early morning patrons all glared at their arrival with condemnation slapped over their haughty faces. Mark knew what they were thinking—Mark with his bed hair, his morning-after-the-night-before glad rags, and Bradley by his side looking like he'd just stepped off the cover of *Attitude* mag.

They're going to think I've paid him.

Instead of mortification surging through him at the assumption he looked the sort of person who had to pay for sex, Mark was startled to discover that it was anger boiling his blood. *Is this how people view Bradley?* As nothing more than a prostitute, someone who accepts money in exchange for his delightful evening company? Damian had said as such and he hadn't even met him. Beady, disapproving eyes glared up at Bradley in his skin-tight vest and jeans, with his tousled blond hair, and his muscles flexing as he snaked through the tables in the dining hall. If he had to squeeze past, he always added an apology, or an, "excuse me, mate," finished off with a dashing smile.

They all tutted, with one family even going so far as to turn their child's head away from view.

By the time he'd reached a vacant table at the back, Mark noticed the distinct slump in Bradley's normally broad shoulders and that his head wasn't held as high. And the smile he offered Mark as he pulled out a chair for him wasn't as bright.

Bastards! Mark had a sudden urge to grab Bradley's perfect face and slap a kiss to his luscious lips, tasting that sweet—*hang on, did Bradley even brush his teeth? Did I?*

"Can I offer you a tea or coffee, sirs?" A waitress holding two silver pots encroached on the moment.

"Tea, tea, please." Mark sat and the sizzling pour from the pot into the cup soon rid him of tension.

"And for you, sir?" The waitress held the pot over Bradley's cup.

"Just an OJ, please, love."

"I'll be right back." She scampered away.

Bradley smiled over at Mark as he sipped. "Feel better now?"

"Indeed." Mark added an *ahhh* because he couldn't not. "Nothing like a fresh cuppa to start your day."

The waitress returned with a glass of orange and Bradley took an immediate slurp, wiping the traces of juicy bits from his top lip with his tongue. He seemed to take his time over it too, allowing Mark to get a proper eyeball of how flexible and long Bradley's tongue actually was.

That could wrap double around my cock. Clearing his throat, Mark wriggled in his seat. Thank God he hadn't uttered that out loud. The family on the next table would be covering their sprog's ears as well as eyes.

"So." Mark clapped his hands and pushed back his chair. "I don't know about you, but I could use a full English."

"Lead the way, Mark. I could be persuaded to squeeze a full English in me." Bradley grinned.

"Perhaps you ought to rephrase that," Mark suggested, tucking in his chair and making his way over to the hot buffet.

Bradley caught up to him. "You're dirty, Mark Johnson." He grabbed a plate and handed one to Mark. "But after last night, I don't think you can shock me, anymore."

"Ha!" Mark perused the contents overflowing from each dish and sizzling under the heated lamps. "I could put you straight there and inform you that I could well indeed shock you further."

Why did I say that? He piled his plate with the usual ensemble that made up a decent brekkie, minus the black pudding because he still hadn't got over the time when his mother had informed him what it actually was. He'd been eight. He hadn't been able to look Miss Piggy in the eye since.

"I'm intrigued. Do tell."

Giving Bradley a look that he hoped would convey that wouldn't be happening any time soon, or ever, if he could get away with it, Mark returned to their table and filled his loose gob with breakfast.

Bradley joined him a short time after, a plate piled high of egg and beans. Protein rich. No meat.

"Do you not eat meat?" Mark asked, tucking into his.

"I do." Bradley spoke out of the side of his mouth. "But not real fatty stuff. I got told that this body has to stay this way if I want to keep up the dancing. So I can only have chicken, yeah, bit of steak sometimes."

"I see." Mark shovelled his fatty meat in. "I don't seem to have that problem. It doesn't matter what I eat, this body remains."

"It's a nice body." Bradley didn't look up from his plate to say that, nor was there any indication that had been a joke.

Still, Mark stared across the table in wait. Bradley finally looked up and held Mark's gaze while stabbing through the scrambled eggs on his plate. "You don't believe me?"

"In comparison to yours, I find it hard to believe." Mark pointed his fork across the table.

"This?" Bradley flexed his biceps. "This is what society says we should look like. This is what happens when you try too hard to please people."

"Is that what you do? Try too hard?"

Bradley shrugged.

Mark pondered the meaning of that while clearing the contents on his plate. He leaned back and rubbed his stuffed stomach. As much as he'd said he would be piling in as much food as he could, he couldn't eat another bite. So he downed his tea, instead. Then had to pick a piece of leaf stuck to his lips.

He stared into the cup. "Huh."

"Something interesting in there?"

"It's loose tea." Mark shook his head. "So there's leaves left at the bottom. I'll need a new cup for the next one." He glanced around, hoping to get the server's attention.

"So there is something interesting in that mug." Bradley's whole demeanour erupted, like a child who had just been told Santa had been. It was rather infectious. Bradley waved his hand. "Pass it over."

"Excuse me?"

"The cup. I'll read your leaves for you."

Mark handed over the mug with a dubious smile. "You can do that?"

"Told you, my gran can. She taught me the basics." Bradley twirled the cup in his hand, held it by the handle, then peered into the porcelain. A look of wonderment flashed over his features. "What question do you want answered?"

Mark rubbed his forehead. "I don't know. I mean, what is it that tea leaves can actually answer? Is it like the eight ball that constantly tells me no? Pretty sure it's broken. Actually, wait, I would seriously appreciate the lottery numbers if that's a possibility?"

Bradley narrowed his eyes. "No, Mark. This is serious. But you need to want an answer to something in your life, or your fortune. Otherwise this is meaningless."

The deflation of Bradley's shoulders caused an instant pang of guilt. Bradley was serious. Deadly serious. And Mark found himself serious too. He sat straighter, leaning forward for a better view into his cup. Not that he had any clue what he'd be looking for, although if a few numbers were spelled out in leaves he'd most definitely take note.

"What do you ask it?" Better to palm off the question on Bradley, because right then the only quandary on Mark's lips was whether he would be getting a second cup of tea or not.

"I've asked the leaves a lot of things in the past. Depending on where I am. In life."

"Like?"

"Am I doing the right thing by leaving Australia? Will I find fortune in stripping? Who will I fall in love with?" Bradley shrugged. "Y'know, stupid stuff."

Mark widened his eyes, intrigued. About all of it. Not just the last question. *Honest*. "And what have the answers been?"

Bradley paused his wistful gazing into the mug and peered across to Mark, unreadable. "Yes. For a while. An older man."

"Ah." Mark's throat was dry and he desperately wanted another cup of tea to at least have something to mask the surprise he knew would be spreading across his face. "And you believe it all?"

"She's mostly right, my gran. She's been doing this for years. Predicted all sorts of stuff for the family."

"Like what?"

"That my sister would marry a man who works with his hands. Her husband's a gardener. That my dad would lose his job at the bank, but find a better one more suited to him. He now works on Bondi, bootcamp trainer for the new mums. And she read my mum's leaves the day I was born, told her I was gay."

"Wow. How did your mum take it?"

"With two sugars." Bradley smiled, returning his attention to Mark's cup.

"Ha ha." Mark leaned back, folding his arms. "Has she ever been wrong?"

Bradley flicked his gaze back to Mark. "No. Well, jury's still out on my last reading. I thought she was wrong…" He shrugged and stared back into the mug.

Those leaves must have been writing *War and Peace* with how Bradley was focusing on them.

"And your last reading, she said what exactly?" *Careful, Mark, it might look like you want to believe this stuff.*

"She said I'd find love with an older man." Bradley did not look up from the mug.

Mark widened his eyes, his voice caught in his throat.

"But, well, that didn't work out." Bradley mumbled, narrowing his eyes as he spun the cup this way and that.

"Oh." Mark willed for something more to say. "Why not?" *Because he's not in love with you, you pillock! Do you really want him to spell that out to you?*

Bradley sighed, clonking the cup onto the table cloth. "Remember the guy I told you about? The one who got me into stripping? The one whose roof I was fixing?"

Mark nodded. *Ah.*

"We were together a while."

"I see." Mark was now grateful for no fluid to add to his curdling stomach and wished he hadn't consumed as much breakfast as he had because it was in danger of being regurgitated.

"I really thought he was the one my gran had predicted. The whole scenario, the roof, the stripping, the older man. But it just didn't feel right."

"In what respect?"

"In that I was just his arm candy. Used me to flaunt around and took control of my food, my schedule. Signed me up for gigs and took a percentage. But when it came to anything meaningful, it just wasn't there. I tried. I did. I thought my gran was right. I thought he was my forever man and I just needed to get past the superficial beginning before the love came. It didn't. For either of us. He thought I was stupid for my beliefs, and I thought he was a controlling bastard. So I asked my gran if I should leave Australia, and him. She said yes. Told me to go see Macy. Now I'm here."

Bradley's wringing hands brought forth an unexpected sympathy within Mark. He knew how the man felt. More than Bradley could ever know. *And I thought we had nothing in common.* Before he could stop himself, Mark reached across the table and placed a hand over Bradley's cradled ones.

"It sounds like he didn't know what was in front of him."

Bradley held his gaze. "Yeah. Maybe." He sucked in a breath. "So you wanna know what's in yours?"

Mark slipped his hand from Bradley's and fell back in his chair. "Um. I'm not sure."

"You don't believe in this anyway." Bradley folded his arms and glanced out of the window at the cars passing beyond it.

"Try me." Now Mark was intrigued. Whether it was all a load of mumbo jumbo or not, the fact that Bradley shone while talking about it made Mark want to know more.

"You're going travelling. Far away."

"Really?" Mark leaned forward and peered into the mug. "Where an earth does it suggest that?"

Bradley picked it up and pointed toward a splodge of black leaves curdled together close to the handle. "There. It's the Earth."

"Is it?"

"Sure. See the circle formed, then the little parts in between? Indicates that world. And as it's by the handle, it's going to happen pretty soon."

"Oh." Mark was a little taken aback. He wasn't sure why. He'd had reading tea leaves down as reliable as those fortune cookies the Chinese restaurants gave away by the bulk load—generic nonsense that could relate to anything. But Bradley seemed so sure. So confident. And now a little pissed off. "I always wanted to go travelling. Made plans for it and everything."

"Why didn't you?"

"Various reasons. Mummy, Pa, money, fear..." *George*. Mark heaved in a breath.

"Well, looks like you now got a chance."

"Huh." Interesting. At least Mark was now certain that reading tea leaves was absolute bollocks. Mark couldn't go anywhere. Not with his house, his lack of funds, his ties to Marsby. "I will most definitely be requiring the lottery numbers for that to happen, so let me just check—"

As he reached over to grab the mug, his elbow bashed on the salt pot and it clanged onto the table, the screw top falling off and spilling a mountain of white grains onto the surface.

"Far out, Mark! That's bad luck. Quick!" Bradley rolled back his chair. "Toss it over your shoulder. Now!"

The fear in Bradley's face caused outright panic in Mark and he immediately gathered up as much of the salt as he could, pinching it between his thumb and forefinger. Without bothering to look, he threw it over his left shoulder. Trouble was, it wasn't the devil waiting there waiting to reap in its blinding qualities, it was the choir-boy-type kid from the next table. The sprog wailed and screamed as he attempted to wipe the grains from his tufts of blond hair.

"Bugger!" Mark leapt from his seat and bounced over to the child, swiping his hands through the boy's hair. "I am so sorry!"

The parents said nothing as they grabbed their son's hand and dragged him crying from the restaurant. Mark turned to Bradley.

"I think I might believe that cup now. I should most probably leave the country."

* * * *

There didn't seem much point in hanging around after that, so they emerged out from the hotel and onto the streets of Shoreditch ready to tackle the journey home. Mark felt every step of the walk of shame. Bradley, however, appeared as natural as ever as he glided among the Sunday-morning tourists, and street sweepers clearing away the remnants of a typical Saturday night in the smoke. So confident with his easy long strides and whistling while he walked, Bradley would be a ray of sunshine on any dreary day. Mark would miss his joviality when he left.

The thought caused an uncomfortable knot to clog in Mark's chest.

They boarded the ridiculously busy Central Line among those all heading out for a spot of Sunday shopping, or traipsing home from an extended Saturday night shopping, and rode the tube to Stratford. As the train screeched into the station, an announcement declared that all trains to Canterbury would be cancelled after the one about to depart from Platform five.

Bradley grabbed Mark's arm and yanked him through the turnstiles, sprinting onto the platform.

"You desperate to get back?" Mark called out through harried breaths.

Mark hadn't run for anything, including a bus, or train, for a good few years. He often looked upon those energetic beach joggers who trundled past his house with varying degrees of pity. But right now proved that although he was a slender man, he wasn't exactly fit.

"Come on, Mark!" Bradley hopped, skipped and jumped.

The whistle for the last train shrilled out around the platform and Bradley, up ahead, swung effortlessly into the last carriage. Mark gasped. That was the first-class carriage!

Mark hadn't ever broken the rules to anything before. He was a bit of a stickler for them, even the really stupid ones, like staying left on the escalator even when it was empty. It just felt more comfortable to know he was doing as expected.

His heart hammered as he approached the closing doors of the first-class carriage, and it wasn't just because his body wasn't used to such a rigorous early morning exercise regime. It was the fear that he was considering breaking the cardinal train rule.

Bradley crammed his bulk between the doors, holding them open, and ushered Mark in. Mark froze. What would his mother say? It would be worse than when she'd found the DVLA letter when he'd been snapped going thirty-five mph down Dover high road. She'd never let him live that one down, either. He'd been forever referred to as a reckless driver after that, and responsible for all roadside deaths.

Bradley practically tore Mark's arm from its socket as he yanked him onto the train. He stepped back as the doors slid shut but Mark, in his hesitancy, got caught in the gap. With shoulders squashed up to his neck, Mark closed his eyes in the horror of hearing the screeching alarm. He was stuck. In first bloody class. Where he didn't have a ticket for.

Grabbing Mark's hands, Bradley tugged him forward. His shoulders were finally released and he toppled, falling splat against Bradley's chest.

"If you wanted a hug," Bradley said, wrapping his arms around Mark. "You could have just asked."

Mark stepped away and checked the seated area of the carriage just as the train shunted out of the station. All seats were occupied by people. First-class sort of people. It was obvious from the broadsheet newspapers sprawled on laps, as well as the sneering glances sent his and Bradley's way.

"We are in first class." Mark gritted his teeth.

Bradley shrugged.

"I don't know what it's like in Australia, but here it's rather frowned upon to be in first class when you have a ticket for standard. We are looking at a two hundred pound fine!"

Bradley gasped, slapping a hand to his chest. "You British." He tutted. "Class system everywhere. Chill, Mark. It's Sunday. No one cares on Sunday."

Mark looked deep into those blue eyes, the swimming green emulating the bits in Bradley's morning juice earlier. His orange juice, that was. He didn't know about his other morning juice. He'd yet to see that. *Wasn't* going to be seeing that. Yet. Not yet. As in he wouldn't be seeing it. Not that he won't *yet* be seeing it. Mark sighed and wished he could buy his mind a gag.

He cocked his head. Maybe Bradley would be into gagging?

"Tickets, please!"

Oh, bugger.

Chapter Thirteen

Mummy, Dearest

"Mark, Mark, Mark."

Mark twisted at the oncoming tutting. "There is only one of me, isn't there?" he asked Bradley out of one side of his mouth.

Mark had called Damian after they'd been thrown off the train at the first stop, unable to even board the lower-class carriages. But having belly-laughed down the phone for several hours, Damian had refused any rescue mission, claiming he couldn't disturb his bedfellow. So after forking out the two hundred pounds each in ticket fines, neither Mark nor Bradley could afford a taxi home that would have cost about the same, meaning Mark had resorted to drastic measures. Now as his mother swaggered ever closer, Mark rather wished they'd walked it.

Grabbing Mark's face with her freezing-cold bony fingers, his mother smacked him with several air kisses to each cheek.

"Mark." She slapped his chest with the back of her hand, her heavy diamond-encrusted rings catching in his shirt buttons.

"I'm sure you like the name." Mark removed her hand and thrust it back at her. "Having been the one to choose it for me, but really just the one use every so often is considered an acceptable amount."

"Don't be so obtuse, Mark."

"Mother, I believe that's the wrong use of the word."

And for that Mark received another slap. His mother's frown turned upside down and merged into a dashing smile as she laid eyes on Bradley behind him.

Mark couldn't blame her. Bradley was rather a delightful morning view, and ever more so now he'd put his best 'meet the mother' act on. Mark shimmied to the side, to offer the formal introductions, until he realised he didn't know how to actually do it. How to explain who Bradley was to him? The fact he stood there, Sunday morning, still in Saturday night get-up, with a man who was eighteen years his junior looked rather reprehensible to say the least. His mother would not be letting that pass. She never let anything pass. So he was desperately trying to rack his brain as to who Bradley could be that his mother wouldn't bat her perfectly curled dark eyelashes at.

"Bradley this is my mother, Vera. Mother, this is Bradley." *Just leave it at that?*

Vera stepped forward and held out the back of her limp hand. She was rather glamorous for her age. In her mid-sixties, she still had a full luscious mound of blonde hair. It used to be dark, like Mark's, but early onset greying in her thirties had made her lighten with each dye job to the point she was now a full-on platinum Barbie doll.

"Charmed, I'm sure."

Bradley offered a beatific smile that made Mark want to throw up. Or, actually, kiss the man's entire face off. When Bradley took his mother's hand and planted a chaste kiss to the blue veins, his mother giggled, Mark wasn't sure which one of them he was more disappointed in.

"He fixed my roof," Mark blurted out with no forewarning.

"Is that a euphemism, darling?" Vera did not take her fluttering eyes from Bradley.

"No, Mother."

"Oh, well, that is a shame. I was looking forward to some sordid tales to make up for this journey into the big smoke." She finally tore her gaze from Bradley and onto Mark, her face falling into the usual disdainful expression it wore for him. "I mean, that is the only reason you ever venture here, isn't it, darling?"

"I worked here last night. Mark came to…support me." Bradley smiled. "And call me Brad."

"Don't you have ladders for that sort of thing? Mark is hardly a hands-on sort of man. Are you, Mark? I mean, look at those arms. They can barely hold up a finger, let alone a safety harness."

"Thank you, Mother." Sarcasm, the lowest form of wit but essential when dealing with Mummy dearest.

"I'm pretty sure Mark's got a firm grip." Bradley winked at Mark, then aimed his dashing smile at Vera. "Besides, fixing roofs is more my hobby."

Mark inwardly grumbled.

"So where do you work, then?" Vera asked with a certain curiosity and a scrutinising look up and down Bradley's attire.

"Macy's Tea Shoppe," Mark blurted out. "Which, speaking of, we really must get on back to Marsby. I'm sure Bradley has a multitude of things to sort out for the shop opening tomorrow, haven't you, Bradley?"

"Sure thing," Bradley replied with a knowing grin. "Although, Macy should be back tomorrow."

"Should she?" Mark swallowed. *Does that mean… What does that mean?*

He didn't have time to ask as his mother cut in. "Macy's? That delightful little tea place on the seafront?"

"Yes." Mark waved his hands, urging his mother to move and show them where she'd parked the blasted car.

"Macy…now there is one reason why I'm thankful Mark is gay." Vera directed her comment straight at Bradley with a tut. "Because if he wasn't, I'm sure he'd marry that disaster of a woman just to annoy the hell out of me."

"Mother!" Mark's clipped tone startled even him.

"No need to shout, Mark. I may be getting old, but hearing is one faculty I do still have."

"But tact is sadly lacking," Mark replied. "Bradley is Macy's cousin."

"Really?" She whipped her head, giving Bradley the once over. "So whereabouts from up north are you?"

"Oh, dear Lord." Mark hung his head. "He's from Australia, Mother. Apologies, Bradley, my mother believes anywhere north of the M25 is northern."

"Fair dos." Bradley shrugged.

"Now if you don't mind." Mark tapped Vera's arm. "We do really need to get back."

His mother obliged that time, not before adding another *tsk*, and sauntered to the station car park. On clicking her key fob, the lights on a black Bentley illuminated like Blackpool at night. Bradley hurried beside Mark and gasped.

"Is that a—"

"Yes." Mark clenched his jaw. "I ask you not to mention it again."

"Are your oldies loaded?"

"It's a long story." That Mark had neither the energy nor the time to retell just then. Certainly not within earshot of Vera.

"And yet you can't afford a roof?" Bradley widened his eyes.

Mark sighed and slumped away from the car, waiting for his mother to slip her slender body elegantly into the vehicle and slam the door.

"My mother is money. Came from money. Always had money." Mark shuffled his feet and tried to tuck his hands in his jacket pocket only to rip the stitching farther. "Pa, unfortunately, gambled most of it away on the horses." Mark held up a finger to stop Bradley from replying. "They lost it all. But Mother likes to keep up the pretence that they still have it all. It wouldn't go down well in her circles to know the car is on credit."

"Right-o," Bradley said.

Mark held open the car door and allowed Bradley to climb in first to the back seat. Mark followed behind. There was simply no way he was sitting next to his mother for the hour and a half drive back home. That would be longer than any time he had been that close to the woman since he'd suckled her breasts. Mark shuddered, so much so that his whole body convulsed and Bradley shot him a concerned look.

"Someone walked over my grave." Mark yanked the seat belt, getting it stuck in his haste.

"So, Bradley, dear?" Vera sailed the car out of the station driveway and headed through the London streets toward the South, with Mark still entangling himself from the seat belt. He could put that down to his mother not caring all that much about his safety, but it was more that her focus was on the stranger in her car. "Were you opening a new tea shop in London? That's something I can imagine my son being a party to."

"No, no." Bradley clicked his own belt into place with the ease of normalcy. "It was another job I was doing here. I kinda have a few fingers in a few pies."

"Well, you are still young, dear, unlike poor Mark. I'll bet the pies quite like it." Vera winked in the rearview mirror. "Wish my Mark could find a pie."

"Mother," Mark warned between gritted teeth. "If we're talking jobs, I have one."

"Being a glorified secretary for that awful man who pays you peanuts is hardly what I consider worthy of my son. I mean for goodness' sake, Mark, you have a degree!"

"You do?" Bradley whipped his head around.

"Yes." Mark nodded at Bradley but returned his exasperated glare on his mother in the mirror whilst still yanking his seat belt free from its constriction. "But graduate-level jobs were hard to come by in a seaside town, Mother. You know that. I got what I could when I came back." *At your request!* Mark would have added that in, but it would just add salt into an unhealed—and surreptitious—wound.

"You could run that place! You could be a top executive in a multibillion pound law firm. But, no, you chose to be girl Friday for a midget!" Vera was clearly on one of her rampages.

"Mother!" Mark finally got the *clunk-click* of confirmation he was strapped in.

"Your problem, Mark, is that you're just lazy. You don't want to work to earn money. You want it given to you, as if it is your God-given right. Like when you asked us for that loan for your house. We refused, because you need to learn the value of hard work. You still live in your pipe dream of travelling the world. And when you ran off to London to let someone else to take care of you… Well, that didn't last, did it, Mark?"

Mark avoided Bradley's open-mouthed stare at him and rather wished he'd forked out for a first-class bloody train ticket. It would have avoided all this painful headache-inducing trip down Memory Lane. At least it reminded him of why he didn't visit his mother with any sort of regularity. If it wasn't for his father, he probably wouldn't at all.

"Anyway, Bradley." Vera smiled. "How long are you in the country for?" She over-pronounced every word, like she did to those who worked in the post office through fear of not being understood.

"Ah, well, not long." Bradley scratched the nape of his neck, which would have been a drool-inducing sight with those biceps flexing and the scent of underarm manliness wafting Mark's way.

Instead, Mark just felt a painful stab in the chest. *Heartburn? Too much breakfast?*

"What?" he blurted. The seat belt acted accordingly to his jerky movement by believing Mark was in danger of hurtling through the windscreen and so pinned him to the seat, restricting his ability to breathe. It was either that, or Mark's chest was painfully constricted with the thought of Bradley leaving. He tested the belt anyway.

"Macy's back soon and I was just standing in..." Bradley hardly looked Mark's way as he spoke. "Anyway, I've got a chance of a gig back in Sydney, earn some more money, then I'll fly off somewhere else."

"Wow." Vera raised plucked eyebrows. "You don't stay in one place very long, do you, Bradley?"

The bastard actually had the audacity to shrug. "Not unless there's a reason. I go where the stars tell me." There was that wistful look in youthful eyes.

Mark felt sick. So very sick. And trapped. He tugged the seat belt again and it released. He breathed.

Okay, he gasped.

"You all right, mate?" Bradley slapped Mark on the back.

Like a mate would. Like someone who was passing through. A travelling companion. Except they weren't any of that, were they? Hardly friends at all, really. *What are we? What is this? What have we been doing?* Mark felt like his life had significantly changed since the Australian's arrival on his doorstep with perfect toes within pink thongs. Did Bradley even feel the same? Had anything changed for him? Or was Mark simply another person met on his intrepid exploration of the world?

"Fine and dandy," was what Mark's frozen brain decided to allow him to utter, along with giving a flippant wave of his hand.

Bradley nodded, once, then held Mark's gaze. Without processing what that look could mean, Mark raised his eyebrows, willing Bradley to say something, anything, else. He didn't. He turned away and glanced out of his passenger-side window at all the vast farmland passing by. Mark's lips parted—

"You'll catch flies, Mark, dear," Vera said.

Mark slapped his mouth shut.

"You know," she continued, her eyes finding Bradley's through the mirror once more, "Mark said he was going to move to Australia."

Bradley gazed back from his idle scenery pondering. Mark was still too preoccupied with the previous conversation for his brain to catch up on the current one, still processing the thought that Bradley was vacating his life for good in a mere twenty-four hours. He'd just started getting used to having him around. *Is that why Bradley's so eager to get his leg over so quickly?*

"It was after his little speech at school."

That snapped Mark from his bubbling emotional turmoil of figuring out what he was more upset about—Bradley leaving or that he'd only been chasing after Mark because he knew it wouldn't be a long-term thing.

"Has he told you about that, Bradley?"

"No, he hasn't, Vera." Bradley smiled, his pure white teeth bursting from behind pink lips so much so that Mark could taste the enamel. "Do tell."

The untold is about to be told! In a desperate attempt to prevent the following detail falling from his mother's treacherous mouth, Mark lunged forward. The seat belt in its infinite wisdom retracted once more, gloating over a job well done. Mark slammed back against the seat, the wind firmly knocked out of his sails, and drank in the sight of the English Channel approaching over the horizon. *Maybe she won't have enough time to tell it all?*

"Mark was chosen to write and give a speech on the last day of term at school. Such a bright boy, lots of potential back then. Most likely to achieve. What? I'm still unsure." Vera waved a flippant hand from the steering wheel. "Anyway, it was proposed he write something about his educational journey, *School – The Best Years of our Lives!* That sort of thing. Mark didn't allow anyone to read it before the big delivery—"

"Mother." Mark hacked out a warning through the pressure of his seat belt slicing into his neck and almost decapitating him.

It came out as more a whimper than an order. He would have tried again had it not been for Bradley's hand laying itself on his knee and trailing upwards to his thigh. That had to have been done subconsciously, because Bradley hadn't moved any other muscle, including his eyes that focused solely on Mark's mother.

"So little Mark, sweet sixteen, stood in front of the whole school and declared to all of Marsby that his school years had been torturous." Vera clutched a hand to her chest and sniffed, as though the memory pained her.

Mark fought for breath, or at least the bravery to go through with the decapitation.

"He explained, to everyone, that he was gay, that throughout his years at Marsby Boys Grammar, he had been made to feel like an outcast. He'd been bullied and ridiculed and singled out, and that finally, on his departure from compulsory education, he was so deliriously happy that he no longer had to conform to their…what was it, Mark?"

Mark shook his head. Bradley's hand squeezed.

"Hetero sadomasochistic rituals." Vera swerved the car, narrowly missing a truck. "Then said he was off to go live in the Australian outback."

"Far out." Bradley grinned. "I'll bet you were a hoot at school."

"Far from it." Mark sank into his seat. "Unfortunately, every word of that speech was true. Except the Australia part."

"Why Oz?"

Mark sucked in a deep, shaky breath. "Because it's very, very, very far away."

"Yeah." Bradley slipped his hand from Mark's leg and turned back to count the sheep outside his window. "Sure is."

* * * *

Mark convinced his mother to drop them both at his house. He didn't invite her in for a cup of tea. She looked relieved at the fact. She hated stepping foot in Pa's childhood home at the best of times. Mark doubted she'd spent much time here during his parents' courting days. Mark didn't dwell too much on those thoughts. He found it hard to believe his parents had ever dated. Or had sex.

Or enjoyed each other's company.

Bradley, however, hovered at his door and although Mark didn't actually utter the words, it was explicit in both their actions that he would at least come into the house before buggering off to, well, who knew where anymore?

Mark bolted through to the kitchen, flicking the kettle on, and Bradley slipped in behind. Whilst Mark wiped off two mugs from the draining board, Bradley opened his fridge and passed over the milk with a sly grin.

"What?" Mark narrowed his eyes.

"You bought OJ." Bradley smiled. "I'm touched."

"Ah." Mark had bought a litre carton the last time he had been at the corner shop, with no suggestive reasoning whatsoever. It had simply been to check out the wonderment that is a sunshine breakfast to see if it could rival his morning tea fix. Less time faffing about with a kettle. The fact it remained unopened in his fridge was neither here nor there. "Well, perhaps you can take that back with you to Australia?"

The words tumbled from his mouth and seared his tongue like a paper cut. Of course Bradley wouldn't be hanging around Marsby forever. It was a retirement destination after all. A young, travel-hungry man should not, by any means, see out his days in a sleepy seaside town whose newest development in fifty years was a Costa Coffee. He should be roaming the world, seeing the wonders on offer, soaking up the experiences that Mark hadn't been able to.

"You okay, Mark?" Bradley slipped up behind him. The water from the kettle spilled out of the cup Mark had been pouring it into and onto the counter, trickling over the edge to the floor.

"Bugger." Mark slammed the kettle down on the counter.

"It seems like you're have trouble making tea recently."

Mark yanked out a roll of kitchen towel, wound it around his hand and bent down to wipe up the spilled water.

"Yes," Mark agreed. "Why might that be, I wonder?" He stood and twisted to throw the wet towel into the bin but collided with Bradley directly in front of him.

Their chests bumped so close that Mark was sure Bradley could feel his hammering heartbeat. Mark felt a fool at being so reactive to the close proximity, and incredibly small and impossibly skinny. Bradley's shoulders were easily a whole other person broader than him and Bradley's chest was a rock-solid foundation that consumed Mark's slender frame. Distracted by the body comparison, Mark hadn't noticed Bradley sliding his large hands onto Mark's hips until Bradley cocked his head and leaned in to brush his lips against Mark's.

"Because of me?" Bradley's sweet, warm, honey-coated breath tickled Mark's lips.

"Pardon?"

He'd forgotten what the question was, or the answer. Whatever it was he was meant to be responding or referring to. To anything. Ever. There were no questions and there were no answers, not at this moment. There was only him and Bradley and—*dear God, those fingers!*

Dry, calloused fingertips ran up into Mark's shirt and stroked along the sensitive skin by Mark's hip bone. Mark shivered and traced the outline of Bradley's full pink lips ghosting his own. *Is this a dream?*

"Mark, Mark, Mark," Bradley whispered his name in a teasing call, tingling Mark's lips with his own. "How do you do this to me?"

"I'm quite sure that I haven't been doing any doing, or if so, I am not aware I have been doing it." Every hair on Mark's entire body stood to attention. "And what exactly is it I'm doing, may I ask? Just for future reference."

Bradley exhaled a low, discerning laugh. The warm breath dried Mark's lips and, as if he noticed, Bradley pressed his down on top, warming Mark's with his own soft, plump cushions.

Mark shut his eyes. He wasn't sure why, as this was most probably the best sight he was ever going to witness in his life. But Bradley would only appear as an oversized blur if he to tried to watch the whole scenario play out—whatever that was going to be. He quite wished he could float out of his own body and gaze down upon it, because he'd never believe himself otherwise.

In a spurt of out-of-body experience, Mark seized the moment and kissed Bradley back. He parted his lips, capturing Bradley's bottom lip between his, and kissed the man's face off. Bradley slid his hands up into Mark's shirt and Mark wrapped his arms around him to squeeze those devilishly pert cheeks that would forever be ingrained in his mind as the arse to rival all others. He dug his fingers in, making Bradley tumble forward and squish him against the counter. *If I die right now, what a way to go!*

Mark couldn't quite believe this was all happening. Maybe he *had* died. An amazing hunk of Australian Adonis was in his dishevelled kitchen and kissing him. Not only was he kissing him, he was devouring him. Bradley's mouth took over his entire face, slurping and slapping at Mark's lips like he'd just been trekking the outback for months and Mark was his only water supply. He delved in with his tongue and Mark sucked in a breath through his nose at the sheer shock of the wide, thick, sloppy muscle entwining around his own. Mark pondered as to how that tongue actually fit in his mouth. He decided, on second thoughts, he didn't care. It did, and it tasted better than tea.

He gasped.

Before Mark's new-found freedom could really be let loose and test how far he could trail his hands up from

Bradley's arse to touch the tense and firm contours of muscles beneath Bradley's top, a strangled inhalation caught Mark off-guard. At first, he thought it was his own, because Bradley would never have sounded that feminine.

Oh bugger!

Mark dislodged his tongue from inside Bradley's mouth and peeped out of the corner of one eye.

Macy, hands clasped over her mouth, stood with eyes wide enough to rival the dinner plates at the Hungry Horse pub, where they gave you a free dessert if you finished your meal.

"Mark Johnson!" She slapped her hands to her floating multicoloured skirt, that if unravelled could be used as the flag for Marsby's first Pride Parade. "What are you doing to my baby cousin?"

"Ah," Mark uttered, wiping his lips.

Bradley stepped back.

"Bugger."

Chapter Fourteen

No, Non, Nein, Nah, Mate…Yes

"This is most definitely not what it looks like," Mark stuttered, wiping his saliva-coated lips.

Bradley stepped away from grinding his erection against Mark's leg and stifled a chuckle. Mark would have preferred he responded with something more confirmatory to Mark's statement.

"No?" Macy folded her arms to underline her scepticism and shook out her fuzzy ginger hair that bunched around each ear in pigtails.

"No." Mark shook his head, his own hair billowing wildly to rival Macy's.

"No?" Bradley folded his arms across his iron chest that mere moments ago had been holding Mark up as if he were a falling building.

Mark could still feel the weight that had been pressed against him and he called out to be crushed again. To ground him. To complete him. But that would only exacerbate the current situation and provide ammunition for Macy not to believe a damn word he dared utter next.

"Well, no," Mark stammered, confidence waning.

"You weren't sucking face with my baby cousin?"

Mark raked his gaze over the Aussie. He did still find it rather hard to believe that he had had his tongue down Bradley's throat, which did make it a tad easier to contest the accusation. He turned his attention to the friend he'd known a fair bit longer. Minus tongues. *Thank goodness.*

"Well, you see, there you go." Mark waved a hand in the air and almost hit Bradley standing over him like a menacing threat of pure sex. "That statement most definitely can be answered with a no. I was not sucking face with a baby."

"Thank goodness," Macy replied. "But you were sucking my cousin?"

"Wh—what? No!" Mark shook his head furiously again.

He was nauseated, his brain spinning as though he was riding one of those godawful summer fairground contraptions. *What was the name of the damn ride?* He'd spent his youth trying to avoid it, no matter if the bigger kids and scrumptiously fit boys all used to hang out there every night of the school holidays. *The teacups?*

No. He probably would have remembered that.

"No?" Bradley repeated again, voice elevating, snapping Mark from his reminiscing.

Mark narrowed his eyes and, although Bradley stood there with that one blasted eyebrow crawling so far up his face it was in danger of joining his head of hair, he was sure Bradley was fucking with him. Or at least Mark hoped that he might still want to. Unable to sustain any more vowels, Mark pffft'd, snorted then grunted. And after that display, he was now fairly certain Bradley would be coming on board with all the nos.

"No," Mark finally agreed. Or didn't agree. He wasn't sure at this point what meant no and what meant yes. So he'd stick to the nos, regardless.

"Shame." Bradley breathed out, unfurling his arms and glancing away.

Mark opened his mouth, accepting that all the flies would set up camp in there for a nice overnight holiday, breed and he'd been spitting out maggots for the rest of his life like some late-night 1970s horror movie.

"I asked you to show him around town." Macy slammed her hands on her hips. "I didn't think you'd stop just at your house, Mark Johnson."

Mark furiously shook his head and attempted to shuffle forward from the kitchen counter. But Bradley blocked his way, refusing to budge an inch. Could Mark slip under his spread legs, perhaps? Probably best not to.

"I did not stop at my house, Macy," Mark declared, rubbing the back of his neck. "I'll have you know, I did indeed show Bradley around town. We have also ventured as far as London."

"Where Mark paid for us to stay in a hotel." Bradley grinned and it was touch and go as to whether Mark would slap him to shut him up. Or kiss him. He was beginning to think those two things were interchangeable when it came to Bradley bloody Summers. "After he tried lap dancing for me."

Slap him, definitely slap him.

"Mark Johnson!" Macy tutted, a smile forming.

"Don't worry, Mace." Bradley shot Mark a wink. "He only got as far as taking his jacket off then gouged some poor woman's eye out."

Mark closed his eyes and proceeded to count to a million in the hope this dramatization would come to an end.

"Sounds like Mark."

He tried to find some vowels to go with the multitude of consonants spluttering out of his mouth, but it seemed they had vacated his memory bank along with his maths ability. How was he meant to explain all that had happened in Macy's absence? Even he wasn't quite sure what had happened, or what was going to happen. He'd spent his life avoiding moments like this. And here he was, slap-bang in the middle of some daytime soap opera. A man nearly hitting his forties, having been single and happy—*pfft*—for the most part of ten years and resigned himself to a life of carefree liaisons that were, frankly, limited to say the least—*as in non-existent*—cavorting in his kitchen with a stripper nearly half his age who was related, by blood, to his best friend!

Bradley grinned, and Mark was unsure whether Macy's clucking of her tongue was out of true disappointment for Mark, or if she also found this whole scenario amusing. Mark could quite use a nice cup of tea. *Is it rude to ask everyone to bugger off?*

"Brad?" Macy said, eyes wide.

"G'day, cuz," Bradley replied. "How was the trip?"

"Awful." Macy sighed. "I begged to get off at the nearest port and managed to get an early flight home. Mum found an even older geriatric to keep her company and after I was locked out of the cabin on the second night with a sock hanging on the handle, I decided it was time to come home."

"Good-o." Bradley still hadn't made any further steps back and it was taking all Mark's strength not to push him away, which would never work as Mark wouldn't be able to move the tank of the man, so he'd settle for a stern lecture on personal space. Or his other option was to ignore Macy and continue where they'd left off when she broke into his house. Which reminded him…

"Er, Macy, you realise this is my house? That you let yourself into *my* place of domicile?"

"Yes, Mark." Macy nodded. "Good thing, really, eh? Lord knows what would have happened, had I not. You can pretend your tongue wasn't in my baby cousin's mouth, but it would be harder to explain where you were hiding your dick."

"Macy!" Mark exploded and he wouldn't have been surprised if his ears blew steam like the kettle.

Bradley cracked out a laugh.

"You're not helping!" Mark prodded an aggravated finger in Bradley's chest and covered the ricocheting pain it caused.

"Sorry." Bradley smiled, all sweetness and light. "But this isn't a big deal."

"Isn't it?" Mark rubbed his brow. He needed an aspirin. Quick.

Bradley shrugged. "Why would it be?"

Mark couldn't answer. Not without reaffirming all the complications that had had Mark keeping Bradley at arm's length for the last few days. *Gosh, has it only been days?* Bradley was young. Too young. And too good-looking. And too flighty.

Mark was old. Too old to be flouncing around with Bradley. He might have let his inhibitions fly away a moment ago, but now Macy was here, reminding Mark of who he really was. And how everyone and everything had a use-by date.

"Brad?" Macy's calming, soothing tone floated along the silent kitchen.

"Yeah?"

"Why don't you go back to the shop? I brought some stuff from my trip and stashed them there to make some cakes for tomorrow. I need a word with Mark."

Bradley narrowed his eyes. "What about?"

"That's private."

Bradley whipped his gaze from Macy to Mark, playfulness dissipating with each passing look.

"Don't make him feel bad. None of this is his fault. It's no one's fault." Bradley smiled. "If you want to blame anyone, blame Gran. Or the stars. This is fate."

"Gran?" Macy rolled her eyes. "Bat-shit crazy Gran? What did she predict this time? That you and Mark are a match made in heaven?"

"In tea leaves, more like." Bradley's whole body radiated pride.

Mark shrank, in stature and in confidence.

"Bradley," Macy sighed. "I know you believe in that stuff, but she got it wrong last time, didn't she?"

"No." Bradley shook his head. "No. *I* got it wrong. This is right." He waved a hand between himself and Mark.

What? Mark should probably attempt to ask that out loud if he was hoping for an answer to his question.

"Okay, okay, look." Macy held up her hands in defence. "Just let me talk to Mark, please?"

Bradley paused in front of Mark and, dare Mark think it, there was a distinct demise in confidence from his stance. Mark wasn't sure what to make of that. Bradley exuded confidence. Was Macy making him realise his mistake?

Then, he was caught completely off guard when Bradley leaned in and kissed him on the cheek. A sweet, delicate peck that tingled along Mark's spine and his lips left a lingering, teasing patch of moisture that Mark never wanted to wash off.

"Listen to your heart, not her," Bradley whispered into Mark's ear before gliding over to his cousin, offering a less romantic kiss to her cheek and leaving the house.

Mark was a little weak at the knees. Was it from Macy's death glare or left over from that chaste kiss of Bradley's? As his gaze met Macy's, Mark swallowed and believed it was the former.

"You owe me an explanation, Mark."

"I need tea, Macy." Mark fell back onto the counter to steady himself. "Quite badly."

"First, you talk to me." Macy grabbed Mark's arm and yanked him into the living room. She collapsed with a huff onto the sofa and Mark lowered into the seat next to her, far more delicately and a tad more cautiously. "You like Brad?"

Mark shrugged. Macy slapped him.

"Ouch!" Mark rubbed his arm with a pout.

"If I find out you have used his faith in astrology, tasseography and whatever the hell his hippyish Byron Bay upbringing and our gran's influence has him believing in next, as a chance for a little slap and tickle, I will…I will…urg! I will refuse you service at my Tea Shoppe!"

Mark gasped. "That's totally unjust!"

"Yes. So be careful what you say here." Macy folded her arms.

"Hang on, you told me he could look after himself."

"He can. He does. But he's got that look in his eye."

"What look?"

Macy lowered her chin, peering up at Mark with sultry eyes. "Love."

"Absurd," Mark mumbled.

"Why?" Macy folded her arms, curled her legs under her bottom and draped her long skirt over the edge of the sofa. "Are you saying a good-looking man like my cousin can't fall in love? Because he's a stripper he doesn't have *feelings*? Is that it?"

"What? No." Mark firmed his lips. "He just doesn't have them for me. He's here in town for a short time—turns out the man who's been sent to make him feel welcome is also a homosexual and he's using the opportunity to pass the time. I could be anyone. And, sorry, but maybe there was a brief momentary lapse in judgement, there, because, well"—Mark waved a hand in the air—"he's the dictionary definition of 'sex'. They may as well forget the words on the entry and insert a photograph of him. But I can't let myself go there."

"Why not?" Macy drew in concerned eyebrows. "We've been friends for a fair few years now and I haven't seen you with anyone."

"I like my life like that."

"Give over." Macy slapped him on the leg. "I think you're about ready to get back on the horse, as they say."

"Bradley is most certainly not a horse." Mark folded his arms. "He is, for all intents and purposes, a stallion."

"Got that close while I was away, did we?"

"No." Mark shook his head. "No, no, no."

"Did you want to?"

Mark met with her gaze and sighed. "It isn't worth the inevitable heartbreak."

"Oh, you are an absolute waste of a gay man, Mark Johnson!"

Macy's lips hadn't moved to say that, and the voice had dropped a few decibels too. On realising it hadn't been Macy uttering it at all, Mark flipped around on the sofa. Damian stood at the entrance doorway, hands on his hips.

"Have you ditched the almighty Australian fuck-god, already?"

Mark pinched the bridge of his nose. This morning had just got a whole lot worse.

"Firstly, the fuck-god is my baby cousin." Macy glared at Damian

Damian held his hands up in apology, with minimal wincing.

"Secondly, Mark is most definitely not having rampant sex with an Australian." Macy turned back to Mark. "Or any other man of any nationality."

"What's new?" Damian perched on the edge of the arm rest next to Macy and kissed her cheek.

"Just a little enquiry, if I may?" Mark asked.

Both Macy and Damian stopped their sniggering to address Mark with their similar sets of raised eyebrows.

"If you're both so eager for me to be finally getting my end away, why have you both let yourself into my house? I'll be having those spare keys back, thank you very much."

"Ah!" Damian hacked out with an accusatory point of his finger. "So you *do* plan on getting all Will Smith behind closed doors, then?"

"I beg your pardon?"

"Oh, come on." Damian huffed. "Getting jiggy with it?" He wiggled on the edge of the sofa, rotating his arms in a dance move to rival Bradley's Adonis Cabaret. "Na, na, na, nana, nanana."

"No," Mark replied a little exasperated. "No, no, no."

"She doth protest too much," Damian said with another eyebrow waggle.

"Actually, I've decided to have a real-life friend cull, rather than just on Facebook. So I am sorry, lady and gent, you didn't make the cut."

"You need us, Mark Johnson," Macy shoved his arm and Mark was beginning to feel like a ragdoll with all the manhandling. "We're the ones who are here to support your foray into uncharted territory."

"It's not quite uncharted."

"They've changed all the rules since *you* last did it." Damian tutted. "Did they even have lube back then?"

"I'm getting confused." Mark scrubbed a hand over his face. "I thought you, Macy, didn't want me…cavorting with your baby cousin. Now it's all, go on, Mark, get jiggly with it."

"I just want to know it's consensual on both sides. And that you both know what you're letting yourself in for." Macy shrugged.

"And I came here for a nice cup of tea and to find out all the details of last night." Damian rubbed his hands together with glee.

"I don't have any bags," Mark admitted with a sullen sulk.

Their gasps said it all. And while Mark listened to the cackling from the other two on his sofa, his mind flickered to what Bradley had said he should listen to—his heart. What was his heart telling him? What was the ultimate pull? Where were the stars guiding him?

Satisfied that the stars were aligning in some sort of order, Mark hefted up from the sofa. "I'll go get the tea."

* * * *

The bell tinkled its welcome and Mark pushed through the door. His hands trembled as he closed it and twisted the lock. Was this a very bad idea? Glancing around Macy's Tea Shoppe, he paused at its stillness. He thought about calling out, but should he allow his mouth to speak, it might not shut up. So instead he cleared his throat, threw his jacket over one of the tables and forced his jelly legs to get him around the counter and into the back kitchen.

Bradley had his back to him, shoving various items from a crate into the large industrial fridge. He had headphones in, which could have been the reason he hadn't heard the entrance bell or Mark's shoes slapping on the floor as he edged closer. Mark lost his nerve. The contours of Bradley's muscles through his thin vest top was enough to give Mark second, third—hell even a bazillion thoughts. None of which were rational. So he abandoned them to enjoy the view of Bradley reaching for each item and shoving it onto a shelf.

Bradley was perfect. If Mark had been told to draw the ideal man, he would forever be sketching Bradley from memory. The fact he couldn't actually draw was neither here nor there. Mark would know who it was.

But Bradley was young. Far too young for this not to feel just a mite icky.

Bradley twisted and stared.

"G'day, Mark." His face erupted into a grin and he flicked out his headphones.

Mark didn't have the first clue who Bradley was listening to, or even what type of music category it would come under. There had only been four genres when Mark had been an avid listener of popular music—rock, pop, classic and heavy metal. Now it seemed there were a multitude of subgenres—and subgenres within subgenres—to explain what type of music any one band played. All bands were now unique and not bunched together under the simple category of popular music.

Mark sighed. And told his brain to shut the fuck up.

"You want a tea?" Bradley asked, turning off the phone and shunting the kitchen into anticipatory silence.

Mark shook his head. "No."

"Right-o." Bradley waved a hand to the delights cluttering the kitchen surface. "Cake? Macy brought some cool choccie muffins back. Sure she won't mind if you fancied a nibble?"

"No. Thank you."

"Okay." Bradley elongated the word and glanced around the kitchen. "You want a coffee?"

Mark snorted. "No."

Bradley chuckled, but was soon rendered to a halt when Mark found his confidence and edged closer.

Bradley straightened. "Do you want"—he cocked his head—"me?"

"Oh, fucking God, yes." Mark surprised himself with how loud that came out. The words ricocheted off the stainless-steel counters and echoed in resigned confirmation.

Bradley smiled. Beamed. Radiated an illuminating glow that sizzled Mark's skin. He leaned forward, brushing his lips against Mark's with enticing fortitude.

Mark didn't move. He allowed the warm breath against his lips and waited for Bradley to take over. Bradley would want it that way. Mark was happy to give it to him. Allow him to lead all this nonsense. That way, Mark could plead ignorance to any seduction techniques that he clearly didn't have in his arsenal.

"Come on, then, Mark," Bradley whispered against Mark's lips. He licked his own and wiped his tongue across Mark's teasingly. "Take me."

Thirty-nine years Mark had been in his own body and mind. He thought he knew himself infinitely well. He'd spent years coming to terms with who he was—a bumbling fool consumed by misfortune. He was fairly certain he could pinpoint his immediate reactions to any given situation and they usually ended in some comedic slapstick fallout.

But this, this was new.

And so Mark decided to forgo his usual reserved reactions and do what Bradley said. *To hell with all consequences.*

He rammed his mouth on top of Bradley's and kissed him—consumed him—no holds barred. This time, he had no desire to stop. He didn't even care if anyone wandered into the kitchen asking for tea—they could watch if they were so inclined.

Mark was a new man.

He sliced into Bradley's mouth with his tongue, entwining it with Bradley's and tasting all the juicy orangey bits still remaining on the roof of his mouth. *So that's why Bradley always has such sweet breath!* Bradley staggered back, falling into the open fridge. He glided his hands onto Mark's hips, whether to steady himself or to tug him closer being debatable. But Mark crushed his body forth regardless. Bradley trailed his fingertips inside Mark's shirt and Mark whimpered. Bradley's hands were cold and Mark's skin erupted with goosepimples rivalling the plucked chicken sitting on the shelf of Macy's fridge.

Bradley tucked his arms up into the sides of Mark's shirt and stretched with such force that the buttons ripped off in one smooth movement and pinged around the kitchen. Luckily, Mark had his eyes closed or there could have been another eye incident to add to his growing list.

Slipping Mark's shirt free, Bradley hummed from the pit of his stomach and floated the shirt to the floor. Mark should have been feeling all kinds of self-conscious then, standing there in Macy's Tea Shoppe kitchen with his skinny body on display for a man who stripped for a living. But for once his conscience switched off. And especially more so when Bradley freed his mouth from Mark's and kissed, sucked and licked down Mark's neck, over his collarbone and to his chest. Mark grappled with Bradley's hair, sliding his fingers in and watching Bradley sink lower. Bradley was devouring him, lapping up every inch of Mark's skin. It wasn't rushed, either—he was taking his time over it. *Enjoying* it.

Bradley licked over Mark's hardened, protruding dark nipple. He nipped a bit, too, which Mark thought was a little uncalled for, but he discovered it wasn't exactly painful and enjoyed the sensation, nonetheless.

Slipping his cold hands down inside the waistband of Mark's jeans, Bradley stood to grin and lick his lips. "I don't feel no taking, Mark."

"God, I hate that grin," Mark purred in a way completely opposed to his words.

"Come get me, Mark." Bradley stretched out his arms in invitation.

Mark cocked his head, holding Bradley's challenging gaze. He'd take that dare. Tucking his fingers into the top of Bradley's jeans, he attempted to unfasten the button. Mark had a lot of experience opening and fastening his own jeans fly, so he would have thought that ripping open Bradley's would be second nature. He flicked his thumb and finger once more around the circular metal and came to the conclusion that Bradley's jeans were clearly secured together by super glue. He had no choice but to drop his seductive eye contact to give his full attention to the bloody task at hand.

Choosing to go in with two hands, he attempted to tuck the metal through the hole. He grimaced, his tongue poking out in concentration. Not a good look for the current moment.

"How on earth do you get these things off so easily on stage?" Mark asked, flapping out his thumb that had dented from the metal.

Bradley chuckled. "Velcro."

Mark glanced up. "Couldn't think about wearing that next time?"

"If this is on the cards, then yeah, sure thing."

Mark's stomach fluttered, which soon turned into curdling mush leaping up his throat. Was there a next time? Would there ever even be a this time if basic clothing mechanics were beyond his capabilities? Bradley's increasing hardness beneath his hands wasn't helping him focus. He blew out a puff of air to waft his hair back from his perspiring forehead, but before he threw in the towel completely and chalked this up to fate, the stars, lack of tea, Bradley wrapped a meaty hand around his and with a quick flick had his jeans open and the head of his cock popped out with an eager hello.

Or rather a g'day.

"Thanks," Mark said.

"You're welcome."

Mark licked his lips on seeing the glistening head poking out of Bradley's now open flies. No underwear. *Beautiful.* Before his feet could catch up with his wrenching gut and leg it out of there, Mark sunk to his knees and yanked Bradley's jeans down with him. Bradley attempted to step out of them, but his trainers caught on the foot holes and Mark had to help him slip out of them by undoing his laces for him. Those were the parts in porn they didn't show. And for good reason.

Mark slung the trainers somewhere in the kitchen that he would no doubt trip over later, and ripped Bradley free of his jeans. Bradley's cock didn't falter and pointed at Mark's face with a blatant come-hither. Mark, for once, obliged and went and hithered with gusto. Gripping the root of Bradley's shaft, he licked up the full length and wiped the sprinkled tip. It tasted a darn sight better than anything he had ever licked in this shop before, including the iced fingers.

Opening his mouth for more, he dived in and Bradley toppled back into the fridge. A few items from the shelves were knocked off and fell to the floor with thick splats. Chocolate custard glooped along the tile ridges, but Mark knew which he would rather be lapping up right then. He trailed a hand behind Bradley to grip at his taut, muscular arse cheek and squeezed him out of the fridge and deeper into his mouth.

"Mark Johnson!" Bradley breathed out, scratching fingernails through Mark's scalp. "You are *dirty*."

Mark let that statement whittle down to its core meaning and continued to prove that, yes, he could be as filthy as the next bloke. Especially when kneeling on a kitchen floor amongst discarded food items and with another man's dick in his gob. Mark couldn't remember the last time he had done this. It had been quite some time ago, and he desperately tried not to allow his mind to linger too long on the whens, wheres and how fors to focus solely on the one he was currently enjoying filling up his mouth. *Just like riding a bike, this!* He could remember how to get a man off with his tongue alone, and swiped it around Bradley's cockhead, trailing the veins and poking it into the slit all to the tune of Bradley's low encouraging moans above him.

"Mark!" Bradley called out. Yelled out. *Groaned* out.

Mark glanced up to catch the pure joy on the man's face above him. It made his toes curl, and *he* still had his covered by socks and shoes. Poor Bradley's perfectly rounded pedicured digits were seeping into the brown custard globules on the floor as he clung to the fridge with one desperate hand and Mark's hair with the other. Mark didn't stop. He was on a roll. He sucked furiously and pumped faster with the hand curled around the root.

Excitement, anticipation and curiosity all merged into one as Mark wondered how far he could take this. *Should* take this. He needed to test the waters, see what he was dealing with there. He glided the hand clutching Bradley's arse to slide into his crack. Would Bradley buck, or tense? Would he even be expecting it?

He did neither. He leaned forward, away from within the fridge, giving Mark better access. *Intriguing.*

Bradley, bent double, watched his dick slide in and out of Mark's keen mouth, allowed, no *encouraged,* Mark to poke inside him deeper.

"That's it, Mark. That's it. There. Oh, yeah!" In between his babbling grunts of gripping pleasure, Bradley let go of the fridge door and it bashed against Mark's back, kicking in his gag reflex.

Bradley's cock fell from his mouth and Mark's legs trembled, trying to keep him steady in his crouch. He peered up and Bradley looked down, both gazes both wondering what to do next.

Should they ask the stars?

"You know what this means, now, right, Mark?" Bradley panted as Mark licked his lips.

"That we owe Macy a new fridge?"

Bradley chuckled. "That you're going to have to finish this. Properly."

"Right, well, let me just—" He went to heft himself up, mentally crossing his fingers his knees didn't crack and remind him no forty-year-old gent should be kneeling down for that long, but Bradley hauled him up and kissed him.

"Fuck me, Mark. I want you inside me. Now. All of you."

Mark swallowed. Hard. And it was a crying shame he wasn't gulping down Bradley's juicy bits whilst he did it.

Bradley cocked his head. "If you want to, that is?"

"Want to? I'd beg to."

Bradley smiled. "So, that's a yes then?"

"You don't mind to... You're a...bottom?" Mark couldn't even begin to fathom the miracle of that. He'd been preparing to give himself over to Bradley. Breaking in the old heave-ho. Something that he hadn't done in… Once, he'd done it once. Many years ago, at the request of—

"Yes." Bradley kissed Mark's nose, cutting off any images slapping Mark in the face. "Told you, Mark, this is fate."

Even with the freezing temperatures bursting out from the fridge behind him, the heat oozing off Bradley's body seeped across into Mark and relaxed those dastardly goose pimples to create a glistening sheen of sweat over his skin. Whether or not he believed in fate or in whatever Bradley believed in, Mark was ready to give this a go. To test the theory for real. To see if they did fit. *Could* fit. And he hoped not just in the literal sense.

Bradley smiled and kissed him, heating Mark exponentially. Mark stumbled back and grappled to tear the remaining clothes from Bradley's impressive body. For a man he'd only known a few days, Mark had seen him naked more than he'd seen him with his clothes on. From the computer screen, to on stage, to lying in a bed next to him, but now Mark could allow himself to properly feast upon the sight. And not just by looking. He was no longer another spectator tuning in to see the Geek God, or standing in a queue to cop a load of the Aussie Adonis. Mark wasn't there for Bradley's alter ego. He was there for Bradley. *Brad.*

Nope, *Bradley* was still much, much better.

"This needs seeing to." Bradley stroked up and down Mark's released dick with a delectable glint in his eye.

Huh, when did Bradley unzip my jeans?

Mark fluttered his eyes to a close, thinking no more of the magic trick Bradley must have performed on his outerwear. It had been oh so long since another set of fingers had fondled his dick that Mark had forgotten just how marvellous it truly was. And Bradley's hand was thick, and firm and slid up and down with agonisingly gradual strokes. His movements were a lot slower than Mark would have done on himself, and that just added to the thrill of it all. To know that he wasn't in control of his own…faculties? *No, no, wait, my destiny!*

Cripes, I'm a new-age hippy!

With a sensual swipe of his thumb across Mark's cockhead, Bradley drove Mark to newfound dizzy heights. Far worse than those he had ever encountered on the tea cup ride thing—

"*Waltzer!*" Mark blurted through a grunt.

"What?" Bradley's grip tightened around Mark's flesh at the sudden outburst. And that felt excruciatingly magnificent.

"Nothing, nothing." Mark shook his head. "Just an old fairground ride."

"You calling me a ride, Mark?"

"Oh, God, yes. I can pretty much guarantee this will be the ride of my life."

Bradley chuckled. "You better strap on, then." He nodded down to Mark's unsheathed penis battling its way out of his pants.

"Right." Mark stepped back and tucked a hand into his back jeans pocket. He could kiss Damian right then for slipping him a condom as he'd left for London last night.

As he fished out the packet, he waved it in triumph in front of Bradley, brandishing it like a trophy. That wasn't the prize though. The man in front of him was, the condom a mere certificate that would be discarded and forgotten, whereas Bradley would remain forever a gleaming beauty to brighten up his dull and, currently bare, mantlepiece. Wouldn't he? *Better not think about that now. Let's at least finish the game.*

Nodding in approval, Bradley snatched the packet from Mark and tore it open with his teeth. Mark lost all train of any type of thought when Bradley unrolled the sheath over Mark's eager cock and sent a distinct aroma of chocolate wafting from the rubber—or was that just the floor? He stared deep into Mark's eyes, as if he was reading his mind, and tugged down Mark's jeans and boxers to his ankles.

Would anyone ever believe this? That Mark, old has-been Mark, was going to fuck a stallion? God, that did things to his balls he couldn't put a name to. Or wouldn't want to. What were words, anyway?

Bradley offered a long, tantalising kiss, sucking in Mark's bottom lip before whipping around and leaning over the counter. That perfectly rounded arse stuck out in an invitation that Mark wouldn't ever decline. He was pretty much ready to self-combust at the view alone and had no idea how he was going to manage the task of sticking his dick inside and pushing in and out long enough to make this rigmarole worth all the hassle.

Oh, God, don't let this be an in, out, done!

"Come on, Mark." Bradley waggled his hips.

"Right, yes." Mark needed to remember the basic functions of sex. *Shit.* "Lube?"

"Jesus, Mark, you not bring lube?" Bradley shot a concerning look over his shoulder.

"I didn't realise I would have a need for it." Mark swiped a hand across his forehead. "I came for tea!"

"Bullshit, Mark. You came here for me!" Bradley's once-confident voice wavered a little.

"No." Mark waved a hand in protest. "No, no, no."

Bradley slapped his hands on the edge of the counter, looking like he might just get up and forget all this.

"All right, yes," Mark admitted, and lowered to drape himself over Bradley's back and kissed the man's razor-sharp shoulder blade. "Yes, I did. Yes, I do want you. Yes, yes, fucking, yes." He finished off a statement with a bite, just in case anything was lost in translation.

"Get creative, then." Bradley's growl was rather demanding. *So, no submissive bottom, then.* "'Cause I need this. I need you. I gotta know, Mark."

He couldn't just use spit, could he? *No, no, that's never a good idea.* He wanted this to be at least a decent try. What could one use within the confines of a tearoom's back kitchen? This was absurd! But one look at Bradley's waggling bare bottom, enticing and inviting, was enough for Mark to use his noggin for once.

Hurrying over to the fridge, he nearly slipped in the custard spilled on the floor but regained composure enough to find the only thing he could think to use. He shoved his fingers into the nearest tub of margarine-style spread that proclaimed itself Better than Butter, shrugged and slicked up his condom-clad dick, battling with his subconscious as to whether he wanted to ever recall this moment or not.

He'd remember. Just with gaps in its entirety.

"Come on, Mark." Bradley's desperate plea thrummed off the stainless steel and through to Mark's raging cock.

"Give a fellow a moment. I'm not as agile as I was." Mark stepped up to Bradley, cupping his greased-up dick and lining it up with Bradley's hole.

Mark, being Mark, paused.

"Get in me, Mark." Bradley growled. "Now!"

"You're rather bossy." Mark avoided the tut that would vaguely resemble his mother's to slide a hand up Bradley's back, grip his shoulder and push through the resistance.

Except there was no resistance. Mark slid in, thanks to the Better than Butter mimicking both butter and absent bodily excretions, and his eyes rolled to the back of his head at the heat engulfing his cock.

Bradley grunted. "Oh, Christ, Mark! That feels fucking fantastic!" He backed his arse into Mark, gripping the side of the counter, giving Mark the courage to get really into it.

He slipped out, enjoying the sensation, then teased back in. Merely watching his dick dip in and out of Bradley's perfectly sculpted arse was enough to send Mark over the edge. How had he gone so bloody long without doing this? He'd been kidding himself all this time that he could go without. Why hadn't he dusted off the cobwebs some time ago and been like Damian?

Mark slammed in and out of Bradley with renewed vigour, fearing Bradley might be getting burn marks from the steel counter on his bare skin with the pace of Mark's thrusts. Bradley didn't complain and Mark chose to deal with that after. Now, though, now he needed to feel…every…single…earthshattering…sensation.

"Bradley!" Mark yelled into the aether, once all the ooos and ahhhs and uuuhs had been used up, then grunted through his climax as it rushed around his entire quivering body and exploded into Bradley.

"Oh, God, Mark!" Bradley raised Mark's orgasm with one of his own that spurted from his dick and landed with a splat to the floor. He hadn't even needed a hand to shimmy that along. *He's one of those!*

Collapsing onto Bradley's back, Mark gave one last thrust and vowed to remain there until he died, or got his breath back. Whichever came first. That had been amazing. No, better than amazing. Perfect. *Beautiful*. And Mark's head floated in a cloud of hazy euphoria that he had no desire to come back down from. Had it ever been that way? Had he ever felt this way before? Like he belonged? Like they both belonged…together?

No. No it hadn't.

Mark inhaled. Time had evidently passed and he was still sprawled over Bradley's back.

"Tea?" Bradley offered over his shoulder.

"Yes." Mark nodded. "Please."

Chapter Fifteen

Tea for Two

"This one is my best yet, I think?"

"Really?" Mark replied, taking hold of the steaming mug of tea Bradley handed down to him. "And what makes you so confident about this particular beverage?"

Bradley smiled that beatific smile of all-white teeth and the green flecks in his eyes sparkled like the speckles glistening in the cup from the reflective lights above the café. Hovering over him on one of the vacant tables in the tea shop, Bradley bit his lip and Mark curled his fingers around the cup handle and lifted it to his lips. The distinct colour was particularly appealing. To put it into its correct category, Mark would say it was leaning toward the Strip Teas shade on the official chart and Mark couldn't help but muse at how apt that was, considering the maker. It appeared to have the correct amount of milk and, as he peered into it further, he couldn't see any remnants left in it that shouldn't be there. Bradley was almost a connoisseur.

"No tea bags," Bradley gloated. "That, there, is made with leaves." He cocked his head. "As I know your aversion to tea bagging."

Mark shot the Aussie a narrowed glare and Bradley chuckled. Ignoring the cheeky wink, Mark took a sip and, as he swallowed, his whole body relaxed from its tense clench. He would have thought that after what he had just done in the back kitchen all those good endorphins would have been released and he'd be smiling for weeks. But as soon as he had ventured out into the seating area, the old Mark had come back to haunt him and the realisation of how dreadful uncomfortable the whole scenario was burst through his every orifice.

The tea was a welcome relief for his ailing body and mushed-up mind.

"It's very good," Mark finally agreed and downed more of the impeccable beverage.

Bradley took up a seat opposite him and sat back, arms folded. He inspected Mark with those sparkling eyes and proceeded to laugh.

"What's so funny?" Mark wrapped his trembling hands around the mug.

"So, you were just flirting with me last week?" Bradley said. "Trying to get into my pants, eh? Tut tut, Mark."

Mark narrowed his eyes. Flirting? He was pretty sure flirting wasn't something he knew how to do.

"You told me my tea was *perfect* last week," Bradley reminded him and waggled a finger across the table. "Now you've downgraded that to 'very good'. You think now you've got me, you don't have to be so complimentary?"

"I'd hardly say I've got you."

The look Bradley shot him across the table made Mark realise that was a rather flippant statement, so he thought best to back it up, add some more, like his mouth always did before his brain kicked in.

"What I mean to say is, that getting you would mean that I get to keep you. Which sounds a lot like a purchase of some description. And I haven't paid for the tea, either." He held up the cup in demonstration. "I am able to pay for the tea, of course. It is, like I say, a rather good cup and one I would be more than happy to offer monetary gratitude for."

He took another gulp from the mug and shut his eyes. On opening them he noticed Bradley was waiting for more. Or perhaps in some sort of trance or other.

"Not that I wouldn't offer a monetary value to you." Mark shook his head with the absurdity of what had just tumbled forth from his mouth. "Sorry, erase that."

Bradley smirked.

Mark sipped his tea. "What I mean to say is that I've *had* you." He confirmed that with a firm nod. "I think. Or if the past hour was simply a dream, then I do apologise and I'll just drink this up and get on home."

"Have you *had* many boyfriends, Mark?" Bradley folded his arms across his rock-hard chest that was unfortunately now covered by a vest top. The question was merely stated, no inflections or raising of eyebrows. Like he was just interested in Mark's previous encounters. None of them had been on a counter of course, just Bradley. *Oh, God, I just fucked Bradley on Macy's kitchen counters!*

Mark fixated on staring at his latest conquest in awe. That top was so delectably tight that Mark could make out the contours of taut muscles, especially when Bradley clamped his arms together and curled his fingers around the bulging biceps. Mark had to bite his tongue, which he should have done some time back. Or at least had it removed along with his tonsils when he was a teenager. A bout of tonsillitis would actually have been a welcome condition right about then as he saw the look of intrigue dancing across the young man opposite's beautiful face.

"That's a rather personal question." Mark slurped the next mouthful of tea. Rather uncouth, he was aware, but his trembling lips and flapping tongue couldn't handle table manners right then.

"Are you saying we aren't at that stage in our relationship yet to learn such things of each other?" Bradley inquired with a tilt of his head. "Because, I'd say we've moved up a notch or two, no?"

He winked and Mark coughed. Loudly. He was rather perturbed he'd finished the tea and there was no bag at the bottom to splat onto his face and move the conversation along to something far less embarrassing. Damn the Aussie and his now decent teamaking ability. Slamming the cup on the surface, Mark stroked a hand through his hair which he was sure had remnants of Better than Butter greased through it and was in danger of looking like those grunge kids who skated along the seafront and who refused to shampoo, claiming that the products were against nature.

"You can give a ballpark figure, if you like?" Bradley offered.

"Ha!" Mark hacked out. "It would be rather an empty ballpark. Not even in the realms of Marsby FC's weekly turnout."

"They get many?"

"Wouldn't know, never been, but this isn't a particularly large town and, from my flick through of the local weekly rag, I believe Marsby has a habit of losing."

"Fair dos." Bradley leaned forward, his elbows perched on the table top. "A handful then?"

"Why are you so blinking interested?" Mark spat. "Did I do it wrong?"

Bradley chuckled and fiddled with the paper sugars in their porcelain pot. "No." He smiled, wistfully. "Far from wrong. Although, margarine? That's ingenious."

"How many boyfriends have you had?" Defusing the question was infantile, sure. But he was losing. And he had never been opposed to cheating. At games, that was. Not relationships.

His heart leapt out a painful spasm of memories and he had to rub it better over his chest.

"Three." Bradley didn't falter his quickfire reply. He stopped his idle fingering of the condiments packets and sat back, rubbing a hand over his stomach. "Had a girlfriend at school once, too. But I was thirteen then so I don't really count her. And we only kissed."

"I see." Mark nodded. "I, unfortunately, went to an all-boys' school. No opportunity for girls there."

"No," Bradley confirmed with a glint in his eye. "Just lots and lots and lots of boys."

Mark snorted and not particularly lightheartedly either. He ended up hiccupping and Bradley leaned back in his chair to watch the pitiful demise with an opposing grin.

"You know, Mark," he said, "I'm getting the feeling you have something to hide."

"Not at all," Mark lied with a firm shake of his head. "Hid the sausage today and that's about the extent of my hide-and-seek abilities."

Bradley burst out a laugh and Mark smiled at the pleasurable release. Bradley was infectious when he laughed and Mark was relieved that for once it hadn't been caused by *his* misfortune. Well, it was, but indirectly so that was a lot easier to take on the chin.

"All right." Bradley inhaled a deep breath, regaining his composure and evidently not waning in his need to continue the inquisition. "Now you tell me."

The tinkle of the bell above the shop door was a welcome saviour. Now Mark knew where that statement might have originated from. Because he'd never been saved by the school bell. But as he turned his head toward the incoming, consisting of two shit-eating grins on Damian and Macy's smug mugs, Mark would have preferred to explain his tragic life-slash-love story rather than have to make pleasantries with those two.

"Good evening, Mark." Damian greeted him with a wink and pulled out one of the chairs next to him. He thrust out an eager hand to Bradley. "Don't believe we've met."

"Brad," Bradley offered and shook Damian's hand.

Damian clung on to it like a cat to a hanging branch, searing his claws in to Mark's man. Bradley attempted to slide his hand away, causing a tug of war over the square table.

"Damian," Mark warned through gritted teeth.

"Possessive now are we, Marky Mark?" Damien released his grip and Bradley fell back in his seat. Damian whistled, bit his bottom lip and mouthed a *wow* over his shoulder. That wasn't the end to his dramatic performance—he flicked out a napkin from the holder and proceeded to fan himself with it.

Mark kicked him under the table.

"We were worried, Mark." Macy scraped out the chair beside Bradley and gave an all-knowing smile to her baby cousin.

I really must stop referring to Bradley as a baby cousin.

Bradley grinned and that pretty much summed up all in the lopsided curvature of his lips exactly why Mark hadn't made it back home yet.

"I am thirty-nine!" Mark declared. "Quite capable of getting around by myself. Certainly in the middle of the day."

"See, you say that as if it's true." Damian waggled a finger so close to Mark's nose he had to bat it away. "Remember that time you got lost on your stroll along the coastal road?"

Mark sighed. "I did not get lost. I merely took a wrong turn."

"And ended up in the middle of Dover docks about to board a freight ferry to France." Damian chuckled. "They nearly locked you up as they thought you were a refugee." He squealed and clutched his stomach. "Until they remembered that refugees rarely try to get *out* of Britain."

The anecdote wasn't that funny, so Damian's over-the-top cackling was merely a way to get some attention on him. His fluttering eyelashes wafted a breeze through Bradley's blond tousled locks and Mark glared at him, then removed his stare to land it on Bradley. Bradley smiled back. He hadn't even given a second glance to Damian. It made Mark a tad uncomfortable, but his stomach liked to indulge him with its warm and fuzzies on this occasion.

"I don't see it." Bradley cocked his head.

"See what?" Mark asked.

Bradley waggled a finger between Damian and Mark. "You two."

He still didn't produce a damn wrinkle with his furrowing brow and Mark wondered which brand of cream the man used as he'd quite like to buy the stuff in bulk. Until he recalled Bradley's actual age and swallowed down the returning anxiety overload. *I really am a cradle snatcher!*

Damian gasped, snapping Mark out of his brief reverie. "Did Mark tell you about our little attempt at being more than *just good friends?*"

"I would delete the word *good,* there," Mark retorted with a sullen grump. "And, no, I hadn't. It's not something I boast about."

Damian scowled over his shoulder, but soon whipped back around to offer a delightful smile to address the Aussie instead. Mark didn't blame him. Bradley was much better to look at.

"I guessed." Bradley shrugged. "So that's at least one then, Mark?"

"Damian was never a boyfriend. Not really." *Would that be misinterpreted?* Probably.

"No, we weren't." Damian cupped his chin in his palm, tapping his fingers on his cheek as he gazed at Bradley. "When we first met, we were both hopeless romantics suffering years of torment at being in love with men we couldn't have and shouldn't want." Damian pointed at Mark. "I told him to just get over it. Move on. We tried, and, well, it was like kissing my brother." He shuddered. "We decided it would be better to just pine over others and be each other's fall-back if we weren't settled by forty." He slapped a hand on Mark's thigh. "Which isn't far off, old fellow!"

Mark's face drained of any colour as Bradley widened his eyes.

"Me." Damian, oblivious to any unrest, splayed his hand across his chest. "I love Tom Hardy. And the man simply refuses to answer any of my fan mail. But he's got one year left before I forget him and become Mark Johnson's bottom. Because that was also the deal, or Mark wasn't having any of it."

"And Mark?" Bradley shuffled forward. "Who does he love?"

Mark opened his mouth. Nothing came out except Damian's voice.

"Oh, Mark, here." Damian waved a hand to indicate that he was aware Mark was still sitting there, although his flapping lips seemed evidence to the contrary. "He just still pines, bless his cockles."

Bradley arched that one damn eyebrow that was probably ever so much fitter than its comrade across the bridge with all its recent lone workouts. Mark decided now was perhaps time to offer some information, even if it wasn't strictly truthful. But before he had the chance to open his mouth, Damian leaned in toward Bradley and lowered his voice.

"I gave Mark all my best moves, but no matter what I did I couldn't snap him from his pining. You'd think ten years was enough—"

"I do not pine, Damian!" Mark nearly toppled out of his seat to yell that.

"No?" Damian thrust his whole body around in the chair. "It's all you ever do. It's all you ever did! It's why that kiss was so bloody deplorable! It was like wading my tongue in a pit of despair mixed with self-loathing and despicable depression. And even when we tried a little beneath-clothing fumbling, it was still riddled with despondency."

"Maybe it was your incessant chatter?" Mark snapped, his blood boiling. *God, is that what Bradley tasted too? My years and years of torment?* "How can one even slip their tongue in you when you keep flapping your lips?"

"Ooooo." Damian sashayed his hips in retaliation. "I do apologise that I couldn't match up to your Mr George, blinking perfect, Carroway!"

Mark glared at Damian. Damian, in turn, glared back. Mark didn't take his eyes off Damian. He couldn't. He could feel Bradley's gaze on him and he wanted nothing more right then than the ground to open up and swallow him.

Macy, bless her mismatched cottons, remained quiet but took the opportune moment to stand and smile.

"Perhaps we could all use a cup of tea?" she suggested.

"Who's George Carroway?" Bradley asked.

Mark didn't respond. He had no idea how to summarise the complexity of the answer to what Bradley assumed was an acceptable question. Mark had spent a long time avoiding having to talk about it. Having to deal with it. Having to come to terms with what George had done to him. He'd accepted. He'd moved on…if solitarily.

Macy skulked off to the kitchen with nothing more than a tip-tap of purple shoes and Damian sucked in a breath that he didn't seem to be exhaling at any given moment, darting his worried gaze from Bradley to him. Mark should say something. Anything. Whatever he said would be so much better than what Damian might suddenly decide to utter should he ever want to breathe out again.

Just when things were getting a trite awkward, with no one speaking and Bradley content to keep his eyebrows having their daily thirty minutes of isometric exercise, Macy's loud gasp bellowed out to the seating area. Mark widened his eyes at Bradley, realisation striking of how they had left things back there. It would be Mark's luck right then that the Health and Safety inspectors would tinkle that bell. Still, least he'd be saved by it.

"Right, well, that'll be my cue to, er…" Mark stood.

"Oh, no you don't." Bradley leaped from his chair, scooted around the table to push him back down to the seat. "I'm not dealing with that on my own."

"It was lovely knowing you." Mark thrust up into Bradley's palms, but got no farther than a millimetre off the seat.

It's all well and good when the sight gets you off, but when you need to make a bolt for it, a well gym-honed muscular system can be such a hindrance.

"What's going on?" Damian asked, narrowing his eyes.

He bundled out of his seat and tottered off into the back kitchen, leaving Mark alone with Bradley. He still hadn't taken his hands away from Mark's shoulders, grounding him or, more like, looming over him in a menacing shadow.

Mark offered one of the best and sweetest smiles he had ever produced in his life. He even fluttered his eyelashes, Damian-style, to soften the blow.

Bradley didn't falter his threatening stance, but did loosen the fingers he had digging into Mark's collarbone somewhat and Mark felt a renewed sense of triumph, going a little way to prove that beauty could win over the beast. Not that Mark would consider himself the beauty in this scenario, but the sentiment was there.

"You two are clearing that up!" Macy stomped out of the kitchen, ripped her straw bag from the back of her chair and gave Mark a stern eyeful, Yvonne-style.

Damian teetered out behind, hands over his mouth, chuckling. "Nice work, Marky Mark. Nice work, indeed!"

Macy yanked open the door, making the bell sound more like the shrill of an alarm as it slapped back and forth on its hook at double time. She shot an embittered look over her shoulder that Mark decided was for Bradley. At least, Mark allowed him to be the recipient of it by glancing down into his empty cup.

Once Damian had vacated the building, Macy attempted to slam a door that was lined in foam pads to prevent such an abhorrence, gave up and growled as she stomped out of sight.

Mark glanced up to Bradley with a shrug.

"Best be sorting that out, then, shall we?"

"Who's George Carroway and why does he deserve your continued pining?"

If Mark didn't know any better, he would say the look in Bradley's eyes bore some resemblance to a little-known emotion called jealousy. It couldn't be, though? Could it? Not if Bradley knew the truth. *Which he doesn't.*

Taking a deep breath, Mark stood, bit down his reserved nature and leaned in to kiss Bradley. Whilst he had hoped that would deter the Aussie from asking any more pressing questions, he soon realised his lips wouldn't be as effective as the memory wipe used in one of his favourite *Star Trek* episodes.

"The answer to your previous question is one." Mark scooted around Bradley's bulky frame and ventured over to the counter. "His name was George Carroway. Mostly known as Mr Carroway in these parts."

Scurrying into the kitchen, Mark glimpsed the leftover mess that proved he had actually managed to double his aforementioned number of conquests. He grabbed the nearest cloth to run under the tap, then cleaned down the surfaces.

Bradley slapped out a bin liner and gathered up the ruined food dregs scraped into the floor. They cleared up in relative silence for a while, Bradley obviously hoping Mark might offer some more information without encouragement and Mark playing a little game to see how long the Aussie would last without pressing for more details.

"Was it a long relationship?"

Mark peered up to the clock on the wall. *Ten minutes. Not bad.*

"Longest I've had." Mark chuckled, but Bradley didn't get in on the joke.

"Did you live together?" Bradley had all but stopped his clearing up and placed a hand on his hips with the bin liner dangling at his side.

"Eventually." Mark scrubbed harder along the surfaces, wishing he could rid the memories as easy as the crusted sperm. "In London."

"How did you meet?" Bradley wasn't moving a muscle, except the ones that enabled his eyes to follow whatever Mark did.

"Mr Carroway was a teacher." Mark twisted and stood opposite Bradley against the adjacent counter.

The counter where he'd banged Bradley into oblivion moments previous. *What a comedown. Better just get it all out.* "*My* teacher, to be exact. It started as a silly crush when I was about fourteen. He was somewhat older, obviously. Being young and naive, I pursued him for a while."

Mark hung his head with the shame oozing through him like the custard still sliding on the floor. "He never returned any of my advances. As he shouldn't. So I made that ridiculous speech at school in the hope he would see I was true to my feelings. My mother left that part out and always does. You can imagine how that would cause a stir around here." Mark peered up and met with Bradley's musing gaze. "Needless to say, I was led from the premises rather prematurely. I enrolled in a college in Canterbury to further my education. One day, I happened to bump into him out and about. Walking his dog along the cliffs. We got talking. One thing led to another and we started up something. I was eighteen, he was forty-one."

"Wow." Bradley had to hold on to the counter for that revelation and Mark didn't blame him.

"Indeed," Mark agreed. "This is a small town. And the fact he had been my teacher sent the rumours around that he must have been with me whilst I was still at school." Mark scrubbed his face with his hand. "He was fired. We left for London where I went to uni, got a job, thought my life was set. Until I got older, and he, well, let's just say, it became apparent that he preferred younger."

"Far out, Mark." Bradley scraped his trainer along the floor, squeaking the sole against the linoleum.

"I had no choice but to leave him. He'd already moved his younger model in by that point anyway.

And things at home were bad with Pa losing the money and not being able to tell Mother. So, I came back here with my tail between my legs, took the first job available at Steinberg's and George remained in London with various younger boyfriends, I believe. Like a revolving bloody door."

"Jesus, mate. What an arsehole. Where is he now?"

Mark sighed. "Marsby graveyard. He died. Heart attack. But what really twisted the knife in was that he left all his stuff to me. I inherited everything but our flat, which went to whoever was on the deeds at time of death. I had a truckload of rubbish delivered in bin bags and boxes, sender unknown. I shoved it all in the loft and haven't ventured up there since."

Mark felt a teensy tiny bit relieved at having said all that, but the feeling soon dissipated as Bradley didn't move, or say anything. He couldn't have expected anything different.

"It kinda all makes sense now." Bradley pushed away from the counter and flapped the bin liner into the swing- top bin.

"What does?"

"You." Bradley waved his hand. "You think you're not worthy of anyone. You think you're too old. *He* did that. What an absolute *bastard*."

Mark smiled faintly at the aggressive insult and thought it best not to remind Bradley that one shouldn't speak ill of the dead. Even if Mark had been thinking ill of George for the better part of ten years. From the moment the man had laughed in his face when linking arms through his new beau with a casual, '*But, darling, we all have best-before dates, and yours was coming up!*'

Well, Georgey, turns out we all have use-by dates, too. And yours was quite some time ago. Maybe it is time to take that rubbish out…

Bradley stood directly in front of him, his looming stance not as threatening this time and just a tad bit intoxicating.

"I think you're beautiful." Bradley kissed him. "Exactly how you are."

Mark smiled, solemnly. It wasn't that he didn't believe Bradley. It wasn't that he thought the man was humouring him after hearing such a pitiful story. It wasn't that he thought Bradley was simply trying to boost him up after discovering that Mark had pretty much been hung out and dried before the age of thirty, and had never been taken down from that washing line in ten years.

It was all down to terrible timing.

"Well, then." Mark hung his head, swiping his forehead across Bradley's. "I guess it's a real shame you'll be leaving soon."

"You'll come with me." Bradley smiled, bright and eager. "Remember the leaves said you would travel. Come with me. To Oz. Then we'll take on the rest of the world bit by bit."

"That's impossible, not to mention ridiculous."

"Why?"

"Because this. All of this." Mark stepped back and really examined Bradley and the wide-eyed, bushy-tailed enthusiasm that dripped off him like a child at Christmas. "I can't *be* him, Bradley. I can't."

Bradley furrowed his brow. "Be who?"

"George. This thing between us, it can't last. It never could. We're polar opposites and not just in distance, although that is a factor here too."

Bradley grabbed his hand. "Mark, this is meant to be. You know it. I know it. We've both been told it. We were meant to meet. I was meant to be here. I was meant to hear you yelling through that open door to this kitchen and come out and set both our lives on a new destiny. Yeah, we're opposites. That's what makes this so right. I'm the yin to your yang. Sagittarius and Aquarius. Fire and water. We're not meant to be the same. But together we can set the world alight! It's in the stars, Mark. It's all written in the stars. You just have to want to read it."

Oh, that beautiful, zestful, youthful faith in humanity! It was such a shame that Mark had to go and bash all that out of him with an unsubtle sledgehammer.

"Bradley, real life isn't like that. Not one bit."

Chapter Sixteen

Good Riddance to Bad Rubbish

Mark rammed his front door shut a short time later having vacated the Tea Shoppe and possibly Bradley's life forever. He hadn't meant to slam the door and flinched when the whole house rattled on its antique hinges. The rickety roof withstood the strain of the completely unnecessary slam—proof once more that the stars weren't aiding him and handing out a perfectly valid reason to run and fetch Bradley back. The few pictures hanging up in his hallway wall did succumb and fell to the floor with remorseful clangs. Thank goodness for his antique carpet as the glass managed to remain intact. Had they fallen onto a hard wood floor, they would no doubt have smashed on impact. There was a reason he kept this house in its original state. Okay, it wasn't so much low beams and open fireplaces that could sell an old-style house these days but more just 1970s décor, but still. It meant he could slam doors and not be too concerned about it.

Except, of course, he was. Not about the house. Not anymore. Heck, let the roof cave in. He'd be quite glad to be buried under a pile of rubble now. He wasn't sure what he had been thinking. He'd spent the best part of ten years avoiding heartache like the one he was now currently experiencing. But enter a particularly appealing Australian hunk and it seemed that all his carefully crafted plans to keep himself from misery had fallen to the wayside. Much like the pictures woefully littering his floor.

Feeling a little juvenile, he kicked the frames to the wall with a huff and a pout then glanced along to his kitchen. *Tea.* There was the answer to everything. Everything, but perhaps not love, regardless of Bradley's attempts to sell him to the contrary. Oddly, he didn't much fancy a cuppa right then. Perhaps it was that he'd had a particularly pleasing mug back at Macy's. That wouldn't have normally prevented his overdose on the English herb—he'd counted up to twenty-two cups consumed in one day before—but something niggled at his chest. Not so much niggled as tightly clenched and restricted his breathing.

He rubbed at the constriction, which was about near where his heart was, and hoped for some relief. Realising it was more of a mental hindrance than any actual heartburn, he huffed. He loitered in the hallway, not willing to venture any farther into the house. It was as if there was some barrier that, if he were to break through, would mean that everything that had happened moments earlier actually, well, *hadn't.* One step more might mean he was going back, resigning himself to being there...forever. Where he'd been buried for the past ten years, wasting away his life that had once been so full of hope and wonderment. How would he ever get out of the hole he was in? Even if he had, momentarily, been in another hole. A beautiful, tight and pleasure-ridden one. Except now he knew that could only ever be a one-off. Like that time he had tasted coffee.

No, that wasn't a particularly good analogy. He had hated that cup and had wanted to spit it out on first glug. But he had been in polite company at the time, so did his best to keep calm and carry on in true Brit style. Because that was who he was, after all. So perhaps a better analogy would be the time he'd ridden the big dipper at Blackpool Pleasure Beach. Mark hadn't ever been one to enjoy the feeling of being out of control, possibly due to the fact most of his life was spent that way, so he hadn't expected to enjoy the roller coaster. It had been Damian who had made him board the tallest ride during their impromptu visit a couple of years back. And, yes, he had screamed like a girl. But the exhilaration at being free was something he still clung on to. Much like he had the pole that had dug into his midsection through fear of falling to his doom.

Yes! Mark nodded profusely. That was most definitely the best way to describe how he felt about Bradley Summers. Ups, downs, flips, turns, tummy butterflies and the fear of falling. And he had fallen. To an almighty crashing end. One time only, too. Because once a person had ridden the Big Dipper, all other rides paled into insignificance. Like, what was the point? They wouldn't match up. So it was the tea cup and saucer ride for him from then on.

"I'm surprised, Mark Johnson, you've managed to make it to thirty-nine without being committed to the nut house." The fact he spoke that aloud to himself confirmed that his statement was indeed one to be marvelled at.

Shaking it off, he slapped a hand onto the banister—wincing when the wood actually wobbled a little—and trudged up to the second floor. If anything, he needed a shower. Slippery remnants of Better than Butter seemed to be everywhere on Mark's body and clothing. The stench was masked a little by Bradley's own alluring scent still noticeable on Mark's skin, which it would be a shame to wash off, but he couldn't linger in that too long. That had been the whole bloody point in the first place. Not to wallow, linger or get infatuated by a man eighteen years his junior and one as flighty as Damian's undergarments.

But by God, it had been good. Bradley was good. *No, great!* So cheeky, so sexy and so goddamn persistent. Mark still wasn't completely convinced Bradley wasn't just using the opportunity. Mark was aware of how he looked, how he acted and was more than acutely aware of who Bradley was. And there was simply no way Mark was going to turn in to George. Chasing after young bloods the way the man had into his fifties before succumbing to a dicky heart. *Ha! Dicky heart. The irony.*

There was no room for Mark in Bradley's life. He didn't fit into it. They couldn't just slot together because his horoscope proclaimed their star signs were a good match. That sort of thing went out with the copies of *Just Seventeen* magazine that Mark had pretended to buy for his mother. *I mean, God, I might as well calculate our chances at successful love by the letters in our name and scribble it in the back of my rough book!* He'd never been one to have faith…in God, in the stars, in tea leaves. Why start now? Rational reasoning was what counted here.

Mark winced as he recounted his parting comment to the Aussie at Macy's. *'I have to be the one to have the sensible head here. I'm older than you. I'm set in my ways. This won't work. You'll find someone new, someone younger, someone who will whisk you off your feet and make you forget this poxy seaside town that everyone does as soon as they get home.'*

It was true. Bradley would. And Mark would be left here to rot amongst the stale, soft pink rock. Sighing, he trudged over to the bathroom where his mirror was waiting to tell him the truth this time. That he was a prick. Mark stuck his middle finger up at it. The mirror reflection stuck his tongue out in retaliation. Mark rolled his eyes and slapped his forehead to the cool glass. He'd officially gone nut house crazy.

He wanted so hard to ignore the look Bradley'd had in his eyes as Mark had kissed his cheek like a sodding grandmother and tinkled the doorbell to leave. He'd been like a little lost puppy, doe-eyed and pouty. Until Mark had proceeded to clamber over the step from Macy's and trip up on the pavement.

Right. Shower. Wash hair. All orifices. Then bed. Tomorrow will always come and will always be the same monotonous cycle of indifference.

And Australia will always be four hundred billion miles away. And sunny. And without English Breakfast!

The shower was rather pleasant. Even if his showerhead was more a trickle of spittle than the full flowing waterfall of the hotel in London. Like his shower had decided it just couldn't be bothered. Maybe spending so much time with Mark Johnson, everything ended up like him? *Pitiful*. Reminded of his laissez-faire attitude to most things, he thought of all the tasks he hadn't managed to do in his boss's absence that would no doubt ping up as reminders on his computer tomorrow. *Bugger.*

Pyjamas and bed followed shortly and Mark pulled the duvet to his chin, staring up at the ceiling like some coma victim in a hospital. He didn't even attempt to get comfy. No bed would ever be comfortable again. Maybe sleep would just creep up on him without any foreplay. It didn't. He tapped his fingers on the duvet and huffed. Perhaps if he closed his eyes? He did. For all of two seconds before opening them again and peering back up at the crumbling ceiling.

It was the weight of it all up there. The plaster tiles dipping from the burden of what lay beyond. Well, like his father had always said—*no time like the present.* Even if it was midnight. Clambering out from under the duvet, Mark shivered at the biting cold, then ventured over to the one place in his house he hadn't been in for years. He felt sick and heavyhearted. He didn't really know what was up there.

Yanking down the rickety loft ladder, he sucked in a deep breath and glanced up at the dark hole in his ceiling. Was he really going to do this now? It seemed for the second time that evening he was going to enter into a hole that scared the utter crap out of him.

"Bugger it." Mark shook out his shoulders, set his bare feet on the first rung of the ladder and made his ascension into the unknown.

He coughed. Spluttered. Fell over a few boxes that had fallen from their stacks, and cursed that brute of a workman who had obviously messed up his perfectly constructed hoard of rubbish. *Crumbs, I really am a hoarder! Book me on that programme now!* Maybe he could earn a few quid down the local car boot with all this rubbish?

It wasn't rubbish. That was the problem. Quite a fair bit of it was made up of memories. Memories that Mark had shoved away long ago, then closed the loft hatch on and got on with his nonexistent life. What had it been that made him want to venture up there now and dredge up the past?

Bradley.

He fumbled along the slanted wall, tapping for the light switch, his bare feet sinking into the rough sponge of the insulation. It was a little damp, with a musky pungency from having not dried out properly. The hole in his roof had been there far longer than he cared to imagine. Luckily, it was now fixed, but wet cardboard would never dry out to regain its job of keeping memories safe from harm.

Flicking the switch illuminated the dark cavity into life. Mark gasped. Christ, it was a mess. Rotten boxes, broken glass from photo frames, mouldy clothing. Mark slapped a hand over his mouth and nose and grimaced. If ever there was a reason to clear this crap, it was simply looking at it. No wonder his house smelled stale and decrepit. Everything up here was rotten.

He rubbed his hands together and got on with the task.

* * * *

He wasn't sure how long he'd been up there, but the twittering of birds and the light ray of sunshine beaming in through the gaps in the roof tiles suggested it had been a fair while. He was in the zone, chucking most things through the hole to his landing where he planned to discard them in the dump later. The other things that he simply couldn't bear to part with were left in the one box that hadn't succumbed to the British weather and his antique roof.

It wasn't until he heard the calling of his name that he stopped at all. He sucked in a breath, which didn't help any if he had wanted to remain hidden, as the dust and mould wafted right up his nose and made him hack up a lung full of disgust.

"Mark?"

He tried to reply, but his childhood asthma came back full force. Now he recalled why he didn't do that much exercise, or visit small, confined, dusty spaces. He spluttered, wheezed and gripped hold of one the wooden pillars to steady himself. His streaming eyes were no doubt bloodshot as they itched like thrush. He pressed the balls of his palms into each eye socket and rubbed. He knew that was a stupid mistake. He should have learned from his bouts of bad hay fever—attempting to scrub the soreness away would only ever make the whole thing worse.

He growled, groaned and sneezed. In one go. Which would have been a sight to witness. Luckily no one else was here. *Are they?*

"Mark? What the—"

Mark squinted through painful eyes. He sniffed up the streaming snot running down his philtrum, ran a hand under his nose and wiped back his hair. He couldn't see. *I'm blind!* This whole mission had become a disaster!

"Jesus, Mark, are you okay?"

Okay? Hmmm, possibly not. Certainly in no state to be welcoming guests into his home. Or grotty loft, as it were. There was one silver lining. His eyes were so sore and bloodshot that whomever had broken into his house and scaled the mounds of rubbish littering his landing and staircase would thankfully not think the tears were all due to having been caught in this precarious situation.

A hand lowered onto his shoulder and Mark blinked.

"Mark?" Concern grew from the voice.

Faint blurry outlines of a person came into focus. He tried to uncross his legs from where he'd been sitting like a child on the floor for several hours. It hurt. He grunted, slapping his legs into life and shook his head.

"Bugger."

"What the hell are you doing up here?"

He blinked again. His mind was detailing a faint outline of an Australian Adonis. Mark, eyes still closed, delighted in that memory. *Such beauty.* Whenever people regained their sight, it should be Bradley they first saw. He represented all that was wondrous in the world. He was like a summer's day, which was basically what his usual attire of board shorts and bright T-shirt were depicting anyway. And his Havaianas. With perfect rounded feet that Mark imagined would look delightful surrounded by warm golden sand between each toe.

"Just a bit of spring cleaning," Mark managed to grit out. His voice sounded like his grandmama's, hoarse from having smoked herself through life and near to death.

"Huh. Often do this sorta thing middle of the night?"

The voice didn't have a hint of an accent. Well, it obviously did, just not one that was like sweet music to his ears, and was harsher in its delivery, as if it was cross at him. Not Bradley, then. He sighed.

"Well, no," Mark replied. "I can't say I often do this thing at all."

"Ain't that the truth."

Mark opened his eyes. Macy smiled back at him. She, too, was a pleasing welcoming sight. Just perhaps not the one his mind had been hoping for. She fluffed up her floral skirt and sat crossed-legged in front of him. Her frizzy hair was left to hope and chance and fluffed up over her round face. She scrunched her nose and sneezed.

"How long have you been up here?"

"Rather a while, I presume," Mark replied. "What is the time?"

"Nine o'clock."

Mark gasped, which made him breath in yet another lungful of putrid stale air. So he coughed.

"I was worried when you didn't come in for your usual cuppa." Macy fished out a tissue from her cardigan sleeve and handed it over. "Thought you may have been avoiding Brad."

"Ah." Taking the tissue with a grateful nod, he then blew, rather fiercely, into it. "Not intentionally."

"Right." Macy squinted at all the mess. "Well, he's packing, so…"

Mark's eyes stung through having to achieve the task of making out what her expression was meant to depict. And her words. And her presence in his home.

"And you are telling me, because?" Mark twirled his hand in the air.

"I don't think I really need to say it, Mark."

That sounded a lot like his mother. And back then, Mark had thought she really should. How was he to know his mother was always so disappointed in him? So Mark waited for Macy to come to the realisation that he wasn't a telepath. It appeared Macy didn't care, as she began wading through the items in the cardboard box between them. She pulled out a framed picture and wiped away the dust and grit that scraped the glass. Mark's teeth hurt.

"This him?" She turned the photo around to show Mark. She needn't have bothered. He knew who it was without having to be reminded.

"Yes."

Macy inspected the image. Smiling back at her would be a much younger Mark, his hair still unruly and wafting around in the breeze of the meadow that he'd been in for an impromptu picnic one summer's afternoon. His arm was draped around a greying George Carroway and Mark was mid-way to kissing the man's cheek. *A miracle really that such an image could have been captured with a clunky digital camera back then.* That look in George's eyes were forever to be seen by all those who gazed at the past. *Look at what I have.*

That had been a good day. A walk in the meadow, a picnic by the river and a meander through a village they had discovered during one of their drives in George's convertible, the car he had bought to recapture his youth. Or to capture other youths with, possibly more accurately.

"Why keep this one?" Macy asked, tucking it back into the box.

"I think I look pretty good in that picture." Mark paused. "Happy. Maybe."

"You could be happy again, y'know? Once you've got rid of all this crap, confronted your parents and all your deep-seated fears." Macy blinked. "And had a haircut."

"I had one recently."

"Really?" Macy squinted.

"Are you one to talk about hair?"

"I like my hair like this."

"You look like Spuggy from *Byker Grove*."

Macy narrowed her eyes and ran a hand through her frizz. "Which nobody below the age of thirty-nine will know."

"True, but I'm not sure she was particularly of fashion back then either."

"Of fashion or in fashion?"

"Neither."

"Fair enough." Macy shrugged and delved a hand deeper into the open box. "If everyone looked the same, the world would be boring."

Tugging out a scrapbook, she swiped the dust from it and laid it in her lap. The book was mouldy around the edges. Although it had been buried deep within one of the boxes, it had still festered among stale rain water, creating little circles of green and black all over the front cover that used to be a beautiful shade of purple. Not his old bathroom *blueberry* purple but more a soft lilac. When Macy opened the front cover, Mark closed his eyes.

"What's this?" She flattened out the bent pages and ran a palm along the stuck-in photos and glossy magazine cut-outs.

"It was our bucket list, I guess. Places to visit. That sort of thing."

"Wow." Macy flicked the pages. "Lots of far-flung places in here. Ever go to them?"

Mark shook his head. "We barely made it out of London. It was all a pipe dream."

Macy stopped on one page and Mark twisted to see which one. Sydney harbour bridge, the Opera House, Bondi Beach, all cut out of travel magazines and stuck in with red circles around the main places of interest.

"Australia, huh?"

"Everyone says they want to go to Australia. Then they find out it's a billion light years away and costs an arm and a leg."

Macy slapped the book shut. "If only you knew someone who, say, lived there?"

Mark grabbed the book, threw it into the cardboard box and gave Macy a stern eyeful, which he was well aware wouldn't have come out the way he hoped, what with his eyes looking as if he'd been on a weekend drug binge and cried for days in the aftermath. Not that he had any clue how one would appear after doing those things. He'd, for sure, be dead if he had.

Macy stood, albeit slouched as her short frame was still too tall for the low-beamed slanted roof.

"Like I say." Twisting, she lowered one foot on the top ladder rung. "He's packing."

"Again, I would ask you to clarify what you mean by your statement."

Macy's fuzzy red hair disappeared down the rabbit hole.

"Just letting you know," she called back. "And shouldn't you be at work, no?"

"Bugger."

* * * *

Bundling through the front reception desk into his office, Mark offered up the best smile he could. Yvonne gave him her first eyeball and grimace of the day. This time, she had good reason. Mark was over an hour late. And he still looked like death warmed up. At least that might gouge some sympathy out of the ice queen.

Nope, no it didn't. Yvonne followed Mark's every move with her unrelenting gaze as he scurried through the office to his desk. Mark shot another smile over his shoulder, followed by a brief shrug and flumped down into his seat. Huh, the thing didn't budge. It didn't collapse on him like it usually did. *Strange.* Mark twisted around in it. Not even a squeak from the old nails and metal. So, obviously, he must try harder. He bounced up and down, but the seat maintained the extra weight and impact in true job-well-done fashion.

"Has this been fixed?" Mark called over to Yvonne.

She shrugged, then answered an incoming phone call.

Mark wasted no more time thinking about how his chair had miraculously managed to repair itself and wondered if it had been the stars in some magical realignment. Things were going his way, or rather not raining down on him with imposing difficulty. He was now able to begin work without all the usual kerfuffle and his early morning call to the *Man With A Van That Can* had confirmed he was available today to clear up the rubbish mound in his house and take it to the dump for him. *Result.*

Things could finally move on.

Mark started up the computer, made sure to check Caps Lock wasn't on, and went through the motions of listening to the cracking dial-up whilst tapping his fingers impatiently on the desk. He yawned. Loudly. A quick peek to Yvonne and the second eyeful came his way. Mark would have been concerned if it hadn't. He mouthed 'sorry', following it up by picking his mug of mouldy tea left from Friday and waggling it. Yvonne rolled her eyes. Some things wouldn't ever change, and that was fine with Mark.

He busied himself making his first morning cuppa in the adjacent kitchen. He made sure to make Yvonne one and was rather pleased at the outcome. Extreme fatigue suited his tea-making abilities. It was like an ingrained thing. He needed tea, therefore his body took over and produced the most excellent versions. Slurping his drink, he sauntered back into the office and plonked Yvonne's down on her desk. He hovered for a bit, awaiting perhaps a spark of gratitude, even a hint that she was impressed. That tea deserved to be in a museum. *No, an art gallery.*

Yvonne grunted, which was the best Mark was going to get. He took another sip and meandered back to his desk. He sat, gulping more lifeblood, and the chair instantly collapsed to its last rung. Of course it did. Mark wasn't even surprised that half his tea sloshed down his chest and soaked through the thin material of his shirt to scald his skin. He didn't even bother wiping it, mainly because he was focused on his computer screen. His emails had opened, with the top one a nice note from his boss he had actually sent on Friday. *Late* Friday.

Mark,

I have a ten-thirty accounts meeting on Monday. I need some pastries and such other to offer to the clients. I believe you know a good tea shop on the High Street could provide? Could you make sure you get some. On the office account.

Regards,

Mr Steinberg.

"Bugger."

Yvonne tutted. Mark smiled.

"You, er, available to head up to Macy's Tea Shoppe for me, Yvonne?" Mark queried, voice elevating hopefully. "Just, I, you know, have quite a lot on and the boss needs some cakes and whatnot…"

Fourth eyeful.

Mark muttered several curse words under his breath. Where was the work experience kid when he could really have used him? Weren't tasks like this designed for teen bods learning the work place? Mark was an executive assistant, for Christ's sake, not a personal bleeding shopper. He had far more important and strenuous tasks to be getting on with.

In a defiant act of protest, Mark clicked down to the next email.

Mark,

Have you managed to process that pivot table I need to use for the meeting?

Regards,

Mr Steinberg.

Mark clicked out of the email, plonked his cup down on the desk and immediately gathered up his belongings.

Pastries, here we come.

* * * *

The tinkling bell signified his arrival to Macy's Tea Shoppe and Mark stepped in, stopped and the door hit his shoulder as it attempted to close.

"Mark." Bradley stood in front him in all his glory.

Well, not so much. His *glory* was, sadly, well and truly covered up by his bright pink board shorts. But Mark licked his lips, nonetheless.

"Hello." Mark tried for more words, but nothing surfaced. What could he possibly say anyway? *So long and thanks for all the sex?*

Bradley adjusted his string bag on his shoulder and peered over to flash Macy one of his dashing smiles.

"Thanks, Macy."

"Take care, Brad." Macy roamed her gaze to Mark before turning her green eyes back on the Aussie. "You're welcome here any time."

Bradley nodded and when his gaze finally met with Mark's, Mark was grounded. Bradley paused. Waiting perhaps. Maybe even expecting Mark to not be quite so British and just say what was on his damn mind.

"You off then?" Mark finally stuttered out.

Bradley confirmed the statement with one nod. And Mark returned that and tripled it, as if his head was hanging on loosely by one thread.

"Well." Mark straightened himself out and racked his brain for something quite profound to say. "Safe trip. Tatty bye."

Mark hung his head.

What an absolute arsehole.

Chapter Seventeen

Revelations

The bell as the door closed wasn't the delightful tinkle that Mark had come to appreciate. Instead, it sounded more like a gunshot to his brain. Or perhaps that was wishful thinking. His voice had also seemed to have vacated along with the Aussie Adonis and so he only managed to point at the dismal pastry display and mime for Macy to bag them. He couldn't be too sure he'd win any games of charades with that effort but, regardless, Macy caught on and slapped various cakes and bits into a box.

She, too, had evidently lost her voice. Or, apparently, any coherent mutterings and should perhaps consider getting her eyes tested as any gaze failed to land Mark's way. Mark coughed, probably a rather obtrusive thing to do so whilst he took the open box from Macy's outstretched hand.

"Many thanks." He wasn't signing off an email, but he might as well have been with all the reply he had received. Or, well, hadn't.

That same bell tinkled out as if it was the local Marsby ringers at a Saturday wedding and Mark whipped around with renewed hope. It was quickly dashed when his mother stepped into the cafe. *Wonderful!*

Firm grimace, nose in the air as though she'd trodden in something particularly repulsive, Mrs Johnson swiped her hands down her white trench coat. It wasn't raining, for once, and was actually rather mild outside, minus the accustomed southerly sea wind. But she did like to add an air of mystery to her attire.

"Mark." She glided around the tables, hands outstretched and air-kissed Mark more times that was socially comfortable. Mark even had to do the hop, skip and jump dance routine through his mother's clutches. She didn't have any grip on him physically. Just emotionally.

"Mother." Mark brought the box of cakes around to his front as a firm barrier to any more mother-son canoodling in public.

"I have just seen that delightful young Australian of yours outside getting into a taxi."

"He's not mine. He belongs to no man." Mark shook his head, his hair bouncing around on top. "He's a free spirit."

"So I hear." Vera peered over Mark's shoulder. "Macy, lovely to have you back."

"Thank you, Mrs Johnson." Macy scrubbed down the surface, avoiding looking the woman in the eye. "I don't think I've ever seen you in here before."

"Yes, well, I tend to bake my own cakes."

Mark was pretty sure he'd never seen his mother in an apron or anywhere near a mixing bowl.

"But Mark raves on about this place so much, I thought I'd make an exception and pick up a few pastries for the gathering I'm having back at home later." Vera tugged Mark's chin, digging her pointy nails into his jawline. "You look tired, Mark."

"Yes. Busy working, Mother."

"Haven't they hired someone else to run all your boss's errands, yet?" She nodded to the box.

"No. Still my job. Anyway, best be getting back."

Mark scooted around his mother and added another rendition of *for whom the bell tolls* by opening the door to make his swift exit.

"Mark, dear?"

Bugger.

"Yes, Mother?"

"Couldn't be a love and pop by after work, could you? Your father's in one of his moods."

"What's wrong?" Mark furrowed his brow. His father had many moods and Mark wouldn't want to assume he knew them all by just the words 'one of'.

Vera waved a flippant hand. "Oh, he's in a sulk. Locked himself in the shed."

"Right. Okay. Will do."

"I told him about your Australian man and he went a bit, well, quiet. Hence, I invited the ladies over from the Conservative women's group and he sulked off to the shed and hasn't come out."

Mark nodded, then gave Macy a slight roll of the eyes, hoping for some of her usual solidarity. She returned a more narrowed definition of hers and slapped the tea towel on the counter. Mark decided to take a more leisurely walk back to the office.

Strolling along the seafront didn't give him the lift that it once had. Not even the sea breeze against his cheeks, or the crashing of waves against wooden pillars of the peer or the sight of beefy men in wetsuits wincing at the pain of walking on the pebbles barefoot could snap him from his sulk. The coastal walkway only reminded him of having cycled along there with Bradley, or having teetered side-by-side with him when a little tipsy, and even the cabin shed selling the two-pound flip-flops served as a reminder of Bradley's perfect feet.

Losing all track of time, he slumped down on one of the recently painted benches and gazed gloomily out at the beach. A family at the sea edge made several laughing attempts at chucking each other in. *Poor kids.* They'd get hypothermia going anywhere near the English Channel this time of year. Or any time of year, for that matter.

He opened the box on his lap, dipped his hand in and grabbed the first thing. Iced ring doughnut. He ate the lot in one fell swoop, mainly so the seagulls wouldn't get their pesky beaks on it, but also because he was miserable. And it looked as though food might be his only comfort on this fine day. Not even the beeping from the out-of-tune horn on the passing empty beachside mini-train could lift his dreary mood.

"Morning, Mark!" Charlie waved out of the driver's cabin.

"Mshffsksppp." Crumbs fell from Mark's lips. Not very eloquent, but who cared? Who would care what he had to say anymore, anyway? He'd had his chance to have someone listen to him and he'd failed, spectacularly. He might as well become a mute.

"Morning, son."

Mark swallowed the doughnut whole and it lodged in his throat to the point he could no longer breathe. There were worse ways to die, he supposed. But the rather harsh slap to his back allowed him to cough up much of the congealed dough and it fell to the floor with a splat. The gulls weren't too picky and decided to swoop in, gather it up, squawk and fly off.

"Dad," Mark spluttered out.

His elderly father, dressed in a similar long trench coat to his mother's but his a torrid brown in colour, a flat cap covering his bald scalp, slipped onto the bench beside Mark with a deep and resonating grunt.

"Mum said you'd locked yourself in the shed."

Henry chuckled then raised one impressive eyebrow. So that manoeuvre hadn't passed down in the gene pool.

"You pretended to do that?" Mark's voice elevated in amusement.

"Of course."

"Why?"

"Because then she wouldn't ask where I am, what I'm doing, could I just do this, that or the other. Or ask for some money for her damn women's fundraiser."

"Right." Mark wiped his hands down his trousers, spilling crumbs on the ground for the less expeditious birds along the seafront. "She's in Macy's, by the way."

"Really?" Henry peered up the High Street. "Bugger."

"Where were you going?"

"To see you."

"Me? Why?"

"Need a reason to see my only son, do I?"

"No offence, but you rarely come to see me. Especially on a weekday at"—Mark checked his watch—"bugger." He slapped his arm down with a sigh. "Eleven a.m."

He certainly wouldn't be winning any employee-of-the-month framed photograph plaque in the office at this rate. Not that he ever had, mind.

"True. True. True." Henry nodded with every muttering of the word. "I am sorry for that."

Mark attempted to arch one eyebrow, Bradley-style. Failed miserably. Both zoomed up and he hadn't been wanting to emulate the wide-eyed stare. *Oh well.*

"I heard something, y'see. From Vera."

Mark rubbed his forehead. "If it's about the Australian, I know he's very young and no, nothing is going on. Don't worry, I'm not having a midlife crisis," he lied. "I am aware of my limitations."

"Are you?"

"Am I what?"

"Aware of your limitations?"

"They being?"

"You said it," his father croaked with a chuckle. "What are they?"

Mark exhaled, wearily. "That a pure hunk of a male dance-slash-stripper who is young enough to be my grandchild could see any reason to be with me, Mark Johnson, still only just thirty-ish and unlucky in everything. Including the looks department."

"Hold up, you got those looks from me." Henry took off his flat cap, scrubbed the balding scalp beneath and grinned his gummy smile. "The hair is all your mother's, though."

"I hope not all of it. Because that would require her to have an awful lot of laser therapy."

"She does."

"Too much."

"I know."

Father and son sat in idle silence for a rather long and awkward time, gazing out at the beach, lost in their own thoughts. A ridiculous death-wish of a man dressed in a wetsuit kicked off his rubber pool shoes and legged it, albeit inelegantly, along the pebbles and dived head-first into the crashing wave. Mark wondered whether to call on the coast guard to watch the poor fellow in case he died of hypothermia. There was no way *he* was going into the freezing sea to rescue the idiot who thought that a morning swim in an ice bath had been a good idea. On reflection, Mark had a sudden urge to run in there himself. He wouldn't, though. Those stones killed his feet. Not to mention his arse. No, he wouldn't mention how he knew what it felt like to be lying bareback on Marsby beach.

"Son?"

"Hmm?" Mark had forgotten his father had even been there.

"I think a little father-and-son chat is long overdue."

The look on the old man's face made Mark uncomfortable. Surely, this wasn't the extremely tardy conversation about the birds and the bees? He recalled the last time his father had tried to have that talk back when Mark had been merely a teen. Mark had been traumatized at thinking the poor seagulls aligning the seafront were attacked by the buzzing pests in order to procreate some mythical beast. And also concerned that it would only have happened in August when everyone tried to come out to the beach with a picnic. Thus, he'd learned about sex the hard way. By having to do it.

Henry patted Mark's knee and his shoulders dropped. "There's a few things I think perhaps you ought to know."

"Really?"

"When I was a young lad, it wasn't as acceptable as it is now."

"What wasn't?"

Henry slipped his hand from Mark's knee to entwine his fingers over his lap. "Being homosexual."

Mark adopted the correct facial expression that time by widening his eyes.

"Yes, Mark." Henry lifted his shoulders and looked directly into his son's eyes. "I had an affair or two with men before I met your mother."

If Mark hadn't already choked on and spat out the doughnut, he would've done it again. His voice was once again caught in his throat and he spluttered, trying to dislodge the damn words that would have been absent of any vowel variety.

Henry chuckled. "I can tell, by your reaction, that you had never suspected?"

"Jesus, Dad, no!" Mark blurted. "You are married to Mother. For fifty years!"

Henry nodded. "Yes. And for a time, I did love her. I still do. She is completely exasperating and has sucked me dry in more ways than one."

Mark held up a hand. "Too much."

"I know." Henry inhaled a weary breath. "We were put together by our parents. What with her being from the upper echelons and my parents trying to make a name for themselves here in Marsby. It was all about money. She had it. We didn't. I married to save our finances."

"And lost it all on the horses?"

Henry coughed into a balled fist. "Exactly. That was *my* midlife crisis." He dipped his chin. "I'd've much preferred your one."

Mark shook his head, his hair raging against the breeze and his mouth for once clamped shut.

"I have always been in love with a man." Henry gazed out to the beach. "One I let go many years ago in order to marry your mother."

"B-b-but…who?" Mark was surprised he'd gotten that much out. His father had always been so quiet. So reserved and reclusive. The very thought that he had a sordid past, one not far from his own, was, quite frankly, a mind fuck. *Excuse my French.*

"His name was Arthur." Henry gazed at the crashing waves, or now Mark came to think about it, was it at the man in the wetsuit swimming laps to the pier and back? "He had come here to Marsby on a holiday with his parents, back when Marsby was a pretty decent holiday town and hadn't succumbed to the current climate. We met, just over there." He pointed at the decrepit pier that stretched out over the water. "I saved him from falling in. I still to this day don't know whether Artie had been attempting to off himself. But, whatever, we became friends. I showed him the sights."

"Bet that took all of three minutes."

Henry chuckled. "Indeed. So for the rest of the two weeks, we spent it necking under that pier."

Mark regurgitated his stomach contents rather barbarously. The seagulls would have a feast today. Wiping his mouth with the back of his hand, he couldn't get out of his head the image of his elderly father under the usual teen hang-out, being all grabby hands with another man.

"We were discovered," Henry continued, unawares of Mark's shudder, or ignoring it. "His parents and my parents. Awful time." He shook his head, his wrinkled fingers trembling on his lap. "Artie ran away from his holiday home, knocked on my door and begged me to run away with him. I was very tempted."

"But you didn't go?"

Henry hung his head. "No. Of course, I was too chicken to say that to his face and I said I would meet him at the train station. Artie had bought tickets to London." Behind the lenses of his glasses, Henry's brown eyes glistened. "I still don't know if he went alone or went back home. I never heard from him again. And soon after that, I was introduced to your mother and, well, it is very hard to say no to her."

Mark nodded. He knew that. But still, this was a revelation he would never have expected.

"But why didn't you go? It's been so long, Dad, and you've never tried to find him?"

"You have to remember, Mark, this was the early sixties. It was still illegal back then. I was afraid. And, if I am honest, I believed Artie to be too perfect for me. He really was beautiful. A free spirit ready to take on the world. I just wasn't like that. I couldn't see it lasting beyond the train journey. I'd forever worry, forever fear, forever hold him back."

Mark paused, staring at his father with renewed fascination.

He then suddenly understood why his father had chosen this moment to confide in him. Although times had changed, what his father had uttered was exactly how Mark had been feeling about Bradley. Mark was too old, too set in his ways, too fearful. And Bradley, probably on a blasted airplane to Australia in the next few hours, would be held back if Mark even had bothered to explain any of that. Bradley would get bored with Mark. Most people did. George had.

Henry held Mark's hand between his and tugged it to his lap. "I was so proud of you when you made that speech at your school. I was even more proud when you went to London. Yes, it ended badly. But you did it. Something I never could have done. And I was so proud."

"But you never said…"

"No, I have learned to keep those memories firmly under wraps. All those feelings are too painful to bring to the surface again. I was upset when you returned. I know it wasn't your fault and what happened between you and George was…unfortunate. I guess that's how I imagined it would have ended between me and Artie. So I thought best to just enjoy having you home." Henry gazed into Mark's eyes with an odd look of…hope? "Can you understand?"

Mark slipped his hand free from his father's and rubbed his eye, the wind blowing into his eye socket making it water. *Blasted sea breeze.* He sniffed.

"Don't make my mistake, Mark." Henry stood from the bench with a hefty grunt and cracking bones. "Try to remember that boy who stood up in front of his whole school and told them who he really was with dignity and bravery. Recapture that man who ran away to London with the man he loved. Forget the fear, the rejection, and live. Because, Mark, there is only one life to live. And it should be yours."

Henry patted his shoulder then gazed over at the pier with a deep hum. He nodded, adjusted his cap and hobbled away from the seafront.

"Oh, and Mark?"

Lost in thought, Mark peered up.

"That house of yours ought to have quite a bit of equity in it by now. If money is an issue, you can always sell up."

"But, Mum—"

"Let me handle your mother." Henry tutted. "I'm used to disappointing her."

Had any of that even really happened? His father? A closet queen all these years? Having lost out on true love due to *fear*? Mark leapt up from his seat, the doughnuts falling from his lap to the ground by his feet. The seagulls instantly swooped in and pecked at the lot. Mark, not caring less, gathered what he could into the box and hurtled away from the seafront.

He rushed through the doors into his office and threw the crumpled box at Yvonne.

"I'm loving this, Yvonne." Mark waved a hand over her attire. "Is that a new blouse? It's simply divine. Brings out the red in your eyes."

Yvonne opened her mouth. She said nothing. Then peered down at the crusty, crinkled chiffon top she had probably worn a thousand times to the office and that blended in with the unadorned surroundings.

"And I have walls in my house just like it." Mark smiled, sweetly, fluttering his eyelashes and bounding over to his desk. He was about to sit on the revolving chair when he thought better of it and kicked the thing away. It slid across the room and bumped against the back of Robert's chair. Robert scowled up at him. Mark shrugged and leaned over the desk to tap his keyboard.

"Mark!" Mr Steinberg stormed out of the meeting room and rammed his hands on his stout hips.

"Hmm?"

"Where have you been? The meeting has started! I need you in there taking notes. And where are the pastries?"

"Oh." Mark waved a hand toward the windows. "The gulls were particularly on form today. But I'm sure one or two survived the journey. Yvonne, be a dear, and plate them up, would you?"

Yvonne, having been admiring her own blouse with a small smile curving her lips, glanced up with narrowed eyes. Mr Steinberg stomped closer to Mark and peered over his shoulder to the computer screen.

"What are you playing at, Mark?" His squeaky voice grated on Mark like the underoiled gears on his old mountain bike. "I need you in that meeting. This is the contract of the century!"

"Ah." Mark wiped his hair away from covering his brow. "I am terribly sorry to do this to you, right now, Mr Steinberg, but it seems I have a contract of my own to fulfil and so, therefore, won't be able to continue with any of your mundane tasks."

"I beg your pardon?"

"Oh, sorry, I should make that clearer, shouldn't I?" Mark stood, shoulders straightening. "I quit, Mr Steinberg. Pretty much, right now. I just have to..." Mark waved at his computer screen.

"Clear up your porn stash?" Robert peered around Mark's battered old chair.

Mark stuck his tongue out. *Wow, this getting in touch with your youth side is rather invigorating.*

"You cannot quit, Mark." Mr Steinberg scrubbed a hand over his balding scalp. "You have to give notice. Two months, as per your employment contract."

"Hmm." Mark rubbed his chin. "See, the thing is, sir. I think I may have work-related stress. It's the lack of decent tea in these offices. I have a high dependency, you see, and I'm afraid that just hasn't been fulfilled here in the workplace. It's a disease. I'll get my doctor to write you a note. Once I just…"

Mark swivelled back to the computer that had whirred into life, frantically tapped on the mouse and typed into an internet search box.

"Mark Johnson, this is preposterous!" Mr Steinberg edged closer to Mark's computer screen and was probably aiming for a looming presence, but it was hard to achieve when he stood a fair few inches shorter than Mark. He came across more as a lingering and irritating fly. "Why are you looking up flights to Australia?"

"Right." Mark scribbled on a sticky note, then bit his lip. "Mind if I take this?" He held up the yellow square, shrugged and shoved it in his pocket. "Seasonal Affective Disorder."

"Excuse me?"

"I'm SAD, sir. I need to chase the sun."

"It's winter in Australia," Robert squawked from behind him.

Mark took delight in sticking his middle finger up that time. "Well, I have been told I do everything in reverse."

Mr Steinberg wrapped his small and stumpy fingers around Mark's biceps. Mark peered down at them and marvelled at how he'd never been touched by his boss before and even though his hands were tiny, they still managed to curl around his slender arm.

"Are you okay, Mark?" Mr Steinberg asked, concern oozing out of his reddened cheeks. "Is this the start of a…" He hesitated, then leaned in to whisper in to Mark's ear. "Early midlife breakdown, perhaps?"

Mark laughed. Guffawed, in fact. So hard that the abdominal muscles he was sure he hadn't felt in years rose to the surface. His eyes watered and he had to grip the desk to compose himself.

"Yes!" Mark finally blurted. "Yes, I am. And isn't it simply marvellous! Now, if you'll excuse me I have to go see a man about a possum."

Mark left the dumbfounded expressions to themselves and pelted out of the office. He had no idea how he was going to make it to Gatwick airport, what with Bradley having had a head start of a few hours, but he had to try. Heck, with this breakdown he was having he'd think about jumping on a motorbike and tearing up the tarmac in true Brit rom-com style. His leather jacket would come into its own then.

Perhaps not, though. Especially after the pedal bike incident. Taxi, it was. *No*. Modern it up. An Uber!

Chapter Eighteen

Mad Dash

Mark was rather thankful that, once upon a time, he'd downloaded the Uber app to his phone but on the company account. Not only because Mark hadn't ever used an Uber before, but also because the cost of one from his home to Gatwick airport had been the price of a small country. With no money to exchange hands, Mark legged it from the car drop-off point toward the sliding entrance doors to the check-in gates.

He'd tried calling Bradley several times on the ride over, but alas, no answer. Mark had even left a garbled message on his answerphone that Bradley would no doubt laugh over when and if he ever turned the sodding thing on. What was the point of a mobile of one couldn't be mobile when answering it? So Mark's only choice was to attempt to catch the flight to Sydney before it took off and convince the Adonis to stay a while longer. Perhaps have a nice chat over a cup of tea? Gosh, he needed a tea. But he supposed that should wait.

Stuck behind a family of holidaying Brits in the revolving doors, Mark reined in his need to kick the little kid pulling her monster on wheels. And yes, it was a monster. A pink one with a face. Instead Mark uttered a *pardon me* and inched past them all into the entrance. He stopped and checked the signs on the screens dotted around the check-in lounge. The Archer Atlantic to Sydney still wasn't boarding and actually, for the first time in Mark's life, he'd caught a break by noticing it was slightly delayed. Thank heavens for that good old Brit lack of timekeeping. There must have been snow on the runway or something. Mark was aware it was May, but that hadn't been unheard of before.

With renewed hope, he marched over to the Archer check-in desk and the beauty behind loosed a welcoming, and somewhat unnerving, grin his way. "Checking in, sir?"

"Um, no, not exactly. I just need to get over into the departure lounge, if you would be so kind as to point me in the right direction?"

"Do you have a ticket?"

"No. I don't plan on flying anywhere. This body in hot terrain is not a good look." He chuckled.

She didn't. "Without a boarding pass, you can't enter into the departure area."

"Right." Mark ruffled his hair. "Are you sure?"

She looked pretty damn sure and rather annoyed that Mark had the audacity to suggest she wouldn't know the rules of her profession and that Mark, the infrequent flyer that he'd just admitted to being, would.

"Sorry, of course, yes."

Mark remained stood at the front, deciding what to do next. The family from the doors approached the queue behind him and waited, impatiently, with their suitcases on wheels ready to board the conveyor belt to go to, well, who the hell knew where? Quite possibly not where they were going. Mark offered up an apologetic smile to the father, then turned back to the Archer's delight. Which, in hindsight, she wasn't. What with Mark being the real Archer here, having discovered that from his brief read of the horoscopes in the paper left in his Uber.

"I've seen it on many a sitcom slash romantic comedy etcetera. The guy runs to the airport, calls the damsel's name just as she's hopping onto the plane and wham bam, Bob's your uncle."

The lady arched a perfectly already arched-in pencil eyebrow.

"Are you saying that's all lies?" Mark gasped, hand to his chest. "Are you insinuating that all those films, television programmes—heck, I'm positive there was an advert who used the running to the airport cliché one Christmas—all have gaping plot holes that not one person picked up on and slammed a one-star review on their Amazon profile?"

"I believe they would have all bought a ticket, gone through the departure gates and got there that way. I'm pretty sure that's how Ross did it in the final episode of *Friends.*"

"Oh!" Mark nodded. "I see! I need to buy a ticket!"

"Yes, sir."

"Great. I'll have a one-way then please. Cheaper, right? And I don't actually have to board the plane, do I?"

"You can't buy a ticket from here."

"But you just said—"

"You'd need to buy a ticket from the ticket booth. This is check-in."

"Right, of course." Mark's head pounded with all this new information. "And would you be so kind as to point me in the direction of the Archer Airways ticket booth?"

The girl smiled, her red lips coating her white teeth. She pointed the tip of her pen over to a booth the other side of the airport. Mark sighed, tapped the counter surface and swivelled. His hips, not anything else. This whole situation was rather laborious, but it didn't require the middle finger salute.

"Sir?"

"Yes?"

"You can buy a ticket from any of the airlines." She waggled the edge of the pen at all the other multicoloured booths ranging from budget to exclusive air travel. "You just need to get to the gate, right?"

"Yes! Oh, gosh, yes! Thank you." He physically phewed. He'd had a hunch that his overdraft would never have stretched to a ticket to Sydney and now thanked his lucky stars that he could venture on over to the Aero Flop or whatever and just spend thirty quid on a flight to Edinburgh and still get through the gate.

"Good luck, sir. She's a lucky woman."

"Oh, no, it's not a woman. A man, actually. A hunky fine Adonis specimen of all male. And a stripper, nonetheless!"

"Lucky you." The lady flushed a little. So did Mark.

"I know." He grinned. "Can't quite believe it myself." The fluttering in his chest went on overdrive and he paused to take in the memory of Bradley. Naked.

"Sir?"

"Hmm?"

"You might need to hurry then." She nodded at the screens.

Mark snapped to and glanced up to the signs detailing that the Sydney flight had landed and was on a quick turnaround, boarding in ten minutes.

"Bugger!" Mark rammed through the family behind him, sending the little toddler perched on her pink trunk falling to the floor and wailing. Mark figured that would be a usual start to a family's twenty-four-hour flight with a toddler anyway and so bolted across the check-in toward the nearest ticket booth.

He possibly should have checked who was working the booth before approaching, as he found he only had a way with certain types of people. The man behind the desk at Budget Airways didn't come into this category. Big, hairy, beefy and most certainly heterosexual. All the things Mark had come to despise of in customer services. He couldn't flirt or find some solidarity with this one.

"Hello." He thought he'd best start properly. "I would like a ticket please. To anywhere, not really bothered. Just need out, y'know." He tapped the desk for good measure.

The man smiled. Or, Mark assumed he did. His beard overtook his lips, so it was hard to tell through the strands of movement.

"When would you like to travel?"

"Now. Right now. No time like the present. The world is my oyster. Don't want to be stuck in old Blighty forever, eh?" He now understood why he got on most people's nerves. Not Bradley's though. *Dear Bradley.* Mark phased out again.

"Sir?"

"Hmm?"

"I've got a ten p.m. flight to Reykjavik, you want it?"

Mark slammed the counter. "Yes, I do!"

The man nodded, scratching his beard and set to tapping about on his computer. Mark drummed his fingernails on the desk surface, urging the man to have some speed. He glanced up to the screen monitors that indicated he had five minutes before boarding commenced. Mark's heart beat faster than the clicks on the bear's mouse. He then marvelled further, regarding the never before used analogy of animals of an airport worker and his electrical equipment. *God, I need a tea.*

"I'm in a hurry, could we..." Mark snapped his fingers. He instantly regretted it as the man stopped his idle tapping on the computer to stare vacantly at him.

"The flight is at ten. You got six hours."

"But I have to get home and pack, my dear boy. I can't very well go to one of the coldest climates in just this leather jacket, now can I?"

The man shrugged. "It's a nice jacket."

"That it may be, but it's impractical for Iceland."

"You would have thought you'd have brought a suitcase with you, what with wanting to hurry to get out of the country?" The man raised his bushy brown eyebrows. "Running from something, sir?"

Mark chuckled, then leaned across the counter covering his mouth with the back of his hand. "The CIA, but that's between me and you."

"What they after you for?"

"Tax evasion."

The man snorted. "All right, if you say so." He turned back to his screen. "That'll be two hundred and fifty-eight pounds."

Mark nearly threw up. But he didn't and fished out his wallet from his back pocket. Worst-case scenario, he could use the credit card then call up the bank to say it had been stolen. Mark handed over the well-used and, thankfully, in date Visa.

"Passport?"

"Excuse me?"

"Passport? You need your passport to buy a ticket and travel. You've got a passport, right?"

"Of course I have!" Mark exploded. "What are you insinuating here? That I am an illegal immigrant. Like one of those blasted Australians!" *Oh, the beautiful Australians!*

"No, just you need a passport to travel. Even pre-Brexit."

Mark slapped the desk. "Bugger!" His voice echoed around the check-in and many gazes darted his way. He twisted, back to the passport-holding tourists and into the eyes of beef-man. "Okay, look, I'm on the run. Can't you just give me the ticket and say I threatened you?"

The man looked down at Mark's scrawny frame and arched an eyebrow. Mark flapped his hands.

"Fine, fine!" He huffed and glanced up to the screen. *Now boarding for Sydney.* "There is someone getting on that flight to Sydney right now that I need to speak to. Can you call someone?"

"Well, that all depends."

"On what?" Mark was losing the little patience he had left.

"Why you need to call this person back."

Mark hung his head. He could not tell this man he was chasing after a stripper who he'd fucked in his best friend's tea shop with the aid of a butter replacement product. He possibly could have got away with it over at the Archer check-in, but here, the man looked like he wouldn't appreciate the information, nor the visual imagery. So, he thought of Damian. Never a good thing. But, what would Damian do right now? He'd lie.

"There's been a terrible tragedy."

"Mmm, hmm."

"Yes, my friend's cat has died. Suddenly. Prolonged cancer. Went on for years."

"Died suddenly after years of suffering?"

"Yes. It's an oxymoron."

"What type of cat is that?"

Mark furrowed his brow. "A tabby one? Anyway, I really must tell my friend. He will want to say his last goodbyes before departing to pastures new. So if you could just put a Tannoy out to call here? Maybe? Would that work?"

Silence. Mark drummed his fingernails harder on the surface. Then he recalled what he had in his arsenal. His doe eyes. He widened them, emulating the imaginary cat. The man huffed and picked up a phone. He held it to his ear and dialled a few numbers.

"What's the name?"

"Oh, erm..." Mark looked around the departure lounge for a sign of inspiration. "Suitcase."

"Suitcase?"

"That's right. Frequent flyer. Airmiles the lot. Cat got around more than most. Perfect name for the little critter. Was a shame he couldn't fly out to Sydney with his owner."

The man gawked at him, but Mark remained poised.

"I meant the passenger's name."

Mark would have palm slapped his forehead, if he hadn't made an absolute tit out of himself already. "Bradley Summers," he mumbled. "Getting on the Archer Airways flight to Sydney."

After a brief contemplation, the man dialled the last number and turned his back to speak to whoever was on the phone. Mark could hear him detailing the most ridiculous tosh of lies he'd just made up, but there was no giggling or men in white coats heading his way, so he assumed he was getting somewhere. Beard put the phone down.

"They've put a call out in Departures. If Bradley wants to come talk to his dear Suitcase, he'll be told to call here."

"Possibly could have given the cat's nickname then."

"Which is?"

"Mark."

The man nodded, handing back the Visa card. "Here you go, Mark."

Mark took the card and decided to slip it away as if nothing abnormal had happened. He just waited. Tapping his fingers against his sides and eyes fixed on the screen. Twenty minutes passed and the Sydney flight flicked up to declare it had departed then disappeared from the screen.

No calls were taken.

"I'm sorry, sir. Perhaps just send him a photo?"

Mark snorted. "Of the cat?"

"No. Of you, and those doe eyes. He might board the first flight home."

Mark narrowed his eyes. The man grinned. Mark could tell as he saw teeth that time. *Well, well, well, turns out one never can tell these days.*

* * * *

Three hours later, Mark slumped through into his house with a resigned feeling of dejection. It wasn't the first time, and that stung infinitely more. He'd spectacularly lost everything. And in the process made himself look even more of a dick than was usual. He'd lost his job and the chance at love in one fell swoop. Not to mention all the crap that had been stored in his loft for a rainy day—the man with a van who can proved that he, indeed, could, as the skip outside was empty. He had, however, gotten the beard man's number. Found out his name was Glen. Recently heartbroken too. Trouble was, he lived in Surrey which was a fair way from Marsby. Not as far as Australia, mind, but still a damn trek.

Plus, he was no Bradley.

He kicked off his shoes, slipped free from his jacket and banged his head against the wall for a while. *Knock some sense into me, perhaps?* And it did. He settled on a new plan. First things first, he needed to sell this house. For many reasons. One being that he couldn't live here anymore. Two being he would do as his father and Macy suggested and go see the world like he had always wanted. And three because he'd need the money to buy a flight to Sydney. It might take months, but he would bloody well do it. At least he could get Bradley's Australian number from Macy in the morning and try at another call.

Actually, that all had to come second. First, he needed tea.

He trudged into the kitchen and stopped short when the light switched on and a cup of the good stuff was held out to him by a muscular arm.

"It's probably cold. You took your time."

"Bradley!" Mark swooned.

"Brad." Bradley winked.

"I've said before, Bradley suits you—" Mark was cut off when Bradley swooped an arm around his waist, tugged him forward and kissed him.

And Mark wasn't surprised that his first thought as his tongue raged inside Bradley's hot mouth was, how the hell had the man even got into his house? Had he scaled the walls in his thongs? Had he used next door's dubious stepladder and broken in through the open bathroom window? Had Mark even locked the damn house in the first place?

He decided, though, having obviously knocked quite a bit of sense into himself through his head banging, that he wouldn't ask Bradley the question just yet.

That could wait until morning at least.

Chapter Nineteen

Best Laid Plans

Mark opened his eyes to what was certainly a splendid sight to wake up to any day of the year and a ridiculous grin spread across his features as he brushed his nose to the bare shoulder beside him. Bradley peeped open one eye, his lips curving into a smile rivalling Mark's.

"G'day, Mark."

"It is indeed." Normally Mark's reserved nature would have wrapped the duvet around his skinny, pasty body at this point and offered the man a brew. But it seemed a continental drift was in occurrence, and instead he edged closer to slap a kiss on the Aussie's luscious full lips.

Bradley hummed, groped Mark's backside and dragged him on top of him. "And it's looking up." He arched that one, now seemingly enticing, eyebrow, wriggling against Mark's growing hardness between his legs.

"It's been a while since I woke up to this." Mark kissed him, because it seemed like a good response at the time. And because he wanted to. *A lot.*

"You could have done. Several times." Bradley swiped his nose down Mark's. "If you hadn't been so bloody…British!"

Mark chuckled. "That, I'm afraid, is inevitable."

"Maybe you need a bit of Aussie in you?" Bradley wriggled his hips, slapping his wide hands across Mark's buttocks.

Rather startled at the slap and grope, Mark pulled away and furrowed his brow. "Who's on top here?"

Bradley bit his lip, his suggestive smirk once again needing to be kissed away. So Mark did, because he'd had enough of pretending that he didn't want to.

"C'mon, Mark, you can't tell me you've not switched it up in your extensive lifetime."

"Extensive?" Mark slid off and propped himself up on his elbow, staring down at the beautiful specimen beside him, hardly believing his eyes. Should he have gone to Specsavers?

Inhaling a deep breath, Bradley grappled for Mark and hefted him back on top. Mark's cock twitched, poking up between them as if annoyed it had been forgotten about. Mark could almost hear it huff.

Bradley, at that point, clearly decided it would be better to address the more persistent of the two of them. And that was Mark's dick. He wrapped his meaty fingers around it and slid up and down, swiping his thumb along the head. It seeped, ensuring Mark that this was real and not a wet dream. Just *his* wet dream, underneath him.

"This dick must have had quite a bit of action in its lifetime. If only it could talk." Bradley pumped a little more vigorously, and Mark's dick whimpered. Perhaps it wasn't so much his dick as his throat, but Mark liked to claim that he had full capacity over most of his body's reactions. His penis, however, had always had a mind of its own. And it seemed, right then, that it was leaning more toward hearing what Bradley might have to offer him. *Traitor.*

"Luckily, I only have one mouth that runs away with itself." Mark grunted as Bradley increased the pressure, firming his hand around the tight flesh.

Mark squashed his legs against Bradley's thighs. He pondered what a sight it must be, his skinny body on top of the gleaming, muscular and tight masculine form below him. If someone, somewhere, happened to chance on the scene via some left-on webcam, they would surely assume that Mark would be the better bottom. Perhaps it would be expected of him now to scoot up on his knees and slam back down on Bradley's cock that looked just as annoyed to be left out of the early morning party.

Trouble was, Mark had never been very comfortable with that. He'd done it, yes, once or twice at the command of George. But it had never been very…pleasant. But then Mark peered down to Bradley, the Adonis, the beauty of the man underneath him. The night previous Mark had ravished him, every single inch. And both had climaxed before either of them made a play for taking the other. Then it had turned all terribly cutesy. *Seriously, cutesy?* And Mark claimed he was a grown-up. So they'd fallen asleep in each other's arms and woken to the sound of gulls chirping. Now this…

Bradley's cheeky, brash and confident nature was nothing like the prickling influence that George had claimed over Mark in their years together. Not that George had authority over him per se—except, of course, when he'd been his teacher—but George had liked to play games. He preferred to switch the status quo in the bedroom and enjoyed being…taken care of. Which was why, Mark suspected, when Mark had matured to an age where it wasn't such a strange notion to be "looked after" by him, George had lost interest and sought a younger model to play the part. The irony of it all that then when George had really needed taking care of during his illness, he had died alone. And that, perhaps, was why Mark had taken in all his possessions and looked after them instead. Well, not so much. They'd succumbed to mould and damp in the leaking loft. And now were headed to some landfill, or probably some fly tipping mound somewhere just outside of Dover only to reappear in the blasted English Channel and featuring on the local news about the carelessness of the town folk.

"You think as much as you talk?" Bradley slowed his hand job, angling his head on the pillow to gaze up at Mark with an odd expression Mark couldn't place.

Mark wriggled, or more *rutted* into Bradley's palm. "I think *way* more than I talk."

"Wow." Bradley lifted up, releasing his hand from Mark's cock to tap his forehead. "It must be real busy up there."

Mark snorted. He shook himself out in the proper manner and slapped his hands to each of Bradley's cheeks and kissed him. "Apologies. I endeavour to keep my mind and my mouth shut from now on."

"Your mouth shut? Really?" Bradley pouted. "I do seem to remember that your mouth was a nice place to set up camp for a while."

"Ha. You and camping." Mark cocked his head. "Do you do much camping on your travels around the world?"

"I'm camp everywhere."

That beaming, bright smile made Mark swoon like a teenager, or like all those women who paid to see Bradley strip. Mark certainly wasn't feeling like the old fuddy-duddy he usually did first thing in the morning. *Huh, maybe that old saying is true, you are as old as the man you feel.* Mark chuckled and ran his hands along the hard ridges of Bradley's back. Bradley shivered, his skin erupting in goose pimples, and he gripped Mark tighter to kiss him.

"Mark, Mark, Mark," Bradley breathed over his flushed face.

"The repetitions of my name are a little off-putting."

"Mark, Mark, Mark," Bradley whispered, then kissed the tip of Mark's nose. "*My* Mark."

"*Your* Mark?"

"Have I made my mark?"

Mark tsked, then couldn't prevent the tingle rustling through his entire body. Bradley certainly had made his mark on Mark. And Mark wasn't sure he'd ever be unmarked. *Christ, I really do think far too much. New day, new life,* new *Mark!*

So with that, Mark wriggled away from Bradley's clutches, and shimmied down his body to once again discover the man who had cracked through his shell. Bradley lay flat, stroking his fingers through the tassels of Mark's unruly morning hair, and writhed on the sheets. Mark planted kisses on every inch of the man's smoking-hot skin, to the point it almost burned Mark's lips. If Bradley had made his mark on Mark, then Mark would ensure he made his mark on Bradley.

Oh, shut up!

Doing just that, Mark licked up the salty sweat glistening on Bradley's taut stomach and swiped through the prickles of fair hair trailing Bradley's belly button. The wax job was growing out and it rasped Mark's tongue. He splayed his hands up Bradley's chest. Bradley's nipples were as hard and raging as both their morning woods and Mark flicked one nipple between his fingers, gently squeezing…testing…

Bradley gasped and his dick twinged as he lifted his hips from the mattress. With a satisfied smile, Mark pinched the other one, twirling around it and trailing his tongue farther down to reach Bradley's cock. It was glorious. Hard, full and ready to be ravaged. Mark's dick huffed again, seething at being ignored, but Bradley needed seeing to first, if only for Mark to prove to this man that he was a changed fellow. He could take charge, he could get his needs met when he wanted. No longer the wallflower waiting on the sidelines to be told what to do. And never would he allow his deep-seated reservations to prevent him from getting what he wanted.

And what he wanted was to suck Bradley's cock. His id set free!

Mark opened his mouth, seducing Bradley's cockhead and not taking his gaze from the blue-green eyes watching him. Mark rather wished there was some hidden camera, as he would have loved to record this moment, if only to have a memento when it all went south. *Down under, maybe? Is Bradley still going back home?* They hadn't talked last night in favour of other things, and now the sun raged against the window, reminding Mark that there were still unanswered questions.

Like how the blinking hell had Bradley even gotten into his house?

Mark almost stopped to ask the question, but Bradley's tighter grip on his hair, urging him to swallow his cock, prevented him from going back to the old Mark ways. And as Mark gobbled Bradley to his root, Mark's nose hitting flesh, he was actually thankful there was no mirror, or camera. He couldn't imagine what he looked like right then, bobbing up and down, Bradley's cock thrusting in and out of his gaping mouth. Bradley's lips parted, inhaling a breath, and his groans of pleasures spurred Mark on. To hell with what he looked like—the man beneath him was loving this.

"That's it, Mark." Bradley raised his hips, lifted his head from the pillow and grunted. "That's how I like it. *Faster.*"

Mark obliged, because he was polite that way, but also because the anticipation had gotten to him. He needed to taste Bradley's explosive glory. And he wanted to taste it forever. Flattening his tongue around the flesh, he sucked harder. His jaw ached and his neck began to seize, but he wouldn't stop. Bradley scratched his fingernails into Mark's scalp, groaning and thrusting.

"Wait, wait, wait!" Bradley yelped.

Mark slurped off, dazed, confused. "What? Did I hurt you? What did I do? Oh, shit. Was I too rough? Teeth? Christ!"

Bradley chuckled. And Mark was nearing the thought of slapping him again.

"No, Mark. I just want you, too. Same time. C'mon. Come here." Bradley beckoned with his hands, then shifted onto his side. "Don't be shy, Mark."

After they'd fumbled into position, both lying on their sides with their heads between each other's legs, Mark's dick finally thanked him for being allowed in on the morning wake-up. Especially when Bradley wrapped his luscious lips around it and, using his beefy hands to massage Mark's arse, gorged on Mark's cock. Mark whimpered, his lips vibrating against Bradley's flesh raging in and out of his own throat. They sucked in unison, almost as if it was a dance routine that Bradley had been practising for his next stage performance. *Now, wouldn't that be a sight for all the drunken hens!*

Bradley hummed, and the sensations rippled through Mark's cock and into his balls. He responded by grunting from his throat—his lips wrapped firmly around Bradley's cock made it impossible for any words to escape into the air. Bradley trembled, his legs quivering, his skin pimpling. He moaned, guzzling harder, faster then trailed along to Mark's balls to pop one whole into his mouth. Mark raised that movement, with gusto, by lapping up Bradley's juicy, firm balls. Not so much in sync now as a battle of wills. Who could go faster, deeper, wider, stronger. Who would win first.

Mark did. *There's life in this old dog yet!*

Bradley exploded into his mouth, his entire body rippling and trembling. Mark drank and swallowed every last drop, lapping it up as though it was his breakfast. *Or morning tea.* Bradley, whimpering against him and the bed, didn't let up on Mark's cock and Mark could now allow himself to pull away and watch, doing nothing but enjoy the moment of Bradley pleasuring him. And by God, he did. With his mouth now free, Mark yelled into the vacant air as his orgasm rushed over him like a tidal wave of torrid emotion. He thrust his hips, raging his cock into Bradley's willing mouth, and exploded a stream of pent-up euphoria that Bradley lapped up like his freshly squeezed orange juice. *With added juicy bits!*

A perfect union. And Bradley claimed he didn't like his morning beverages hot. *Snicker.*

Falling onto his back, Bradley caught his breath, panting, and wiped the sweat from his brow. Mark manoeuvred away, lying beside him like when he'd been a teenager and had to top and tail his bedfellow during those awful summer camps. Except for the glistening sweat covering both their bodies and taste of semen on their breaths, that was. Mark blushed.

"So…didn't want to top after all?" Mark tapped his fingers to his chest. For some reason, that fell from his mouth. Because for the very brief few moments he wasn't concentrating on sucking the semen from the Aussie, he had been thinking about what it would be like for Bradley to take him. Would it be different? Would he enjoy it?

Bradley tucked his chin into his chest to meet Mark's gaze. Mark raised both his eyebrows, because he still hadn't figured out how to do just the one.

"You know how long it takes to clear Better than Butter out of your arse? I thought we'd give that a miss this time."

Mark laughed, his whole body lifting from the sheets. "I do own lube."

"Really now? And there I was thinking you just preferred dairy products. Dual uses and all that."

Mark smiled. His chest fluttered, and the spreading euphoria swam through his veins to put him on a real, natural high. *Gosh, I might not even need tea!* He then laughed at himself. Tea had never been about need, but want. And habit. And because it tasted good.

Much like how he felt about Bradley.

Bradley perched up on his elbows. "You thinking about tea?"

"I think you might now know all there is to know about me."

Bradley winked, then slapped Mark's leg. "C'mon, Mark. Get dressed. We're going to Macy's, 'cause you haven't got any OJ here."

Mark scooted to sit. "Yes, I have."

"No, Mark. I drank the entire contents of that waiting for you last night. You could probably taste the pulp in my spunk."

Mark wriggled his tongue and licked his lips. *Yes, yes I can.*

* * * *

When Bradley led Mark through into Macy's Tea Shoppe, the CLOSED sign was hanging face out, but the door was open and the scent of baking pastries sailed around the vacant surroundings. It gave Mark an odd sense of reminiscence, this being how he had first met Bradley all those…days ago? Mark flushed. *Days? Really? Days?* He'd only known Bradley for a few *days* and yet here he was in lo—

"Morning, you two." Macy peered around from the kitchen, wiping her hands on a tea towel. "Wondered when you'd be stopping by."

Mark cleared his throat, shaking off the thought he had almost allowed himself to have. Bradley grinned and pulled out a chair for Mark. *Gosh, such a gentleman.*

Mark sat and Bradley slipped into the seat opposite him.

"Usual, Mark, love?"

"Please, Macy. Make it a bit stronger than usual. I need a wake-up."

"Bet you do." Macy chuckled and set to making the tea. She sloped over to their table with a pot for one and a large glass of clean, crisp orange juice for Bradley. She then parked her arse between them and folded her arms over her flowery, fuzzy, jumper-dress ensemble. "Well?"

Mark took his time pouring the tea from the polka dot pot into the china cup. He hummed, stirring the real leaves and adding a splash of milk from the tiny jug. Bradley glugged from his glass. *Looks like the poor fellow is rather parched.* Mark chuckled to himself.

"Well, what?" Mark asked, sipping the tea. It pinched his lips from the burn, but as he was attempting nonchalance, he didn't respond to it.

"Oh, bloody hell." Macy flicked her frizzy ginger bunches with a huff. "Yesterday, you let him walk out." She flapped her hand toward Bradley, still silent, and pointed an accusatory finger at Mark. "Then you walked out of here like you'd died."

"I hardly think—" Mark avoided looking at Bradley just then.

"Then I got a call from Damian. He's on his way, by the way. He's helping in here for a while."

"Why do you need help?"

"Because he quit." Macy flapped her hand at Bradley.

Bradley shrugged.

"And I realise I do need help and he hates working at the theatre, so he's coming to work here for a bit."

"But he lives in Canterbury." Mark drew in his eyebrows. How much had happened in twenty-four hours? He checked his watch. Was he in some time warp? Was he forty already? *Bloody hope not*. He had a year left to claim he was still in his thirties.

"Yes, so he needs a place to stay." Macy leapt up to grab a spare mug from the counter, then poured out Mark's second cup from his pot into hers.

The utter travesty! No bother, Mark had had his fill of hot stuff this morning. His stomach fluttered so he shut it up with another gulp of English Breakfast, 'cause he'd already had an Aussie one. *Oh, for fuck's sake, how old are you, Mark?*

"So he's going to buy your place." Macy sipped her tea, ginger eyebrows rising.

"What?" Mark slapped the cup onto the saucer. "And where do you suppose I shall live?"

Macy uncurled her pinkie finger from around the handle of the cup. "With him."

Mark looked at Bradley. He in turn stared back at him with an odd look of someone who was in on a secret but had no interest in sharing it among those who were obviously on the periphery.

"I beg your pardon?"

"Oh, we sorted it all out while you were rushing to Gatwick yesterday. How much did that cost, by the way? An Uber?" Macy chucked her head back while laughing like a hyena.

"I put it on the work account," Mark admitted with minimal wincing.

"Nice."

"And what, may I ask, did you all sort out about *my* life and *my* house, all whilst I was rushing across counties like I was in some Richard Curtis movie?"

"Awww." Bradley tilted his neck and wrinkled his nose like a cute bunny rabbit.

Mark tutted. Then swooned.

"That you are going off around the world, like you always wanted." Macy said that as though it had been posted in the *Marsby Gazette* and had already become the chip paper for a freshly caught cod supper. "With Bradley. First stop, Sydney, right?"

"Yup." Bradley nodded and slammed his glass on the table. "Gotta meet the folks, Mark."

"Good luck with that." Macy snorted, holding up her cup.

"Whoa, hang on, *what*?"

No one answered Mark's very valid question as the bell tinkled and Damian entered the cafe. He grinned, fell into the spare seat and fluttered the oversized scarf around his neck. It was glorious sunshine outside, so the scarf thing was all just one of his bold theatrical entrances.

"Good morning." Damian reached for the pot of tea.

Mark slapped his hand away. "Get your own. I think I'll be needing this." He slurped the dregs in his mug, the leaves forming shapes around the china. "What is going on here?"

Bradley reached for the cup, swirled it three times, anti-clockwise then turned it upside down on the saucer. He leaned back, crossed his arms and winked.

"Does he know the plan?" Damian angled his head toward Mark, eyes on Macy.

"He's getting there," Macy said.

"Right." Mark shifted in the seat, his gaze on Bradley. "Care to fill in the fuzzy gaps for me?"

"Okay. After you walked out of here, Macy called me," Bradley replied.

"You answered *her* calls?"

"Yes. Then my phone died. I popped back here, we had a chat. Macy loaned me the money and I managed to switch my ticket to Sydney for next week instead. And, I got two tickets."

"Birthday present from me and Damian." Macy waved off Mark opening his mouth to speak. "For your fortieth. Don't ask for anything else."

"So, you're coming with me to Sydney." Bradley grinned with those perfectly aligned white teeth. "You'll meet my folks. We won't stay with them. I can find somewhere, no probs. I spoke to an old contact and there's a few jobs I can do out there. Roofing in the day, stripping at night. You"—Bradley pointed at Mark—"can get a job in some English tea shop or something. We earn some cash to then start travelling. Where do you want to go, Mark? Uluru? Then onto Thailand? Wherever you want, I'm taking you. And you'll have the money from the house sale to Damian—"

"How on earth can you afford to buy my house?" Mark ignored all the other announcements in Bradley's speech and lurched his gaze on Damian. Why that was the most pressing out of all the rest, he wasn't sure. But it was still a valid question. Am Dram paid nothing, and box office ticket sales clerk even less.

"I have quite a bit saved for the deposit. We'll do a private sale. I know an estate agent." Damian winked. "I need out of Canterbury. The men there are terribly…extra."

"Hmmm." If anyone was extra, it was Damian. "And what about Pete?"

"Who now?"

"Never mind." Mark shook his head and glared at the upside-down cup. He really wanted a refill. "Care to..."

"Oh, right." Bradley leapt forward and picked up the cup. He stroked his chin all the while staring into it as if it was some crystal ball. "You got rid of something recently, Mark?"

"My sanity?"

Bradley smiled, eyes still fixed at the dregs in Mark's mug. "There's a lot of stuff in here, but it's all in the past." He showed the cup over the table at Mark. "All those shapes are to the left of the handle. At a guess, I'd say it was your burden. And the wings signify it's flown away. Gone. The clusters, there, look like it had been weighing you down and so the bits heading up to the edge are showing you it's leaving. Gone."

"Right." Mark still wasn't sure he believed in any of this mumbo-jumbo, but Bradley looked so intrigued, so wide-eyed, so blinking beautiful. So he peered in closer. "What's that by the handle?"

Bradley shifted in his seat, his cheeks tinging pink to match his flip-flops. "Well, what does it look like to you?"

Mark, Damian and Macy all leaned forward, staring into the abyss of the cup.

Surely not!

"Looks like you were right all along, Mark." Damian sat back in his chair. "Tea is your one true love." He formed a heart with his hands and bumped it against his chest.

"The shapes by the handle are the ones that are the present, the now, and what's affecting you at this moment." Bradley didn't look at Mark while he spoke, instead fixating on the cup. "But it can be interpreted how you want it. That to the right of the cup is your future."

"What on earth are two circles meant to mean?" Mark swiped a hand over his perspiring forehead.

"Rings, Mark." Bradley dropped the cup to the saucer. "I'd say they were rings."

Mark lifted his gaze to Bradley across the table. Bradley shrugged.

"Mark, I can see your brain cells ticking." Macy slid her hand on top of Mark's and patted. "This is good for you. To get away from all this. To do what you always wanted to do. To sell that blasted antique house of yours—"

"Mine!" Damian waved his hand in the air like a child with the right answer.

"And to start fresh," Macy continued. "Forgetting the past and moving forward. Like the leaves, *your* blasted tea, is telling you. You are not too old. You are not past your prime, yet. And now you have Bradley."

"That you do." Bradley grinned. "It's why you've been so miserable, Mark! You've not been following your true destiny. You've been stuck here. You're a traveller. An adventurer. You need fun and excitement to make you feel whole again."

Mark inhaled through a distinct fluttering in his chest. That was remarkably...*accurate*? But he turned his attention back to Macy to address the less floaty reasons. "What about all that stuff you said about him being so young, your cousin no less?"

"I admit I was a little shocked. But to be honest with you, Mark, he's good for you. I see a little sparkle in your eyes and he put it there. And he's told me how he feels about you."

Mark shifted his gaze back to Bradley, cocking his head. "And how is that?"

"I'm in love with you, Mark." Bradley shrugged, as if that was the most natural thing in the world to utter over the breakfast table amongst his nearest and dearest.

"You're *what* now?"

"I'm. In. Love. With. You." Bradley enunciated each word, raising his voice, probably in mockery that Mark might have been hard of hearing. "That moment you stepped in here, with that hair, and the tea bag on your face, I knew it. I was told I would. I read it everywhere. Tea leaves, the zodiac, I even tried the eight-ball. We're perfect for each other. It all fits, Mark. This time, it all fits. Every sign pointed us this way. The tea bag, the roof, the bike, the gulls, the hair, the *airline*. Go back. Check it. You'll see I'm right."

"Because the stars, the tea leaves, tell you you're in love?"

"No." Bradley leaned across the table and grabbed Mark's hand to pull it toward his chest. "Because, this time, I feel it too."

"But it's been days, only days!" Mark had no idea why he felt the need to shout that. But he did.

"I fell in love with Tom Hardy immediately." Damian slapped a hand to his chest with a whimsical flutter of his eyelashes.

"You've never met him!" Mark declared, losing his resolve. Not that he had any, mind.

"And that, my dear Marky Mark and the funky bunch, is his problem." Damian pouted. "Because the day we do meet, I'm taking him up that aisle."

"Dirty." Bradley snorted.

"Better believe it, darling."

Mark held up a hand, shaking his head to release some words. "I'm…I'm at a loss. I have no idea… How did you even get into my house?" Yes, because they were obviously the most pressing words to utter right then. *Way to go, Mark!*

"Macy had a key," Bradley replied, deadpan.

"And not one of you lovely people, oh solid friends of mine, thought to call me back yesterday?"

"How could we have achieved all this with you flittering around?" Macy cut in. "Dithering on and on that you can't leave, you're too old, you need to keep the house for your parents because your dad gambled away all the money. Blah, blah, blah!"

Mark pinched the bridge of his nose. *My parents!*

"Now stop that!" Macy slapped the table. "They are not for you to worry about. Your mum is perfectly capable of downsizing that house, selling that car, if things are really as bad as they make out. Which, by the way, I don't think is true with the amount of cakes she bought for the Women's Institute yesterday."

"Maybe," Bradley mumbled, head bowed, twiddling his thumbs in tiny circles. "You don't want this? Me? Maybe you don't see that symbol the same way I do?"

That grazed through Mark's heart like one of Macy's bread knives, carving away on his stale, crusty organ to spill crumbs through his veins. This was all such a shock that he had no idea what to do or say. Only a few hours ago he had come to terms with how he felt and accepted that Bradley could *like* him. Now it was more than that. Bradley had just admitted he *loved* him! Enunciated it, in perfect English no less. And he wanted to travel the world with him. Mark! The thirty-nine-year-old blubbering idiot. All the plans that Mark had painstakingly made in his youth, that he had wanted to do with George, that had never amounted to anything other than a destroyed paper file, was now in his reach. And he could do it with someone he lo—

"Mark?"

"Hmm?" Mark bit his lip, darting his gaze to all three eager faces staring at him. *Oh, bugger it!* He let out a shallow laugh, wiped his eye and shook his head, contemplating his next move.

He stood, pulled down his leather jacket and cleared his throat. Bradley's gaze followed him up, those blue-green eyes wide and the fear in them unmistakable. He thought Mark was going to walk out. Mark had a sudden evil urge to do just that. *That'll show the Aussie and his practical jokes.*

He didn't, though. Instead, he lowered to one knee, took Bradley's hand in his and forgot for one single moment that he was British. "Bradley?"

"Brad."

"Shut up." Mark rotated his shoulders. "I do love you. Quite a lot, really. And that shape in there of congealed leaves *does* look like a heart to me. And it's right. My heart is yours. I believe in this. I believe in you. And I would be honoured to travel the world with you."

Bradley opened his mouth to speak but Mark cut him off by raising a hand.

"On one condition."

"Which is?"

"We take our own tea bags."

Bradley grinned, then leaned down and kissed him. "I'd be honoured to provide you with constant tea bagging."

"You little bugger." Mark reached up, wrapped his arms around Bradley's neck and snogged his face off.

Because he wanted to, and he could. *Forever.*

Okay, well, not forever, because at one point or another one of them was going to die. *And what a lovely happy ending to finish this little anecdote on.*

"Right, now that's sorted." Mark stood, ignoring the gaping faces and faraway looks in his friends' eyes. "Who's for more tea?"

Chapter Twenty

The Big Four-Oh!

Six months later…

"Gerrem off!"

"Show us your hose!"

"Strip, strip, strip!"

Mark settled back along the empty bar area, cup of tea in hand, and watched the commotion play out. He didn't always come along to these things. But today was a special occasion and he'd been railroaded into at least having some sort of celebration to honour the event. Mark would rather it was forgotten. And the sight of his boyfriend up on stage, wriggling his hips and thrusting his groin into the hundred or so females screaming at the front for him to get on with the primary task, aka shredding the remains of his clothing, wouldn't have been Mark's first choice for commemorative shenanigans. He'd much rather have been the only one here. At least he'd gotten a solitary preview earlier that morning. Just for Bradley to ensure he knew all the dance steps, of course. *Snort.*

The stereo system blasted out some fad tune epitomising the moment, and Bradley regaled the audience with his varying grinding moves whilst sliding out of the minimal sheathing he had left. Today he'd gone for the more traditional fireman's ensemble. The words "I Need a Hero" rang out and Bradley went on to prove he could be such that person, to the crowd's utter enthusiasm. At a distance, though. The audience weren't allowed to touch, unless they'd been summoned. But Bradley had always forgone those parts of the act. The other members of his strip team often allowed such sordid atrocities, but Bradley had insisted his parts were for Mark to touch only.

"You want something stronger, mate?"

Mark swivelled, acknowledging the pretty much starkers barman in only tight-fitting boxers and a dickie bow, by holding up his mug. "No, thank you." His British accent almost cut the porcelain against the Aussie twangs. Six months travelling most of the outback and Mark hadn't shed his stiff upper lip.

"Come on, Mark. You're forty today. Brad says you need to get sloshed."

Jaxon, barman and occasional stripper himself, had met Mark the last time Mark had been made to come to one of Bradley's hen night stripping gigs. That time, however, had been largely due to Bradley's over-consumption of whisky and Red Bull that had led to him being incapable of walking the couple of miles from the bar to their flat overlooking Bondi Beach. And whilst it should have been a pleasant stroll through the late-night streets with Mark propping Bradley up and having him whisper in Mark's ear over and over about how much he loved him and wanted to ravish every inch of him on return to their poky apartment, Bradley had crashed out on entrance and snored into a coma.

Mark had had to clear the man's sick from the sheets the next morning, which was a lot less satisfying than the usual sticky remnants that Mark often had to wipe clean the morning after the night before. So after that, Bradley had insisted he wouldn't drink when on duty. And Mark had been rather grateful that his milestone birthday had landed on one of Bradley's gig nights, which meant Bradley wouldn't be drinking. But, as it now transpired, Bradley would quite like Mark to partake in a beverage or two.

Mark arched one eyebrow. At least that was something he'd learned to achieve over the months of travelling. "Did he now?"

"Long Island one?"

Raucous, yet feminine, screams burst out and Mark twisted once more to check on the hullaballoo. Oh yes, there was his boyfriend's package out on full display, band wrapped around the root to emulate a semi and elongate the length. Mark tutted. Bradley shot him a wink then rushed to cover the beast with the Australian flag, the corner Union Jack propped up by whatever Bradley used to make it look like his cock poking through. The Queen would be so proud.

"Actually, on second thoughts." Mark pushed over his empty cup to the barman. "Fill that up with rum."

"Rum?"

"Please. Spiced."

"Like it spicy, do you, mate?" Jaxon chuckled and nodded up to Bradley on stage.

"Indeed." Mark had to agree. He couldn't not. *Look who I'm here with.*

Jaxon passed over his drink. "You staying on tonight? Brad's arranged a heck of a do for ya, once all this lot go onto the nightclub next door."

"Ah, yes. I'll be spending my milestone birthday with a bunch of strippers, two drag queens and no one over the age of twenty-five. It's like someone read my wish that I threw into the Trevi Fountain last Valentine's Day."

Jaxon furrowed his brow and sloped off to wipe some of the bar, probably wondering if that was good old Blighty sarcasm. It wasn't. Mark twisted once more, catching the end of a delightful performance from his boyfriend, Bradley's body glowing under the spotlights. Mark still found it hard to believe that the Adonis up on that stage, with a perfectly sculpted six-pack and the moves to really make it work, was his. And he was.

For six whole months, he and Bradley had been together. When Mark had crossed continents with a man nearly eighteen years his junior, Mark hadn't really been one hundred percent certain that it would work out. He'd expected Bradley to come to his senses and wonder why he was dragging a middle-aged Brit around the world with him. But as time went on, Mark had started to believe that Bradley might actually be a tad smitten. With him. He still explained to him their signs, which all pointed to their perfect union, and Mark had occasionally indulged in the read of the daily horoscopes, too.

They'd been to and fro from Australia, to Thailand, to Europe. They'd camped, they'd bathed in luxury and they'd shared hostels like true backpackers. And Bradley hadn't once shown any desire for Mark to not be there. Waking up most mornings with Bradley's arms wrapped around him in a firm embrace confirmed that Bradley might be in this for the long haul. And not just the flight.

But alas, the equity Mark had received from his house sale to Damian had dwindled and they'd chosen to return to Sydney for their halfversary, earn some more money then jet off again to somewhere new. Bradley had been doing odd jobs in the day, stripping at weekends, and Mark had become an office temp, his tea-making abilities really coming into quite good use for continued employment. All was going rather pleasantly. Even Mark's meeting of Bradley's parents had gone down particularly well. Only one comment had been muttered about Mark being a filthy old man from Bradley's father, but Macy had assured him prior to leaving the country that her uncle liked to piss about with people. So Mark had taken the comment with a pinch of salt, and added it to Bradley's father's tea during preparation. *Accident, total accident, meant to have been sugar.*

Turning forty wasn't as bad as Mark had thought it would be.

Leaping from the stage and into the throng of screaming women, Bradley ended his performance by giving away a few kisses, allowing a stroke of his abs or squeeze of his biceps, then sauntered up the aisle with the Australian flag wrapped low on his delectable hips. On approach, he slid both hands either side of Mark's face and kissed him. The catcalls increased to pierce Mark's eardrums.

"Steady on." Mark held the cup in the air as a way to prevent a spill, until he remembered it wasn't tea in there anymore, so brought it back to behind Bradley's back. He didn't mind wasting a bit of rum, but tea...*nooo sirree!* Licking his lips, Mark grimaced. "Is that the new oil?"

"Sure is. Too flowery, right?"

"I'd say so. Stick to the pure olive stuff. That doesn't have quite the potent aftertaste."

"Will do." Bradley nodded behind to Jaxon. "Red Bull please, mate. And shove a little vodka in it."

Mark arched one eyebrow. Because he should, and could.

"It's your birthday, Mark. We can both drink. And I'm off-duty now." Bradley angled his head to the swarm of girls all now being led out of the main bar area and into the basement nightclub. The cackles and catcalls dissipated as the gaggle teetered away and Bradley turned his grin back on Mark.

"Fine, have your deathly concoction." Mark slurped from his mug of rum, wondering if this was how the pirates used to drink it. Maybe an eyepatch might be more fitting than the reading specs he was surely about to have to start wearing from today. "But it's my birthday, so that means I get carried home this time."

"Fair dos." Bradley grabbed the glass from Jaxon, knocked back a hefty amount with an elongated *ahhh,* then slammed it on the surface. "Right, you want your birthday present now or later?"

"I hardly think this is the most appropriate time for that. If it's what I asked for, that is."

Bradley bellowed a laugh, then leaned in to whisper in Mark's ear. "That's later. I got the outfit off Tony. He had one lying around."

Mark blushed and curtailed it by downing more of his rum. Which was rather stupid, as alcohol always gave him a scarlet glow. Least he could blame it on that rather than the thought of Bradley dressing up as one of Mark's all-time fantasies. *Ah, life really is grand when my boyfriend has no qualms about roleplay and his embarrassment levels are zero.*

"I got you something I can give in public, too."

"Well, in that case." Mark plonked his mug on the surface and rubbed his hands together with glee.

Jaxon and a couple of the other male strippers, along with the two drag queen hosts, came over to watch the show. By the shit-eating grins on their chiselled faces, Mark believed this wasn't going to be a DVD or a book, or something equally as traditional a birthday present one could open in front of others. He feared for the following proceedings.

Bradley cleared his throat, and his usual cocky brashness flickered away. And Mark thought for all of a millisecond that Bradley was also somewhat nervous. Embarrassed maybe? *No, he couldn't be. Not Bradley.* Not Bradley 'he who dares to bare all' Summers? Bradley shuffled the wraparound flag on his hips, tucking the ends in so he was fully covered with no chance of a slight slip, then ever so gradually sank down onto bended knee.

Mark lurched forward, grabbing Bradley's arms. His fingers slipped through the gooey remnants of tan oil, base oil and whatever the heck the man used to slather himself up to a beautiful sheen, and had trouble pulling him upright.

"Mark—"

"No, nope, no!"

"Mark, I just—"

"Christ, oh buggering, Christ." Mark wiped his hands down his jeans, ridding them of the sticky residue, then without thinking, ruffled his hair. The oil made it stick up and Bradley snorted a laugh. *There truly is something about Mark.*

"Mark—"

"No, wait. Just wait." Mark pointed a finger. "You do not get to do that."

"Do wh—"

"Shit."

"Mark, listen—"

"No, you listen! Oh, for fuck's sake. Why do you do this? Why do you buggering do this?"

"If you could just let me—" Bradley waggled a finger at behind Mark.

"Sit!" Mark pointed to a vacant chair by one of the tables cluttered with an array of concoctions left by a hen group.

"Mark—"

"Now!"

Bradley glanced over his shoulder at the naked onlookers, then shrugged and stumbled back to sit on the chair. Mark inhaled a deep and fearful breath. He closed his eyes, bowed his head and pinched his nose. "Jaxon?"

"Yes, Mark?"

"The song."

"Now?"

"Please."

"Okey." Jaxon stumbled off and a short time later the speakers blasted out the song of choice.

Mark opened his eyes. Bradley sat, Australian flag draped over his legs and arched that one perfect eyebrow. It was rather poignant that he was encased in that material, and that Mark could even do this here. The stars *had* aligned. If only he didn't have an audience of more than one. He'd planned to do this in private.

But the Aussie never did allow Mark to do anything by the book.

The music continued from its introduction, and Mark closed off his mind and tapped along to the beat with his trembling fingers. He now regretted he had made this stupid decision. *But in for a penny…or a cent.*

Not faltering his gaze from Bradley, who had clearly cottoned on to what was happening as his grin could not have been wider, Mark dragged down the zip on his leather jacket. He attempted a sway of his hips, just getting into the rhythm a little. He was fully aware he was doing this in front of four professionals. Not only could Mark not really dance in any type of capacity, let alone seductively, but also his body beneath his attire wasn't to the standard one would expect of someone who would be stripping off his clothes. But he had no choice now. *Sod it.*

Thank heavens he'd consumed at least some of the rum. He continued, ruffling free of his jacket. This time he just let it drop to the floor and avoided any health and safety hazards by flinging it around his head. Then started on the buttons to his shirt.

The three onlookers all whistled and clapped, probably giving their own hip wiggling from behind. But Mark closed them off to focus on the one he needed to. Bradley sat straighter in the chair and cupped his hands in his lap. What for, Mark chose not to think about right then. Perhaps Mark wouldn't need a band to temper his girth.

Discarding the shirt, after a bit of a tug over his wrist—he probably should have loosened the buttons on the cuffs beforehand—he danced forward, bare chest on display, and added a hip wriggle, a tushy thrust, which he believed was called a twerk in the industry, and unclipped the belt holding up his jeans.

"Far out, Mark!"

Mark twisted, setting his back firmly to Bradley, and swayed. Bradley grabbed Mark's hips, tugging him down. Mark honoured that, until he realised he was now facing the other three strippers and so quickly whipped around once more.

Mark laughed it off, because what else could he do? Then grabbed Bradley's hands and slapped them around his arse.

"I think I might need some help lowering these." Mark tucked Bradley's fingers into his back pocket.

Bradley sucked in a breath, then tapped around and found the bulge. In Mark's back pocket, not the front one. He ripped out the box tucked inside and Mark lowered to his knees in front of him. The music seemed to fade, whether Jaxon had decreased the volume or Mark had managed to drown it out in favour of focusing all his energy on the man sat in front of him, he couldn't be sure. Bradley stared down at the box, then flipped it open to reveal a solid band ring.

"That's not for professional purposes." Mark licked his lips.

"I should hope not, or you're seriously underestimating me." Bradley grinned and tugged out the ring from the foam inners.

"Bradley Summers…" Mark waited for Bradley to correct him. He didn't, so Mark continued with a smile, "Will you make an honest man out of this middle-aged, crazy-for-you, tea-obsessed Brit?"

Bradley inhaled, sharply. "Are you kidding?"

"No. Are you Laughing Your Fucking Arse Off?"

Bradley met his gaze. "No, I'm not."

"Then, will you?"

Bradley smiled. Grinned. Then cupped Mark's face and kissed him. "You bet."

Mark exhaled, placing the ring firmly on Bradley's finger and stood to do back up his trousers.

"Hey." Bradley furrowed his brow. "Don't I get the whole lot?"

"Maybe later."

Bradley jumped up and kissed him. "You bet, again."

Mark picked up his shirt and slipped his arms through. Jaxon handed him the rest of his cup of rum and Mark downed it in one gulp. He needed that.

"So, can I give you your present now?" Bradley asked.

"Well, there's hardly any point now is there?"

"Why?"

"Because I did it first."

"Did what first?"

"Proposed."

"Oh." Bradley bit his bottom lip, then winced. "You thought I was going to…"

The blood drained from Mark's face and probably left a pool of goo to rival the oil on the sparkling flooring. "Were you not? You were going down onto one knee!"

Bradley chuckled. Then pointed behind Mark. A brown bag sat beneath the bar area. "Nah, I was just lowering to pick that up."

If there ever was a time that Mark felt like an utter fool, it was right then. The plan had been to do the strip back at home, after borrowing the CD from Jaxon, and this would all have been a private show. Once again, Mark had been thwarted. By the Aussie. At least the stars have realigned back to their normalcy.

Bradley lowered, grabbed the bag and handed it to Mark. Opening it, Mark laughed. At least that really was the perfect present.

"Now I don't have to get up and make you tea in the morning." Bradley ruffled Mark's hair. "Teasmade does it for ya." He winked, then bit his bottom lip with a suggestive smirk. "Don't worry, though, I'll still give you morning tea bagging."

Turning forty wasn't all that bad.

Want to see more from this author? Here's a taster for you to enjoy!

St Cross: Won't Feel A Thing

C F White

Excerpt

"You want my opinion?"

"Yes."

"My honest opinion?"

"Yes," Ollie repeated. "Please."

"Brutal honest opinion?"

"Yes."

"Even if you don't like it?"

"Even if I never want to talk to you again." Ollie took a sharp slurp through the straw of his smoothie and winced, his glasses tipping to the end of his nose. "Until tonight, anyway."

"Then leave well alone."

Ollie sighed. He sucked up another mouthful of his daily fruit and veg intake, flicked back his blond hair that had lost its vigor after a twelve-hour night shift and glanced away from Taya's wide brown eyes. The eyes that signified she meant every damn word. *Bitch.*

"Told you."

Taya freed her dark, waist-length hair from its curled bun and stroked it over one shoulder. She wrapped the band around her slender dark-skinned wrist then sipped her dainty cup of pink hot chocolate. The blue edges of her lips, caused by the freezing weather, were subsiding back to their usual reddish tinge with each guzzle of the pink cream and rainbow of chocolate candies scattered over her ridiculous sickly concoction. She hadn't even offered a spoonful to him. Twelve hours straight on night shift clearly meant she needed the sugar all to herself.

"He's not worth your time, your worry or your respect." She clanged the cup down onto the glass surface of the table, pulled her winter trench coat over the scrubs she hadn't bothered to change out of and reached for her packet of menthol slims.

"Neither are they." Ollie pointed to the cigarettes.

Taya glared across the table. She unhooked the top of the packet, took one of the white sticks between her teeth and lit it with her pink lighter. Blowing the smoke into the freezing cold air, she waved her hand.

"We all have our vices, Oliver."

Ollie stuck his middle finger up. He slapped it back down and shoved it into his jacket pocket. It was freezing, and Taya had to bloody sit outside the corner coffee shop in order to smoke her way out of the trying night shift. She was right. Everyone needed their vices, especially with what he and Taya did for a living. He sighed.

"I think he needs patience."

"He's got plenty of those." Taya pointed her two fingers clutching the death stick at Ollie.

"Har fricking har. Patience with a *c*."

"He's a *c* all right." Taya took another drag. At Ollie's glare, she sighed and rested her elbow on the tabletop. "What? He is."

"I think you may be the only female in the entire hospital who doesn't like him." Ollie slurped the dregs of his raspberry-ripple smoothie and shivered. He should have gone for a hot drink, but it was hard enough to sleep during the day as it was. Caffeine would only make it infinitely more difficult.

"That's because I know him," Taya replied.

"Urgh. Not you, too?"

"Ew." Taya grimaced around her cigarette. "No, thank you."

Ollie leaned back in the chair. He waved a hand to waft away the smoke drifting into his face. To give her some credit, Taya was trying to blow it out of the side of her mouth to avoid him, but the icy-cold January breeze from the earlier sleet downpour blew it straight back. Ollie zipped up his puffer jacket, folded his arms and jiggled on the cold metal chair.

"You nearly done?" He nodded to the half-full cup of violently pink chocolate.

Taya blew another puff of smoke into the air, stubbed out the remains of her cigarette and downed the rest of her drink, leaving a foam mustache on her top lip. She licked it away. "Yeah. Home to bed, miss the snowfall, back at eight. You?"

They scraped back their chairs and Ollie tucked a five-pound note under the ashtray for the servers. Anyone willing to come outside and serve drinks in this weather should most definitely get tips, even if his wages would no doubt be far less than those of the coffee baristas working this part of London.

"I should go see my dad," he replied.

Taya linked her arm in with his, curling her slender fingers around his quilted sleeve. Checking both ways along the crossroads lined by independent boutiques, high-class restaurants, unconventional cafés and health-food shops, she steered him across, narrowly missing a black cab speeding over the mini-roundabout. The glass-enclosed bus stop's bench overflowed with waiting passengers, so he stood, his freezing toes within his inappropriate-for-the-weather slip-on loafers numbing with each passing second, and checked the time on the electric board for when the next bus was due.

"How's he doing?" Taya asked.

"Good days and bad days." Ollie sighed. "Keeps calling me Tilly."

Taya tried to hold in the chuckle but failed miserably. Ollie didn't mind so much. A good sense of humor was always best in these situations, not to mention their line of work. He pulled Taya in closer. It was fricking freezing and snowflakes fell from the overcast sky. How would he get back to work later that night? London came to a standstill if even one flake hit any mode of public transport. Him living in the other end of the city—the cheap end—would make it all the more difficult to travel across town. On occasions when there wasn't a downfall, he would have cycled in. But that was out of the question with the ice on the roads. And the fact that he hadn't woken up in his own bed last night. Ollie shuddered at the memory.

"Right." Ollie bounced to keep warm while awaiting the number 252. "It's January. So that means New Year's resolutions. What's yours?"

"Quit smoking."

"Good luck." Ollie meant it.

Taya stuck out her tongue.

"Well, we both know mine—"

"Which you broke last night." Taya was a bitch like that.

"I don't believe New Year's resolutions should start until the second week of January." Ollie rubbed his hands together, digging Taya's arm into his side, and wondered why he hadn't thought to bring gloves. Ah, yes, he hadn't had any where he'd been before his shift started. He wasn't allowed to leave any trace of his existence there.

"Riiight," Taya said. "So that means from today, you'll be steering clear of arsehole men?"

"Sadly, no. Unfortunately, I will no doubt encounter many of them in my time without realizing until it's too late."

"Amen." Taya saluted.

Ollie wasn't sure what the salute was about. But he wasn't particularly religious, so maybe that was how it was done in church these days? Or temples, considering Taya's family were Hindu.

"So, what *is* your resolution, then?"

"No baggage," Ollie replied.

"Baggage?"

"Yep," Ollie confirmed.

The gleaming new red Routemaster bus edged along the narrow High Street, bumping over the speed mounds meant to slow the traffic down, which Ollie thought ridiculous as the morning rush-hour pileup tended to last all day in central London. The streets were filled with scuttling people carrying takeout coffee cups, cyclists braving the ice, and the occasional honking of a taxi horn. This time of the morning, most people were trying to get to work and not home from it like Ollie and Taya. He was never quite sure who was keener to reach their destinations.

"I don't mind a complete arsehole—"

"Obviously." Taya cut Ollie off with a raise of her smoothed-out eyebrows. That new rainbow hot chocolate had clearly contained one too many e-numbers and sent her loopy. That and the long night shift. Not that she hadn't been a little bit loopy to begin with.

"Ha ha." Ollie pushed her forehead. "Like, I can handle a dickhead—"

"We all know."

"Jesus Christ," Ollie muttered. "No more white hot chocolate with pink dye for you, okay?"

"Sorry." Taya pressed her lips together. She rose up on her tiptoes to check on the bus's progress but needn't have worried, as it had traveled all of a millimeter since the start of their conversation. At this rate, Ollie might get home in time to have a shower and come straight back.

"What I mean is—"

"You don't want a man who can't commit because of circumstance," Taya finished for him.

Ollie was capable of finishing his own sentences, but Taya was getting warm from flapping her lips, so he allowed it. "Exactly. I'm married to my job. I love my job. Therefore, I should have the occasional fling and become the arsehole myself." He pointed a finger at Taya. "Don't fricking say it."

Taya shrugged and mimed zipping her lips up.

"What do we nurses say daily?"

"'No, you can't have McDonald's'?"

"Not that one."

"'You're going to feel a little prick'?"

Ollie sniggered. "Not that one either."

"Oh, I know. It's 'Of course I'll change your TV channel for you—it's not like I have anything better to do with my time.'"

"No! I mean the big one—'You won't feel a thing.'"

Taya nodded. "So?"

"So, my resolution is to no longer feel a thing."

"Good luck." Taya smiled. *Bitch.*

The bus pulled up and Ollie jogged on the spot, waiting for the doors to open. They hissed to the side, and even though he and Taya were standing correctly at the hop-on part of the Routemaster with the exit farther along the double decker, a tall man with floppy dark hair jumped straight off and bashed Ollie's arm as he rushed up the high street, heading toward the gleaming glass frontage of St. Cross Children's Hospital.

"Ouch." Ollie pouted and rubbed his arm.

"Ha!" Taya jumped the step onto the bus.

"What?"

Amusement shimmered across Taya's face as she bleeped her Oyster card onto the yellow reader. "You just felt something."

"Oh, bog off."

* * * *

Ollie jangled the keys in the lock of his third-floor flat and burst in out of the freezing cold. He slammed the door, wriggled free of his coat and slipped out of his comfortable loafers. Rubbing his numbed hands together, he hurried up the corridor and decided to forgo the shower in favor of sinking under his fluffy down duvet instead.

He stripped out of his jumper and jeans, threw his glasses onto the bedside table and collapsed onto the bed. Grabbing the side of the duvet, he wrapped it around his shivering body, rolled onto his front and made a human sausage roll out of himself. He shut his eyes. Of course, that would be when his house phone decided to ring. He wasn't going to answer it. That time of the morning, it'd only be personal-injury-claim chasers or some double-glazing salesman. The answer phone clicked on and Ollie's recorded voice wafted down the hallway into his bedroom.

"Hey, you've reached Ollie," it sang out. "I'm way too busy and important to come to the phone right now, and if you're not with me then you're missing out! So leave a message, and I'll decide whether to call you back. Oh, and if it's PPI, I've claimed four times and turns out I'm still not owed anything. Oh, and I haven't had an accident in the last three years. Oh, and I'd simply luuurrvve to take your survey on local facilities I use in my leisure time, if I had any. Much love—bleeeeep."

Ollie chuckled. Until the caller's voice boomed down the phone.

"Oliver?"

It seemed like a question, especially with the pause. Ollie held his breath.

"Oliver?"

Ollie hoped he'd either hang up or get to the point before Ollie passed out from asphyxiation. And considering he was naked, wrapped in a duvet, he could just see the local paper headlines misconstruing his accidental death as some sort of sex game gone wrong.

"Right. You're not there. Or ignoring me."

Bright man, this one.

"You left your watch here."

Ollie scrambled to get his arm out from under the duvet and checked his wrist. *Bollocks.* He shut his eyes.

"I've had to throw it out."

Ollie shoved a hand over his mouth, adding to his suffocating possibilities, and ignored the sinking feeling in his gut.

"I'll get you a new one."

Ollie shook his head and sank farther into the duvet to cover his face.

"Don't call me back. I'll see you later."

The answer phone bleeped, indicating the end of the message and signifying the beginning of Ollie's New Year's resolution.

The one where he wouldn't feel a thing.

PRIDE
PUBLISHING

About the Author

Brought up in a relatively small town in Hertfordshire, C F White managed to do what most other residents try to do and fail—leave.

Studying at a West London university, she realised there was a whole city out there waiting to be discovered, so, much like Dick Whittington before her, she never made it back home and still endlessly searches for the streets paved with gold, slowly coming to the realisation they're mostly paved with chewing gum. And the odd bit of graffiti. And those little circles of yellow spray paint where the council point out the pot holes to someone who is supposedly meant to fix them instead of staring at them vacantly whilst holding a polystyrene cup of watered-down coffee.

She eventually moved West to East along that vast District Line and settled for pie and mash, cockles and winkles and a bit of Knees Up Mother Brown to live in the East End of London; securing a job and creating a life, a home and a family.

Having worked in Higher Education for most of her career, a life-altering experience brought pen back to paper after she'd written stories as a child but never had the confidence to show them to the world. Having embarked on this writing malarkey, C F White cannot stop. So strap in, it's gonna be a bumpy ride...

C F White loves to hear from readers. You can find her contact information, website details and author profile page at https://www.pride-publishing.com